MURDER in the HOUSE

MURDER
in the
HOUSE

MARGARET TRUMAN

RANDOM HOUSE NEW YORK

"Trees, though they are cut and lopped, grow up again quickly, but if men are destroyed, it is not easy to replace them."

—PERICLES

MURDER in the HOUSE

PROLOGUE

"The chaplain will offer the prayer."

"We ask you, the creator of all men and institutions, to generously dispense this day the wisdom and courage necessary to do the nation's business. And we seek your divine counsel in order that we may govern wisely, and with compassion. Amen."

The Speaker pro tem, named by the Speaker to rule that day over the House of Representatives, next announced, "The gentlelady from Florida will lead us in the pledge."

Two dozen right hands pressed against two dozen bosoms as the Pledge of Allegiance was spoken. Few members attended opening ceremonies. The first vote of the day would bring the rest running from their offices across the street.

The day's Speaker brought down the gavel sharply: "The Chair will entertain morning-hour speeches. For what purpose does the gentleman from Oregon seek recognition?"

"To address the House for one minute, and to revise and extend my remarks."

"Without objection. The gentleman is recognized for one minute."

The representative from Oregon stepped to "the well"—a podium and microphone on his side of the aisle; the other political party had its own well—and spent his allotted sixty seconds praising the University of Oregon's baseball team for having won the state's collegiate championship. Other speakers would follow, taking advantage of morning hours, during which any of the 435 members of the House were free to speak for a minute on any subject, even baseball.

Later, more serious debate would take place, with each side having an hour to present its speakers' views on a pending bill that would, if passed, strengthen environmental laws. Not that the debate would change anyone's mind. Each member's vote on the legislation had been determined days ago, along strict party lines. But emoting with passion on one side of the issue or the other played well back home, especially now that C-SPAN carried the business of the House of Representatives into millions of homes across America.

The visitors gallery contained a hundred or so people watching the proceedings in person. They included Jack Marx, retired from a large insurance company and a Republican, and his friend and neighbor Oliver Jones, a retired schoolteacher and lifelong Democrat. They'd traveled to Washington, D.C., from North Carolina with their wives, and had obtained passes to the House chamber from their congressman.

They left after an hour and went downstairs, where they hooked up with a tour group. Eventually, they wandered outside and sat on a small bench in a pocket park, a few hundred feet from the Capitol Building.

"Whew!" Marx said, wiping sweat from his brow and lowering his large camcorder to the grass. "Some hot. Hot air."

"Inside," his friend Jones said, laughing.

"Yeah. They're all full of hot air."

"But they eventually get things done."

"If it suits some lobbyist, some big-money contributor," said Marx. "I don't trust any of 'em."

"Push for term limits. Write a letter to the editor."

"Lot of good that would do. Jesus, Ollie, how can you watch those guys on C-SPAN all the time?"

"Keeps him busy," Diane Jones answered for him. "Out of my hair since he retired."

"Amen," Roberta Marx chimed in.

"All they do is talk," Marx said.

"Just some of them. Notice how few were there?"

"Yeah."

"Most of them work behind the scenes. Work hard," Jones said. "There's that small group who spend all their time on the floor making speeches. Same ones every day."

"Blowhards."

Oliver Jones laughed, slapped his friend and neighbor on the back. "You'd agree with Mark Twain," he said.

"I liked him."

"Mark Twain? You know what *he* said about Congress."

"What did he say?"

"Something like 'There's no distinctively native American criminal class, except Congress.' "

"I always liked him."

"Ready to go?" Roberta asked.

"The House really does represent us. America," her husband said as he picked up his camcorder and slung it over his shoulder. "Think about it. Four hundred thirty-five men and women. We send them up here to make decisions."

They slowly walked in the direction of their hotel.

"Good guys, bad guys," Jones continued. "Drunks and womanizers, religious zealots and do-gooders. Black and white. Hispanic. Men and women. Wife beaters and devoted husbands. Left wing, right wing. Middle-grounders. America."

Marx pondered his friend's comment.

"And I'll tell you one thing," Jones said as they waited for a traffic light to change.

"What's that?" his wife said.

"As dumb as the system seems sometimes, there's no better one on earth. Ask any Russian about that."

CHAPTER ONE

MOSCOW—EARLY SEPTEMBER

It was a sour morning.

Yvgeny Fodorov, naked, looked through his crusted apartment window to the British Embassy across *Ulitsa Solyanka*, near where Moscow's infamous *Khitrov* meat market had once festered.

He tasted bile; his eyes, open only a few minutes, itched. His fingers went to them, rubbing. A headache pounded at his temples, causing him to place his fingertips against them as though it would help.

A trim young woman dressed in a navy suit and red high heels entered the embassy. He'd seen her before, an employee, certainly British. She showed her pass to the guard and disappeared inside.

The kettle whistled from the pullman kitchen at the other end of the long, narrow room that had been his home for six months. He made tea, sliced two pieces from a loaf of black bread bought the day before at his local *khleb,* one of a chain of recently privatized bread stores, and made a sandwich of tongue and tomato.

After slipping into a pair of stained white gym shorts and eating his sandwich, he returned to the window, teacup in hand. The sun was rising like a hot orange; the city's pollution, now visible in daylight, blanketed everything, gauze over the lens through which Yvgeny observed the city of his birth that morning.

People came and went on the street below his window. He sat on a rickety wooden chair and watched them impassively, the raising of the cup to his thin lips his only motion. But his thoughts were on last night. Not pleasant thoughts.

Considering the importance of this day, he was stupid to have stayed out half the night. Too much vodka. The incessant beat and blare of the rock music, so loud it hurt. And then the argument with Sofia to top off the night. He'd wanted to be alone with her, discuss things, bring her back to his apartment to make love.

But she wanted to be with her friends, damn them. How he detested their arrogant, trendy ways, so influenced by the rush of Western values and styles since the collapse of the Soviet Union, vapid creatures whose only interests were clothes and dancing and drugs. He'd put up with them for most of the evening at Night Flight, one of Moscow's many discos.

At two in the morning—or was it three?—he'd tried to convince Sofia to leave with him. She'd just laughed, and continued gyrating on the dance floor. The others laughed, too. "The night is just starting," one said.

He hadn't planned to hit her. But the rage had been building inside all night as she and her friends taunted him. "Don't be such an old man," one had said. "Loosen up, Yvgeny. Smile. You look like you sucked on a lemon." More laughter. And then Sofia came to where he stood at the edge of the dance floor, tossed a hip in his direction, held her face inches from his, and said, mirth in her voice, "What are you, Yvgeny? An *apparatchik*? *B-o-r-i-n-g!*"

He'd lashed out with his fist, bloodying her lip and knocking her to the floor. She'd scrambled away from him on all fours, screaming, cursing so loud her voice was heard above the music, dancers tripping over her.

Fearing an attack from Sofia's male friends, Yvgeny ran from the club and went home, where he sat shaking and finishing what was left of a bottle of vodka, hearing their jibes over and over: "Apparatchik?" Yes, and proud to be. What were their loyalties? To decadence. Softness. Wasted, narcissistic lives.

His continued commitment to the Communism that had been pushed aside by Yeltsin and other so-called reformers was a source of pride. It had been since he was a teenager, enthusiastically joining *Komsomol*, the youth movement of the Communist Party, in which the drinking of large amounts of vodka proved one's comradeship, and by extension political unity. That wasn't long ago; Yvgeny was only twenty-two.

Yvgeny Fodorov had volunteered in Gennady Zyuganov's campaign for president, and shared with his fellow believers the bitter disappointment of losing to the fat fool, Yeltsin.

"There will be another day for us," Zyuganov had said to a rally of campaign workers following his defeat. And he repeated what he had written in his book, *Beyond the Horizon*, which Yvgeny had read so many times he'd virtually committed it to memory: "Capitalism does not fit the flesh and blood, the customs of the psychology of our society. Once already it caused a civil war. It is not taking root now, and it will never take root."

Yvgeny was determined that Zyuganov's words would hold true. Communism had made the Soviet Union a great power. Capitalism had destroyed it, turned it into an impotent Third World nation adrift without moral compass or dedication to a common, shining goal.

He finished his tea and lifted weights, observing his efforts in a mirror. He'd always been ashamed of his thin, pale, undefined body and the thick glasses he was forced to wear. But since beginning his exercise regimen four months ago, there had been a discernible hardening of his arms and stomach. At least it looked that way to him in the glass. The stale hot air in the apartment caused sweat to run freely down his face, chest, and back. He added an extra weight to each side of the dumbbell, resumed his prone position on the bench, and struggled to lift it. He managed to do it once, lowered it into its stand, got up breathing hard, and posed for the mirror, the way bodybuilders posture during their competitions. He knew he would look funny to others. But in his eyes, his efforts were succeeding. He was readying himself for the great tests he'd been called upon to face.

Beginning today.

An hour later, after a bath, and dressed in his favorite outfit—black suit, pearl-gray shirt, black tie and shoes—Yvgeny Fodorov walked to where he'd parked his battered Lada around the corner, on *Ulitsa Varvarka*. He settled in the driver's seat, pulled a 9-mm semiautomatic pistol from the waistband of his trousers, and placed it on top of a large wrapped package in a thick red shopping bag. Reflecting sunglasses were taken from the glove box and placed on his small nose, the positioning of them carefully checked in the rearview mirror.

The engine came to life with a series of coughs. Yvgeny pulled from the curb, cutting off a Mercedes speeding down *Ulitsa Varvarka*. Its driver, who was speaking on the car phone, leaned on his horn and cursed loudly out the window. Yvgeny placed his right hand on the revolver and smiled. "Go ahead. Make my day," he muttered in English. He'd learned the words from the American actor Clint Eastwood, who'd spoken them in a *Dirty Harry* movie Yvgeny had seen with Sofia. His aversion to all things American didn't extend to the imported gangster and cop movies proliferating in Moscow theaters.

He'd managed to displace his anger of the previous evening by focusing on the day ahead. But as he drove through Moscow, swerving to avoid gaping potholes or to give way to large red-and-white buses, it returned, as it did with regularity these days. Everything he saw caused his belly to churn and his throat to burn. Gone was the Soviet red flag with hammer and sickle, which had once flown proudly over the city, replaced by the Russian red, white, and blue tricolor.

He passed American fast-food outlets with long lines of customers, gaudy billboards touting American products and services, men on every corner holding cell phones to their ears. A traffic light stopped him in front of G.U.M., the department store, which had recently extended its hours to accommodate more of the fashionably dressed women passing through its doors. At another corner, a knot of teenagers, ears pierced, hair colored purple and orange and green, stood in defiant postures, openly smoking marijuana and making fun of passersby.

Yvgeny's anger elevated to fury; he wanted to get out with his gun and blow them away.

As he reached Moscow's northern outskirts and the Yaroslavl Highway, the city's oppressive, humid heat was gradually replaced by cooler air coming through the Lada's open windows. Traffic thinned. His anger abated, replaced by a growing anxiety that caused him to roll his fingertips on the steering wheel, and to hum the melody of an old Stalin-era song, "My Motherland Spreads Far and Wide," over and over.

He'd been driving more than an hour when the cathedral domes of Zagorsk, also known by its pre-revolutionary name of Sergiev, told him he was close to his destination. Once the center of Russian Orthodoxy, Zagorsk still drew thousands of the faithful each year, bearing bottles to fill with holy water.

Yvgeny slowed as he passed a procession of black-shrouded women shuffling slowly along the highway's shoulder. Old fools, he thought. That was the problem with the Communist Party. There were too many old people at its core, feeble, ineffective old people. That was why Yvgeny knew he was important to the party. It needed dedicated youth like him, willing to do whatever was needed to set the nation back on the right track.

He turned onto a crumbling asphalt road and slowed to spare his aging car's shocks and tires. Ten minutes later he left that road to take a narrow dirt lane running through farmland until ending at a river. He stopped beneath a clump of trees and turned off the engine, lit a cigarette, and fixed his eyes on a small cottage at the river's edge. The air was cool and moist. The sound of singing birds merged with the gentle rippling of the water.

He sat there for five minutes, finishing two cigarettes, which he tossed through the open window. If she was watching, she'd probably criticize him for littering the land near her house. If not for that, for something else.

He exited the Lada and stretched against a dull ache in his back. The Lada was no fun to drive for long periods. But that would soon end. He'd been promised. Hopefully a Zhiguli. Red, if he had his say.

After a few deep breaths, Yvgeny opened the passenger door and removed the shopping bag. His back to the cottage, he slipped the weapon into his waistband, secured his jacket over it, and slowly walked to the front door. He peered through the screen, saw no one. He knocked on the door frame. *"Zdrastvuitye?* Mother? Hello?"

He saw her shadow before she came into view. She opened the door, stood back, hand on hip, head cocked, small smile on her lips: "Well, well, look who's here."

"Hello, Mother. I said I was coming."

"That's right. You did. Sorry. Come in. You'll have to excuse the mess. I was working all night. This morning, too." She stepped back to allow him entry.

Yvgeny entered the large, spare room that served as living room, dining room, and kitchen. There were few windows, and no lights were on. It was cool inside, and still.

Vani Fodorov went to the kitchen and busied herself at the sink. Yvgeny stood in the center of the room, unsure of where to move next. She turned. "How have you been?" she asked, wiping her hands on a towel.

"Good. Fine. You?"

"Working hard. I'm finishing a novel."

"Oh?"

"Perhaps you'd like to read it when I'm done."

He didn't respond. Instead, he put the shopping bag down next to a chair and went to an open door at the opposite end of the room. It was his mother's office. A computer screen glowed blue. The desk was piled high with books, some open, some closed. Others were on the floor, surrounding a green office chair. Free-standing bookcases sagged under the weight of the volumes they contained. One wall featured framed photographs.

"Go ahead." His mother had come up behind; the closeness of her voice startled him. "Afraid to enter my capitalistic den?" She laughed.

Yvgeny faced her. "I'm not afraid—of anything."

"Of course not. Look at the photos on the wall. They're some of your favorite people." Her tone was sarcastic.

Yvgeny pushed past his mother into the living room, her laughter following. Then, silence. She came to him and placed her hands on his arms, looked into his eyes. "Yvgeny, Yvgeny, poor Yvgeny. Don't you understand the wonderful thing that has happened to us? We're free now, Yvgeny. Free."

"Free to do what?" he said.

"Free to—"

"Free to starve? Free to let the Americans and the British and all the rich bastards of the world own us? You call that freedom?"

"Yes, I do," Vani said. "You don't remember what it was like under Stalin and Lenin, under the Communists. Your father was arrested and sent to the camps because they didn't like what he wrote. I had to write in secret, with pencil and paper because they refused to register my typewriter and took it away. Don't you see? We're free to be who we are and what we wish to be. You're young, Yvgeny. There is now such promise in Russia for young people."

He guffawed and pulled away.

"Communism is over, Yvgeny. It is finished. Gone. Things are hard because we've never experienced freedom and capitalism. But in time—"

"Capitalism does not fit the flesh and blood, the customs of the psychology of our society, Mother. Once already it caused a civil war. It is not taking root now, and it will never take root."

"Good God," she said, leaning against a table. "You're still spouting that garbage. And look at you. The way you dress. You want to be a Communist? Dress like one, like a Communist peasant content to work for the State. What are you, a gangster now? That suit. Is that what you take from our new freedom, to join a gang? To be a criminal?"

Yvgeny turned from her and clenched his fists, breathed against the heaviness in his chest. He couldn't look at her. She was dressed in a thin white T-shirt; no bra kept her nipples from pressing against the fabric. Her jeans were tight over her lithe figure, American designer jeans with the name on them. She didn't look Russian. She looked to him like some French trollop or American prostitute.

Writing a novel! he thought.

Trash, undoubtedly. Like the articles she and her friends wrote for rags like *Moskovskiy Komsomolets* and *Nezavisimaya Gazeta*. She had such pretensions about her writing. Vani Fodorov idolized the iconoclast Soviet writer Ivan Turgenev, who'd indicted serfdom in his writings and was banished to exile in Europe as a result. Yvgeny's father, also a writer, preferred the writings of Gogol; as a child, Yvgeny sat through nightly dinner table debates of the relative merits of those writers and others.

Yvgeny was a young boy when they took his father away. He didn't understand it then—something about having written things that were illegal. He never saw him again. From the moment his mother told him his father had died, less than a year after he'd been arrested, everything about Vani Fodorov changed in Yvgeny's eyes. New friends seemed always to be at their Moscow flat, secretive people drinking all night and talking in hushed voices, most of them members of the Soviet Writers' Union, of which his mother was an active, enthusiastic member. Some became her lovers, the sounds of their copulating causing him to hold the pillow over his ears.

When the painful process of *perestroika*, the restructuring of the Soviet Communist system, commenced in 1988 under Gorbachev—and *glasnost* followed, allowing free discussion of all issues without fear of State reprisal—Yvgeny again saw his mother change. He was fourteen, a sullen, angry teenager who viewed his now gay and vibrant mother as the cause of all his problems, his lack of friends, slowness in school, and wan, sickly looks.

It was as though she'd been reborn and he had begun his death spiral. They fought. He dropped out of school and stayed away from home for days at a time.

On his seventeenth birthday, Vani confronted him with an ultimatum: either he change his ways and begin to build his life, or he could live elsewhere.

Yvgeny moved in with an older friend, Felix, who shared his views of what was happening all around them in Moscow. Felix earned money by running errands for local mobsters, who promised he would move up in the ranks one day. He introduced Yvgeny to his employers, and they gave him chores to do.

Yvgeny rarely saw his mother during the ensuing five years. She kept the apartment in Moscow, but bought the *dacha* in Zagorsk, where she spent most of her time, returning to the city only when the winter became too foul to enjoy the countryside.

This visit represented the first time they'd seen each other in almost a year. Vani had been surprised when Yvgeny called to say he intended to visit. Had she been totally honest, she would have said that she did not want to see her only child. His involvement with the burgeoning criminal element of Moscow—of every Russian city—disgusted her.

Still, he was flesh and blood. Was he coming to Zagorsk to announce a change of heart, to tell her that he realized the error of his ways and intended to set a new course in his life before it was too late?

"I would love to see you, Yvgeny," she'd said. "Yes. I look forward to it very much."

And now here he was, as defiant as ever, dressed in his silly black suit and mouthing tired Communist clichés.

"Yvgeny," his mother said, "why did you come here today? Would you like to have lunch and talk about pleasant things? You can tell me about what you've been doing with your life. I'll tell you about my novel, what it's about and why I have such high hopes for it." Her laugh was forced. "I suppose you won't agree with its . . . politics . . . but there's much more to it than that. It really isn't a political novel, although there is some. Yvgeny, I would like this to be a happy visit. I haven't seen you in too long a time. You look well. I must admit I do not like that sort of suit, but it's your choice. You are an adult. I've met someone. He's an artist, a very good one." When he said nothing, she added, "I mean I've met someone I'm falling in love with. His name is—"

"I brought you a present," Yvgeny said.

"Oh?" She looked to the red shopping bag on the floor. "Is that it? May I open it?"

"Da."

She removed the wrapped gift from the bag and took it to the kitchen, where she slowly began to undo the green ribbon, out of habit not wanting to cut it, to save it for another day. As she did, her back to him, she said, "It was sweet of you to bring me a gift. I think, Yvgeny, this might be the day we put our lives together again. I mean, as mother and son.

There's so much I want to share with you. I was thinking just this morning that you come from the blood of two writers. You showed writing promise in school. I wish you hadn't dropped out, but it isn't too late to go back."

She was as careful and deliberate with the wrapping paper as she had been with the ribbon.

"What would you think if I suggested that we—?"

Her fingers stopped peeling the tape from the wrapping. She sensed that he'd come up behind her, that something was wrong.

She started to turn but never had the opportunity. Yvgeny touched the 9-mm to the base of her skull and pulled the trigger, causing Vani Fodorov's head to erupt in an explosion of blood the color of cardinals.

CHAPTER TWO

WASHINGTON, D.C.—A FEW DAYS LATER

"I don't care what the Chinese ambassador said, Sandy. The fact is they're trying to do an end-run around the treaty and I'll be damned if they'll get away with it. Put it in the strongest possible terms at the press briefing. Put it in Chinese if you have to. . . . What? You don't speak Chinese? I suggest you remedy that as soon as possible. . . . Sure. Thanks. Check in with me after the briefing."

Joseph Scott hung up on his press secretary and pushed a button on the intercom. "Is Congressman Latham here yet? . . . Good. Send him in."

An aide opened the door, and United States Representative Paul Latham strode into the Oval Office. Scott got to his feet and came around the desk to greet him. "Welcome back, Congressman."

"Thank you, Mr. President."

The two men were tall, but that was where physical similarities ended. Joe Scott was a strong, beefy man, six feet five inches tall and solidly built, with brown hair tinged with red and just the right touch of gray at the temples. Everything was oversized about him; people on the receiving end of his handshakes often commented on the size of his hands.

Paul Latham was six feet tall, but slender in body and face. Although both men needed glasses to read, the president was reluctant to wear them, especially when in public or facing a camera. Latham's half-glasses were perpetually perched at the end of his aquiline nose. "Professorial" was the term often used by the press to describe him, causing him to laugh and say, "If that's true, anybody wearing glasses would automatically be smart. And we all know that's a crock." He looked more professorial than he sometimes spoke.

"Sit down," Scott said, settling into his leather chair and indicating the seat he wanted Latham to take. "Coffee?"

"No, thank you," Latham replied. "It might keep me awake."

"We can't have that. So, Congressman, how did things look to you on your latest jaunt to the riddle wrapped in a mystery inside an enigma?"

"Pretty much as Winnie said it, Mr. President. The Russians may have officially opened up to the rest of the world, but that doesn't translate into letting it all hang out. Depends on who you talk to. Yeltsin's people say everything is fine. But our intelligence people at the embassy have a different take."

"I spoke to Yeltsin last night," the president said. "He sounded drunk."

"He doesn't drink anymore since the surgery."

"According to the press releases. How's Ruth?"

"Fine. Mrs. Scott?"

"Complaining that the White House is aging her prematurely. Other than that, she's top-notch. Always asks for you."

The president of the United States and the California congressman went back a long way together. Both Democrats, although not always in agreement, they'd been through the political mill. That Joe Scott would one day run for and win the presidency was never a surprise to his friend. He had a bigger-than-life quality about him, star power that drew people to him, made them want to touch him, lose their hand in his, be the recipient of his engaging smile and fast, firm slap on the back. Paul Latham, eight terms in Congress and going for his ninth, had backed Scott at every step of his rise from Chicago ward politics to the House of Representatives, then on to the Senate and finally, firm possession of the White House.

Latham had been especially helpful a year ago when Scott ran for the presidency. The towering Joe Scott was known as a domestic candidate, comfortable and effective with issues at home, but lacking experience—lacking understanding, according to his opponent—of foreign affairs. Latham's leadership as chairman of the House International Relations Committee, and his special interest in that committee's Subcommittee on Economic Policy and Trade—coupled with his being in the enviable position of having Scott's ear—helped balance the voters' perception of the man who would become president.

Naturally, there was speculation that Scott would nominate Paul Latham as his secretary of state. But once Scott became president, there were other debts to be paid. The nomination went instead to the distinguished international attorney Jacob Baumann, who was easily confirmed by the Senate, and who'd done so far what most Washington pundits felt was a credible job.

What most people didn't know was that President Scott had approached Latham first about the job, and that Latham had politely declined. The odd fact was that Paul Latham loved his position in the House of Representatives. Chairing a committee as important as International Relations, with the particular emphasis he placed upon economic policy and trade, was immensely fulfilling to the former college professor, attorney, and think-tank advisor.

"I appreciate the confidence behind the offer, Joe," he'd said, "but it's not for me. Go with Baumann. He's a good man, will sail through confirmation and do the job for you."

That was the last time he'd called his old friend "Joe." From that moment on it was "Mr. President," even when they shared quiet moments together and the president suggested Latham drop the formality. Formality, ritual, and precedence were important to the congressman from California.

"So, Mr. Chairman, tell me about your trip," the president said.

Latham pulled a sheet of paper from the inside breast pocket of his conservatively cut blue suit and consulted it while giving the president a thumbnail report, ending with "The single thing I found most disturbing, Mr. President, was what our intelligence people told me at a briefing just before I left. It's their opinion that an unholy alliance is being forged between the Communists and the *mafiya.* All those out of work KGB types are becoming Russian mobsters. The ranks are swelling."

Scott's eyebrows went up. "Why would the Communists and the blackbread mob join hands, for Christ's sake?"

A small shrug from Latham. "Desperation. The Communists are becoming increasingly desperate while Yeltsin bullies the economy into some semblance of success. He may be the duly elected leader of Russia, but he runs things like he was still a Communist bureaucrat. A few embassy people feel there's a calculated reason for the Russian mob to hook up with the Communists. Here it is: Yeltsin's biggest problem is crime.

You can't do business there without paying off some goon or gang. They call it *krisha.* 'Cover.' Built into the budget like rent and paper clips. The more crime, goes the theory, the harder for Yeltsin to make things work. The bigger he fails and the worse off people become, the better the chances for the Communists in the next election."

Scott grunted. "You buy the theory?"

"It's as good as any I've heard lately."

"The FBI's East European unit briefed Justice a couple of days ago. Here's a synopsis." He slid it across the desk to Latham.

"Can I take this?"

"Sure. Anything devious going on over on the Hill I should brace for?"

Latham smiled. "I'm sure there is, Mr. President, but I haven't been back long enough to tap in. If there is, you'll be the first to know, as usual."

"Glad you're back, Paul. Staying in town a few days?"

"Exactly. Just a few. I'll be heading back home for the election."

"If you need anything, let me know."

"Things are good there," Latham said, standing.

His district in Northern California, which included a large area of San Francisco, was known as one of the more solid districts in Congress. There had been an occasional threat to his reelection over the years, but nothing to cause him sleepless nights. Still, you couldn't take anything for granted. The voters wanted to see you on your home turf, press the flesh, hear your answers at town hall meetings and on TV debates with your opponent. Local issues. That was what it was all about. The minute you lost sight of it, you lost elections. Paul Latham believed in what President Harry Truman once said about running for office: "When there's a hundred people applauding you, look for the one who isn't, and find out why."

"Thanks for seeing me, Mr. President," Latham said. "You're looking good. Rested."

Scott laughed and came to where Latham stood. "I wish I could say the same to you. You look like you need two days of sleep."

"As usual, you're right. I—"

The door opened, causing Scott to scowl at the intruder. It was a senior aide. "What is it?" the president asked.

"Sir, this just came in. It's . . . very important." He crossed the room and handed Scott a piece of paper.

The president frowned as he read it, lowered his head, and mumbled an obscenity.

"Mr. President?" Latham said.

"Thank you," Scott said to the aide. "I want the crisis group together in a half hour. Fifteen minutes. Get Sandy in here now!"

The aide left the Oval Office. "From Hopkins in Ops," Scott said, handing the paper to Paul Latham. He read its terse message: URGENT. AIR FORCE AIRCRAFT CARRYING SECRETARY BAUMANN AND GROUP REPORTED DOWN IN CHINA. CAUSE UNKNOWN. INITIAL REPORT NO SURVIVORS.

CHAPTER THREE

THE NATIONAL CATHEDRAL—FIVE DAYS LATER

Secretary of State Jacob Baumann's funeral was held in the cathedral's tenth-of-a-mile-long nave. It was attended by six hundred people, two dozen of whom eulogized him.

The religious portion of the service was conducted by the Right Reverend George St. James, bishop of Washington and dean of the cathedral, imposing in his purple, black, and white clerical garments, a pectoral cross resting comfortably on his chest. St. James spoke directly to God on behalf of Baumann's soul.

Those who stepped forward wearing secular attire directed their flowery comments to Baumann's family, friends, and to the television cameras and sizable press contingent among the mourners. In Washington, D.C., you grabbed your photo ops where you found them.

Members of President Joe Scott's cabinet spoke, as did leaders of the House and Senate, and close personal friends of the deceased secretary.

"Go in peace," St. James said, sending the temporarily bereaved out of the cathedral and back to their busy lives. Baumann would be buried in the presence of a small group of people, immediate family and specially invited friends, which included Congressman Paul Latham and his wife, Ruth, a short, trim, neat brunette with well-turned calves, testimony to her pre-Latham life as a dancer. It was virtually impossible for her to wear anything that didn't look good on her.

Baumann's body was lowered into the ground with appropriate ceremony. The honored few left the gravesite and walked across the peaceful, verdant cemetery to waiting limos. Baumann's wife, Patricia, guided Latham away from the group.

"Anything I can do, just call," Latham said.

"I know that, Paul. You've been a good friend."

"There'll be hearings into the crash," he said, seeking words of encouragement to offer. "I thought after Ron Brown died, the air force would get its act together and upgrade the navigational equipment on its planes. It's been over four years now. It's just not happening fast enough. If Jake's death has any meaning, it will prompt them to—"

"Paul," Patricia Baumann said, hand on his arm, "I know that. What I wanted to say was that if the president asks you to replace Jake as secretary of state, I hope you'll accept. It's what he would have wanted."

"The president hasn't offered anything, Pat."

"But he will. That's what I hear. All I ask is that if he does, you seriously consider it. For Jake. Please?"

"I will."

"So much good has been initiated by the Scott administration. It would be a tragedy if that work isn't carried forward."

"I understand. I'll keep in touch."

"I know you will, Paul. Thanks."

They hugged, and climbed into their respective limousines.

"Are you going back to the Hill?" Ruth Latham asked her husband as they headed for Washington.

"Yes. I have a committee hearing at one. I'll be late tonight. Two fundraisers to drop in on, and that reception for Giles Broadhurst."

"When does the president get back from the G-Seven meeting?"

"Tonight. He hated to miss Jake's service. I'm glad the veep was there."

"Will you have a chance to speak with the president tonight about—?"

"I don't think so." Latham visually confirmed that the partition between the driver and passenger compartments was closed. He whispered to his wife, "I promise, Ruth, I won't make a decision about the nomination until we've had a good long stretch of time to discuss it. I won't do anything without your support."

"I know." She managed a small smile and gripped his hand. "We'll talk."

Congressman Latham's administrative office was in the Rayburn House Office Building, south of the Capitol Building at Independence and First

Street, N.W., built in 1965, the newest of three buildings accommodating the offices of the 435 elected members of the House of Representatives. Shortly after its completion, *New York Times* architectural critic, Ada Louise Huxtable, described it as "profligate, elephantine . . . the apotheosis of humdrum," concluding her review with "to be both dull and vulgar may be an achievement of sorts."

Paul Latham usually agreed when friends commented negatively about the building's jumble of columns, pediments, cornucopias, and other marble overkill. But the Rayburn Building, named after famed Texas House Speaker Sam Rayburn—whose statue greeted you when you came through the main entrance—provided the most modern facilities of the three buildings. The statue of Rayburn had originally been installed with its back to the entrance, perhaps to mirror the former Speaker's disdain for ostentatious, expensive, and complicated architecture. (The Rayburn Building was one of the most costly public buildings ever constructed in the nation's capitol.) But enough people complained about the deceased Speaker's apparent rudeness, and he was turned.

Because Latham had sufficient seniority, he enjoyed one of the building's 169 suites, giving him and his staff room in which to function. His suite was situated on the north side of the building, its splendid view of the Capitol more than making up for the suite's drab, tan walls, the color of all offices on the north and west sides of the building. East- and south-side offices were painted robin's egg blue. It was the rule. Why? No one knew. The Congressional Building Committee operated behind closed doors, answering to no one.

"How was the funeral?" Bob Mondrian asked as he followed his boss into the imposing office.

"Tough," Latham replied. He tossed his jacket on a leather couch and, standing, scanned papers neatly arranged on his desk. Mondrian hung the jacket on an antique coat tree.

"What's this?" Latham asked, holding up a sheet of paper.

Mondrian came around the desk and looked over Latham's shoulder. "Jack Emerson brought it over this morning," he said. Emerson was staff director of the International Relations Committee, chaired by Paul Latham.

"Where did *he* get it?" Latham asked.

"Kelley at Ops and Rights." International Operations and Human Rights was one of five subcommittees under control of the full committee.

Latham sat heavily and directed a stream of air through pursed lips. "The Commies won't give it up, will they?" he said.

"If the analysis is correct," Mondrian said.

Robert Mondrian had been Latham's chief of staff for twelve years. He was considered by other congressional staffers to be one of the best in the House, bright and insightful, hard-nosed when necessary, conciliatory at other times, and fiercely loyal to his boss, one of the most powerful members of Congress because of his chairmanship of the International Relations Committee.

Mondrian was divorced, his marriage a casualty of the often insane demands of the job. The father of two teenage daughters, he was a short, squat, swarthy man who'd suffered male pattern baldness at an early age, and did nothing to compensate for it. His square build rendered suits shapeless; he never took offense at jibes by fellow staffers that he'd been voted worst-dressed by a nonpartisan House panel.

Prior to joining Latham as chief of staff, Mondrian had worked for the Export-Import Bank in its international business development division, and had put in six years as a Washington lobbyist. He'd been around, and knew how to get things done on the Hill. More important, he knew how to keep them from happening. And he was fully aware of his importance to the legislative process. Every survey of Washington lobbyists confirmed that their number-one target was always congressional staff members, so potent was their input into their elected bosses' decisions.

Latham's appointment secretary, Marge Edwards, entered the office. "Good morning, Paul," she said, handing him his schedule for the rest of the day. Latham glanced at it. "How did this Asian-American group get on the slate?" he asked.

Mondrian answered: "Just five minutes, Paul. A quick give-and-take, a shot or two, they're gone. They carry a lot of weight back home—in California."

"All right." He looked at the antique grandfather clock, a gift many years ago from his mother-in-law. One o'clock. He was due at his committee meeting.

They turned their attention to side-by-side color TV sets. One was tuned to C-SPAN 1, offering gavel-to-gavel coverage of the House of Representatives. The other, C-SPAN 2, carried debate from the Senate. Mondrian turned down the sound on the House, and boosted volume on C-SPAN 2. Republican Senate minority whip Frank Connors, a three-term senator from Southern California, had stepped into the well: "It is no secret to any of my colleagues in this body, on both sides of the aisle, that while my personal admiration and respect for Jacob Baumann was great, my view of this administration's foreign policy, as carried out by the secretary of state, was not as generous. The president will soon nominate someone to replace Jake Baumann. I take this opportunity to extend my sincerest sympathy to Secretary Baumann's fine family—and to put the White House on notice that the soft policy generously granted our enemies in this volatile world will not be allowed to be repeated. . . ."

"Great timing," Mondrian said. "Baumann isn't even cold."

"The meeting," Marge said. As she left the office, both men cast admiring glances at her nicely turned body, and long, shapely legs extending from a black leather miniskirt.

Latham grabbed his jacket from the coat tree and headed for the door, saying over his shoulder, "Get me a list of who'll be at Broadhurst's reception tonight. And check up on Molly, see if she moved into the page dorm. She was supposed to this afternoon." Molly, the Lathams' youngest daughter, had been accepted as a House page for that session of Congress. Because he was a prudent man, believing in protocol, he'd asked another member, close to the House leadership, to arrange for Molly's appointment. In return, that member's son was granted an internship on Latham's International Relations Committee. *Entre nous.* The way of the House.

He went to the Rayburn Building's basement, where the subway connected all House and Senate office buildings, and with the Capitol itself. He was the only elected representative in the open car, sharing it with a dozen tourists. A woman recognized him: "You're Congressman Latham."

Latham grinned, said, "For better or worse. Enjoying your visit to D.C.?"

"Sure are," her husband replied, " 'cept for the heat. Hottest damn place I've ever been."

The short ride ended and Latham bounded off, papers under his arm, a farewell wave for his fellow passengers. A few minutes later he came through the door of H 139, on the southwest corner of the Capitol's ground floor in a cluster of House committee offices. Jack Emerson was waiting.

"Sorry I'm late," Latham said. "The funeral."

"Everybody seems to be running late today," Emerson replied. He was a veteran of House and Senate committee staffs, minority or majority, depending on which party dominated Congress during any given period. Latham knew he'd hired a top staff director in Emerson; the young man's reputation was pristine.

"Did Bob give you that report from Russia?"

"Yes. I have it with me. It's shocking—if true. Is it? True?"

"No reason not to think so," Emerson answered. "The four murders happened, Mr. Chairman. That's fact. All four were members of the old Soviet Writers' Union. Still exists, different name—Russian Writers' Union."

"All of them shot?"

"Execution style, according to the report."

"Why the assumption it was the Communists? Sounds more like the mob. I don't recognize any of these names, Jack."

"No reason you should, Mr. Chairman. None of the four were widely published. Wannabe writers, I suppose. Mr. Stassi wants to hold hearings on it."

Congressman Mario Stassi, a Republican, was the ranking minority member of both the International Operations and Human Rights Subcommittee and Latham's International Relations Committee.

"It doesn't warrant a hearing," Latham said.

"I told Stu that," Emerson said, referring to Stassi's subcommittee staff director.

"And?"

"He says Mr. Stassi is adamant. He's talking about going to the floor to ask for a resolution calling for hearings on human rights abuse in Russia. Widen the scope, but use these four killings as the pivot."

"I'll talk to him. He still wants the tariff reduction for that manufacturer in his district. If he pushes for hearings, he can kiss that good-bye. Who are we meeting with this afternoon?"

"Mr. Brazier's advisors. They have reservations about some of the provisions the policy and trade staff want included in the bill."

"Can't staff resolve it?"

"We've tried, Mr. Chairman. I think it needs your direct input at this point. Frankly, I don't see it getting out of subcommittee without you putting on the screws."

"Are they here?"

"Yes."

"Then let's get on with it."

An hour later, Latham rode the subway back to his office. He'd no sooner arrived when Molly called.

"Hi, sweets," he said. "You get moved in all right?"

"Uh-huh."

"Sorry I couldn't help. Mom get you settled?"

"Uh-huh. Are you coming with us to the shore this weekend?"

"I can't, sweets. All tied up. But you and Mom enjoy yourself. Maybe in a few weeks when things slow down."

"I understand. I think I told you before, Dad, but I really appreciate your getting me into the page program. It'll look great on college applications."

"And it's good real-world experience. Or as close as Washington ever gets to the real world. Besides, I'll be able to see you every day."

She laughed. "So you can keep your eye on me."

"That's my job, isn't it? I'm your father."

Bob Mondrian poked his head through the open door. "The A-A group is here, Paul."

"Got to run, Molly," Latham said. "Picture time with some voters. Love you."

"Love you, Dad."

He spent fifteen minutes with his Asian-American visitors, the session ending with a photo taken on the Capitol steps. He had just settled back behind his desk when Marge Edwards appeared. "Here's the guest list for Mr. Broadhurst's reception tonight."

Latham perused it. Quickly. "Oh, Mac Smith will be there. Good. Time we scheduled a little tennis to let me get even for the last match. Nice man, wicked backhand. Probably illegal. Thanks, Marge. Everything good with you? You don't look happy."

Her lovely, full mouth broke into a smile. "Considering my love life is on hold, everything's great."

"I thought you were dating that exec from Brazier's office."

"Anatoly? I am. I mean, we go out now and then. But nothing heavy. Russian guys are strange."

Latham laughed. "They come out of a very different experience, Marge."

"I know. Which makes them strange. Hear from Martin?"

Latham's son, Martin, who now crafted wood furniture in upstate New

York, as distant geographically and philosophically from politics as he could take himself, had briefly dated Marge when she first came to work for Latham. Latham wasn't especially pleased with that arrangement, convinced that Martin had done it deliberately to nettle him. But he did nothing to get in the way of the relationship, which ended abruptly two months after it had commenced when Martin moved away. Being dumped, as Marge put it, had upset her. But she had seemed to bounce back quickly, much to Latham's relief.

"Yes, as a matter of fact. He'll be in town for a week."

"Say hello for me."

"Say hello yourself. He'll be stopping by the office."

Don't count on it, she thought. She said, "Okay. I will."

"Well," Latham said, "any time you want to vent, come on in, close the door, and let it all hang out, as they say."

"I just may do that."

"By the way, Marge—now that Molly's going to be here on the Hill every day, and I never know where I'll be, I thought you wouldn't mind keeping an eye on her. You know, sort of be the one she can come to if she has a problem, and I'm not available."

"Happy to, Paul. Don't worry about it."

Latham thought about Marge Edwards after she left.

She'd been his scheduler for almost two years. It was one of the toughest jobs on the Hill, keeping track of members' hectic days and nights, fielding requests for "just a minute of his time," and managing the office as well, juggling the $900,000 budget allotted each House member.

Most of Latham's colleagues complained about their appointment secretaries, not because they didn't do a good job; they blamed them for their busy schedules. A no-win situation was the way Latham viewed it.

Marge Edwards was good at her difficult job, and Latham knew it. He also knew firsthand how volatile she could be when under personal stress. Her emotions seemed always to be on the edge, or out in the open, and he'd ended up becoming her father-confessor on more than one occasion. He never resented that additional duty. Marge reminded him in some ways of his oldest daughter, whom he seldom saw these days.

Did Marge view *him* as a father figure? He assumed she did.

Did counseling her about her personal trials and travails, including some highly personal aspects of her life, provide him with a psychological substitution for the time he didn't have for his own daughter? Help assuage his guilt?

He hoped not.

He just wished he had more time to figure it out.

CHAPTER FOUR

Annabel Reed-Smith pulled the blue Chevy Caprice up to the curb in front of the National Democratic Club on Ivy Street, S.E. The Republican hangout on the Hill was the Capitol Hill Club on First Street, S.E. The two clubs were closer in geographic proximity than political philosophy, but Mac commented that the top-shelf liquor served in both was distinctly nonpartisan.

"How late will you be?" Annabel asked her husband.

"A few hours," Mackensie Smith said. "I'll be home before you, unless the concert drives you out early."

"Not likely. The National Symphony seldom disappoints."

Smith smiled, leaned over, and kissed his wife on the cheek. It was one of those moments that occurred for him with regularity since marrying Annabel Reed. He was immensely grateful to her for having said yes to his proposal.

They were practicing attorneys when first introduced at a British Embassy party, she specializing in matrimonial law, he one of Washington's most respected criminal lawyers.

Annabel had never married. (How could this be? Mac mused after that initial introduction, and a long, pleasant conversation over glasses of white wine.) Her face was open and lovely, framed by hair the color of burnished copper. Her five-foot-seven-inch figure was nicely proportioned. Most appealing at that first meeting was her ready, wide smile and sincere interest in everything he said. An impressive package, Mac thought at first.

No. More than that.

Annabel Reed was quite simply the most beautiful woman he'd met since losing his wife and son years ago in a Beltway head-on collision, a drunken Agriculture Department employee crossing the line to take from him everything that was good and precious.

That defining moment in his life changed Mac Smith forever. His passion for criminal law dimmed, and he began to question whether he should continue to pursue it. What would he do instead? Retire? Politics? Teach? The last became increasingly appealing.

At the time of their introduction, Annabel, too, had started to wonder whether the practice of law, especially her emotionally wrenching specialty of divorce and child custody, was worth the pain. Deciding to become a lawyer had been a pragmatic move. Prior to law school, she'd been an art major, focusing on the pre-Columbian. Launching a career in the art world as an assistant curator in some small museum—if she could even find such an entry-level job—would not, she knew, provide the material things she wanted at that stage of her life.

Law proved to be a good choice in that regard. Her practice flourished, she surrounded herself with well-chosen, lovely things, and eventually there was money in the bank for her future, no matter what it held.

But there was, at once, an emptiness inside. She suspected it could be filled only by following her dream: opening a gallery specializing in pre-Columbian art. Now that she was financially secure, that goal was certainly reachable.

After Mac and Annabel fell in love—it happened surprisingly fast, considering they were lawyers—and as their conversations dug deeper into their inner selves, their mutual dissatisfaction with their profession increasingly took center stage. One night, over succulent Maryland crab cakes at La Chaumière, they made some fateful decisions.

"I just feel that since I don't want to do it anymore," Mac said, "I can't do justice to my clients."

"Of course you can't. I feel the same way."

"What's your dream, Annabel?"

"To own a gallery. To surround myself with artifacts I love."

"Might that include *this* artifact?"

"Mackensie Smith?"

"Yes."

"Hmmmm."

"I've been offered a teaching position at GW. In the law school, of course."

"Of course."

"I don't know much about art," Mac said. "But I know even less about pre-Columbian art."

She laughed. "You don't have to know anything about it. *I* have to know about it. All you have to know is what your law students need to know."

"But I wouldn't want to appear stupid about what you do each day."

"The one thing you could never appear to be, Mackensie Smith, is stupid. About anything."

"Thanks for the vote of confidence."

"It isn't that. I believe that if two people are satisfied with their individual lives, they stand a better chance of being satisfied in their relationship."

"No argument. But you're leaving the law. I'll still be involved with it. Granted, as a teacher, not an advocate. But your life will revolve around art, and I'll—"

"Mac, I think what we each do with the rest of our lives doesn't mean a damn thing, as long as we respect what it is that each of us does."

"I can be cantankerous."

"I can be difficult. But adorable."

"The older I get, the more liberal I become despite knowing I'm supposed to become more conservative because I have more to conserve."

"And?"

"And, I become more accepting of the human condition with each passing year."

"I like that."

"Annabel."

"Yes, Mackensie?"

"Would you consider a contract? Would you consider marrying me?"

"Be more direct."

"More direct? All right. *Will* you marry me?"

"Of course."

"Why?"

She sat back and laughed. " *Why?* You sound like you're back in the courtroom. *Why?* Because I love you, about-to-be former counselor and soon-to-be distinguished professor of law at George Washington University, pipe, bow tie, and all, I assume. I love the image."

"You're beautiful, Annabel."

"Thank you. You're handsome."

"Thank you. Let's do it. You open your art gallery—with my enthusiastic encouragement—and I'll become a mentor of future Supreme Court justices."

"It's a deal." They shook hands across the table.

"And we'll be married. Soon."

"Of course."

"Of course."

Annabel watched her husband enter the building and experienced her own twinge of gratitude. Although Mac was decisive and self-assured, he moved his angular, fit, and lanky frame with appealing modesty. Entering a room on his arm was always a pleasure.

She pulled away from the curb and headed for a night of Mozart, Haydn, and Bruckner at the Kennedy Center. But she was on his mind as Mac came through the door of the National Democratic Club and went to the third-floor O'Neill Room, "Mac, hello," Congressman Paul Latham said as he spotted his friend.

"Congressman," Smith said, shaking Latham's hand. "I see you're still spending your life on airplanes."

"Fortunately, planes with more up-to-date navigation systems than Jake Baumann's. Did you know him?"

"We shook hands a few times. Any word on who the president will nominate to replace him?"

"Your guess is as good as mine."

"I doubt that," Smith said, smiling.

Latham went to greet other arrivals, leaving Smith to make his way to where the reason for the gathering, Giles Broadhurst, talked with well-wishers. Next to Broadhurst was an attractive, big-boned blond woman in a yellow suit. She spotted Smith approaching and came directly to him, hand outstretched. "Professor Smith," she said. "I heard you were coming. How great to see you."

"Always nice to see one of my favorite students again. How have you been, Jessica?"

"Terrific. I'm coming with Giles to the CIA."

"Really? Congratulations. Life there will be a lot different than over at ITC."

At the U.S. International Trade Commission, Giles Broadhurst headed up its Office of Executive and International Liaison. He was leaving that position to establish a new division within the CIA, devoted to using the spy agency's intelligence-gathering ability to enhance America's overseas industrial competitiveness. In actuality, such a division had been in operation for years, ever since the Cold War ended. But the spy agency had recently gotten caught on two occasions doing industrial espionage, and decided it would be politic to, as Le Carré put it, come in from the cold.

"I'm braced for it," Jessica Belle said brightly.

Smith laughed. "At least you won't be spying on spies anymore. Makes sense, using our intelligence agency to help American industry—legitimately."

"That's the way Giles sees it. Me, too, of course. How's Mrs. Smith?"

"Tip-top."

She plucked a miniature quiche from a fast-moving tray, took a tiny bite, and said, "Are you still teaching the class?" She'd been a nonmatriculated student in a special six-session course Smith had taught on the difference between systems of jurisprudence in the United States and Russia, a recent and compelling interest of his.

"No."

"Then I was lucky I took it when I did. I learned a lot."

"Glad to hear it. That's what you were there for."

Broadhurst joined them, looking every bit the academic he was: floppy red-and-white bow tie, natural-shoulder tweed jacket despite the city's heat, modified crew cut, and horn-rimmed glasses. He was considerably shorter than Mac Smith and Jessica Belle, and had a tendency to bounce on his toes while speaking.

Jessica introduced the men.

"My pleasure," Giles Broadhurst said. "Jess says you taught her everything she knows."

"Fortunately, that's not true," Smith replied. "Congratulations on the new post. I've been reading about it, followed the House hearings pretty closely."

Broadhurst launched into a discourse on why such an economic intelligence gathering division was officially needed, and what he hoped to accomplish. His youthful enthusiasm was pleasing to Smith. This was a smart guy, Smith knew, as evidenced by what he'd crammed into his forty-five years—attorney, Ph.D. in economics, a master's in sociology. Quite a résumé.

Others gathered about Broadhurst, freeing Smith to head for the bar, where he ordered a single-barrel bourbon and soda and wandered to an unoccupied corner to enjoy it. As he sipped, he was able to observe the hundred or so people milling about the large room. What a remarkable city, he thought, politics its major industry and seemingly only topic of interest at such gatherings. Along with a little sex and real estate. He wished he'd gone to the concert with Annabel. He'd reached a point in his life where the sort of intrigues routinely played out in Washington didn't hold the interest they once did. Annabel was intriguing enough to last him the rest of his life.

He checked his watch. Another half hour, say hello to a few more people, and he could make his escape, go home and walk Rufus, who'd appreciate the gesture, and wait with the Great blue Dane for Annabel to return.

He was considering a refill from the bar when three latecomers arrived. Smith recognized the group's leader from his picture on the cover of newsmagazines and on television. He also knew a few things about the man, learned from Paul Latham.

His name was Warren Brazier, out of Northern California, one of the country's richest and most influential business leaders and a Latham backer since Latham's first run for Congress sixteen years ago.

But Brazier's notoriety was not limited to the billions he'd amassed from his far-flung industrial empire. He'd become a potent political force in America. There was constant speculation that he would one day use his wealth to launch a third political party, à la Perot, although his denials were consistent, and forceful, like everything else he did. Those close to him were quick to point out that Warren Brazier reveled in his behind-the-scenes power, supporting elected officials in whom he believed, and devoting energy—more important, money—to ridding the nation of others whose political philosophy butted heads with his own.

Brazier was a small man, almost diminutive. Smith judged him to be no taller than five feet four, five-five at best. But he exuded largeness. He was accompanied by two younger men, whom Mac took in with interest. One was clearly not American. Eastern European, perhaps, judging from the cut of his suit and hair. The other man had the distinct look of government; FBI? INS?

Brazier went directly to Congressman Latham. He laughed at something Brazier said. After a few seconds of banter, Latham looked past Brazier to where Mac stood and waved for him to join them.

"Mac Smith, say hello to Warren Brazier."

"Mr. Brazier. A pleasure."

Brazier took Mac's outstretched hand and shook it with energy. The industrialist's smile displayed good, strong white teeth, made more dazzling against a muddy tan. "The pleasure is mine," Brazier said.

"Mac was this city's top defense lawyer," Latham said. "Get in big trouble, call Mac Smith."

"*Was*? What do you do now, Mr. Smith?"

"Teach law."

"Where?"

"George Washington University."

"Well, all I can say is I'm glad I didn't have any reason to meet you in your earlier career. I've devoted my life to staying out of trouble."

"And staying clear of lawyers," Mac said.

"That, too."

"It was nice meeting you, Mr. Brazier," Mac said. To Latham: "I have to run, Paul. Another commitment."

"How's your stroke these days?" Latham asked.

"My stroke? Oh, tennis?"

"Yes. Steal some time this weekend?"

"Sure."

"I'll call."

"Look forward to it."

"Play golf?" Brazier asked Smith.

"No."

"Shame. Thought we could put together a foursome."

"I'll teach him," Latham said. "Safe home, Mac."

As Mac turned to leave, he glanced at the young men standing slightly behind Brazier. Their faces were blank, lacking affect. Humorless young men, Smith thought as he snaked through the crowd to say good-bye to Jessica Belle and Giles Broadhurst. Unpleasant young men.

Mac took Rufus for a long walk that night after returning to the house he and Annabel shared in Foggy Bottom, near the exciting Kennedy Center, the infamous Watergate complex, the enigmatic State Department, and Mac's benevolent employer, George Washington. As usually happened, he fell into a dialogue with the dog—he considered it a dialogue despite its one-way nature—about many things on his mind, glancing about from time to time to make sure his conversation with an over-sized canine wasn't being observed.

The walk lasted a half hour, ample time for Smith to make all the points he wished to make without argument from the Dane. That's what made Rufus "Great," he thought. Once back in the house, he poured himself a brandy and turned on the television set to CNN. Rufus sprawled at his feet.

President Scott's arrival back in Washington from the G-Seven meeting in France dominated the news. Scott gave a brief statement at the foot of Air Force One's boarding stairs, stressing the need for the United States to become a full partner in the burgeoning global economy of which it was an intrinsic part, despite those who would wish otherwise.

Mac smacked his lips and shifted position in the red leather chair. The president was an impressive speaker, which had served him well during his campaign for the White House. Mac had voted for him, but not without reservations. Scott's Republican opponent, the governor of Texas, was a good man with a number of views with which Smith agreed. Still, Scott possessed a leadership quality the law professor considered important in moving the country forward. That Paul Latham, for whom Smith had nothing but unbridled respect and personal fondness, believed fervently in Scott helped tip the scales in the Democrat's favor.

A reporter asked the president whether he'd given more thought to who would replace Jacob Baumann as secretary of state.

Scott said, "I can't give it more thought because I'm always thinking about it."

"Who's on the list?" another reporter asked.

"I'll have an announcement soon." He started to walk away from the cluster of microphones.

"Congressman Latham still your first choice?" he was asked.

The president leaned back and said into the mikes, "He'd be a great one, wouldn't he?"

Annabel arrived home and gave her husband a lingering kiss on the lips.

"How was the concert?" Mac asked.

"Wonderful, although Bruckner takes some getting used to."

"Brandy?" Mac asked.

"Love some. I'll get changed."

Mac joined her in the bedroom. They returned to the study in pajamas and robes and toasted each other, as was their custom: "To us."

"How was the reception?" she asked.

"Typical. I'm impressed with Broadhurst. Paul was there."

"And how is he?"

"Fine. We're trying to schedule a tennis match this weekend."

"Sounds like fun. You beat him last time."

"Barely. Paul's benefactor, Warren Brazier, was there, too."

"You met him?"

"Yeah. Pleasant enough guy, although I suspect he can turn on being pleasant when it doesn't pose any threat to him. He had two dour young guys with him. Why do young people today have such trouble smiling?"

"I suppose because they aren't happy."

"Why aren't they happy?"

"You'll have to ask them. I am."

"Happy?"

"Very. You?"

"Happier than usual. Taking a sabbatical this semester was a stroke of genius."

She laughed. "You're so modest."

"Realistic. I'm really looking forward to the project, the trip to Russia, all of it."

Smith had been granted a sabbatical to research and develop further his course on the differences between the American and Russian justice systems, especially in light of Russia's halting, painful struggle to democratize. Accompanied by Annabel, he and a half-dozen other law professors from around the country were scheduled to take a three-week trip to Russia in October, during which Mac and his colleagues would meet with Russian lawyers, judges, and bureaucrats charged with bringing the system in line with the nation's desperate need for legal reform.

"I'm excited, too," she said. "Want to practice?"

"Sure."

"Vy govoritye pa angliski?"

"Ya nye govoryu pa russki."

"Not bad," she said.

"We'll have to learn more Russian than that before we go. Asking whether I speak English and saying you don't speak Russian won't hack it."

She giggled. "We'll get by. You and me, we go to bedski now?"

"Bedski? To sleepski?"

"*Nyet.* To fool aroundski."

"*Da.* You betski."

Communicating those needs—in any language—had never been a problem for Mr. and Mrs. Smith.

CHAPTER FIVE

Mac Smith and Congressman Paul Latham met for their tennis match at seven o'clock Saturday morning at Mt. Vernon College, on Foxhall Road. Ted Koppel and Maria Shriver were playing on the adjacent court. Latham and Shriver eked out victories.

"I should say I let you win," Smith said, "your being a congressman and all. But I didn't."

"That's good to hear. We should do this more often, then." They walked to their cars.

"How about coming back to the house for some breakfast?" Latham asked.

"Thought I'd grab something at home," Mac said. "With Annabel. She was sleeping when I left."

"Ruth and Molly are down at the shore for the weekend," Latham said. "I'm tied up this afternoon and tomorrow. Sure I can't entice you? I make a world-class omelette, Mac. Besides, there's something I'd like to discuss with you."

"All right. I'll call Annabel from there."

The Latham family home in Washington was one of the more modest houses in the predominantly wealthy Foxhall section of the city, north of Georgetown and Glover Park. When he'd first come to Washington as a freshman congressman from California, Latham rented a small apartment on Capitol Hill, seeing Ruth and the kids only on occasional weekend trips home, and during congressional recesses. But as his personal finances grew along with his political clout, they purchased the Foxhall house and virtually made it their permanent home, keeping the house in Northern California and adding to their real estate holdings later by purchasing a two-bedroom condo on the Maryland shore. Paul Latham had not become rich on his congressional salary of $133,600. But, as he sometimes said, "We're not missing any meals."

After calling Annabel to tell her he'd be home in an hour, Smith settled at the kitchen table with a cup of coffee while Latham put together the makings of a cheese and mushroom omelette.

"Where are you off to next?" Smith asked. "Good coffee."

"Thanks. California. Do a little politicking. Ruth's coming with me."

"What about Molly?"

"She's now officially in the House page program. Living in the page dorm."

"Good for her," Mac said.

"Yeah. She's a good kid. Wish I saw more of her."

Latham served them and joined Mac at the table. After tasting his breakfast—"You're right, Paul. Olympic-class omelette"—Smith said, "There's something you wanted to discuss with me?"

"That's right. I've only shared this with Ruth and a few close advisors. It'll stay in this kitchen?"

"If you've shared it with others, I can't promise that. Ben Franklin had it right: Three people can keep a secret if two of them are dead. It won't come from me, Paul."

"The president wants to nominate me to replace Jake Baumann as secretary of state."

Smith took another bite of omelette. "I hope you weren't hoping to surprise me, Paul. You haven't."

Latham laughed.

"The bigger question is whether you'll accept."

"I have to make that decision this afternoon. I'm meeting with the president at five."

"You're still undecided?"

"Not really. Ruth's behind me if I decide to do it."

"What's keeping you from just saying you will?"

"I don't know. The Senate confirmation process can be tough. You heard what Clarence Thomas said the other day when asked whether he'd consider becoming chief justice."

"One confirmation process was enough for a lifetime."

"That's right."

"You aren't concerned, are you, that you wouldn't be confirmed?"

"A lawyer asks me that question? Since when is anything certain? Never been surprised by a jury?"

"Too many times. Well, Paul, all I can say is that if you decide to say yes, the country's foreign affairs will be in exceptionally good hands."

"Thanks. Mac, would you consider being my counsel if I'm nominated?"

"At your confirmation hearing?"

"Yes."

"Why me?"

"Stature. You don't carry a brief for any party, as far as I know. You're my friend. That's why."

"I'm not sure I'd have the time, Paul."

"I thought you were on sabbatical."

"I am, and never busier. Annabel and I head for Russia in October. Three weeks there. And a ton of book research."

"I understand."

"That's not to say I couldn't be your counsel. From where I sit, you'll breeze through. Your staff will do all the preliminary work. All I'd have to do is sit there and look lawyerly."

"Does that mean you will?"

"What that means, Paul, is that I'll think about it, run it by Annabel, mull it over. But I won't start that process until you decide to accept."

"Will you be home this evening?"

"I expect to be, unless we run out for dinner."

"I'll call you after I meet with the president."

"I'll look forward to hearing from you. Hell of a breakfast, Paul. If the nomination doesn't work out, you can always open a ham-'n'-egg joint. Have to run. Good luck with your meeting."

Latham and the president of the United States sat in the Oval Office.

"Well?" Scott said.

"I'd be honored to serve as your secretary of state, Mr. President."

"Good. I'll announce it Monday morning. I have a press conference scheduled at ten. This should spice it up. You'll have a statement ready?"

"If you wish."

"I wish. Run it by Sandy tomorrow night."

"All right."

"Ruth's onboard?"

"Yes, sir."

"We've been friends a long time, Congressman."

"That we have."

"We know a lot about each other."

Latham nodded.

"But we don't know *everything* about each other."

"We can't know everything about *anyone,* Mr. President."

President Scott swiveled in his chair so that he looked out the window.

"Mr. President, I know what you're getting at. Is there anything in my life, personal or professional, that might be used against me during the confirmation process?"

The president again faced his friend. "Is there?" he asked, his face without expression.

"No."

"No pretty little girls coming out of the woodwork to claim you dipped their pigtails in the inkwell?"

Latham laughed and snapped his fingers. "I forgot about them, Mr. President," he said, his voice still carrying the laugh. "Ruth and I planned to go back to California on Monday. I suppose we'd better cancel."

Scott nodded, stood, stretched, and came around the desk to shake Latham's hand. "Welcome to the cabinet, Mr. Secretary."

"A little premature."

"Piece a cake. Love to Ruth."

"Mac. Paul Latham."

"Hello."

"Where did you have dinner?"

"How did you know we did?"

"Got the machine."

"There was no message."

"I didn't want to leave one. My meeting went well."

"We ate at Pesce. The rockfish with artichoke and escarole was wonderful. Glad to hear it. It's all set?"

"Looks like it. Ruth's coming back from the shore first thing in the morning. I'll be huddled all day with staff. Writing a statement, that sort of thing."

"When's it being announced?"

"Monday morning at a press conference."

"Well, all I can say is congratulations. Deeply felt."

"Thank you. What did Annabel have to say?"

"Nothing. I didn't mention it."

"You didn't?"

"No. But now I will. Feel like stopping over? I pour a mean brandy."

"Another time. We've canceled the trip home. I'll stay in touch. Let me know what you decide."

"I certainly will. Again, congrats, Paul. It's much deserved. You'll make a world-class secretary of state."

Smith's conversation with Annabel about functioning as Latham's counsel during Senate hearings lasted five minutes.

"I think it's wonderful," she said.

"No reservations?"

"None. It's great that Paul will be secretary of state, and I'm excited you'll sit with him during the hearing. I may even see you on C-SPAN."

"You see me in person all the time."

"But TV has a certain cache. I always wanted to be married to a media star."

Rufus plopped his large head on Mac's lap. "What do you think, my friend?" he asked the Dane.

Rufus pulled back, leaving drool on Mac's pants.

"That's what I love about Rufus, Annabel. He lets you know exactly what he thinks. Come on, big guy, time for a walk. She's too easy. I need to discuss this further with you."

CHAPTER SIX

FOUR DAYS LATER

A white stretch limousine with darkened windows delivered Warren Brazier and two of his aides to the sector of San Francisco International Airport servicing private and corporate aircraft. The industrialist set a brisk pace across the tarmac to his private jet, an Airbus 300A model commercial aircraft that had been modified to carry enough fuel to reach almost any point on the globe. BRAZIER was emblazoned in red along both sides of the black fuselage. A red *B* rose up along the vertical tail surface.

When the aircraft was in commercial use, its spacious interior accommodated more than two hundred passengers. Brazier Industries' transformation of it for private use took advantage of the space to create two large bedrooms, a boardroom, a dining room, two marble baths, a kitchen, and conventional airline seating for twenty. Its interior was a rich amalgamation of lemon and orange wood, leather and gold.

At various times during the flight to London, aides were summoned to meet with "the boss" to discuss specific business issues. Executives of Brazier Industries learned early on to have their facts straight, and to present them concisely and speedily; leave the adjectives at home. Brazier was equally terse and quick with his decisions. He hadn't built one of the world's most prosperous industrial empires by being indecisive.

After a two-hour layover at Heathrow for Brazier to meet onboard with staff from his London office, the group, augmented by two employees of the London office, left for Moscow, where they were met at Sheremetevo-2 airport, twenty-five miles outside of the city, by three men in

Mercedes limousines. Besides the drivers, there were three armed plain-clothes private security guards. Brazier and entourage were driven to the National Hotel, on the corner of Tverskaya Ulitsa, across the street from Red Square. The National, built in 1903, was reopened in 1995 after years of painstaking renovation. Whether it or the venerable Metropole represented Moscow's finest hotel was the subject of ongoing debate. Brazier preferred the National because of its top-floor fitness center and swimming pool. He was fond of swimming there late at night when the crenellated top of the Kremlin and the cupolas and domes of its multiple cathedrals were awash in light.

The Brazier contingent always reserved rooms on the same high floor, with Brazier occupying a corner suite. The security men took up positions in the hallway. After an hour of freshening up, everyone met in the rococo lobby at the foot of the sweeping marble staircase, climbed into the waiting limos, and were driven to a modern high-rise building across from the new American Embassy, on the banks of the Moscow River near Presnia Station. Brazier Industries had been a major partner in an American-British-Canadian consortium that had financed the building's construction in 1994. Prior to moving into its new quarters, Brazier Industries' Moscow office, and its hundred employees, had been housed in an old brick building near Red Square.

People stood at their desks when Brazier stepped off the elevator and strode through the offices of the company bearing his name. He greeted them warmly but quickly—"hello" or *"zdrastvuitye"*—not stopping to chat. The staff who'd traveled with him kept pace, eyes straight ahead, smug authority dispensed with each step.

Brazier's private Moscow office was kept vacant in his absence. Knowing he was coming, his staff had placed vases of colorful flowers in it, as well as a tea and coffee service, and a plate of *blinchiki s'varenem*, jam pancakes, for which Brazier had developed a taste. There was never any alcohol served in his presence. He was a teetotaler. Nor did he smoke, presenting an especially difficult situation for his Russian employees, for whom tobacco was an integral part of life. They sneaked their cigarettes outside, out of sight.

He secluded himself in his office, allowing staff members who'd traveled with him to catch their breath. They were bone-weary from the long trip. Brazier, who'd just turned sixty, operated from a seemingly bottomless well of energy. He'd trained himself to stave off fatigue with frequent catnaps—no longer than ten minutes—an ability those on his staff had not been able to master, although God knows they tried. For them, staying awake and alert on such trips was more a matter of dogged determination than acquired skill.

Twenty minutes after arriving, Brazier buzzed for Elena, his personal assistant, a solidly constructed middle-aged Russian woman who'd sat poised outside his door. "Get everyone in the conference room," he said. "Ten minutes."

It wasn't a difficult directive for her to follow. Brazier's traveling staff had already camped in the conference room, joined there by four of the Moscow office's senior execs. But her announcement prompted them to remove their feet from chairs and the edge of the twenty-foot-long leather-inlaid conference table, check their clothing, and sit at attention.

"Good afternoon," Brazier said crisply as he took his seat at the head of the table. "Everyone feeling fresh?"

There was muffled laughter.

"I suggest you suck it up. We have a lot to accomplish in the next twenty-four hours."

A half hour was spent with Brazier receiving updates on company projects underway in Russia. The reports were short and to the point. a new shopping center on *Tverskaya Ulitsa*, the road from Moscow to St. Petersburg; a hotel in the *Kitai Gorod* area of the city; a joint oil-drilling venture with the French and Russians on *Yuzhno-Sakhalinsk*, a Russian island north of Japan and site of the Russian Far East's only known offshore energy field (it wasn't going well; the report on its progress was a few minutes longer than the others); and assorted smaller ventures.

Brazier listened passively, interrupting only to ask an occasional question delivered with the sharpness of a surgical knife. After everyone at the table had had their say, Brazier issued a series of orders. He looked at his watch, stood abruptly, and walked from the room, four of his staff following, two who'd traveled to Moscow with him from San Francisco, and two from the Moscow office. They were joined by four heavyset men carrying automatic weapons under their suit jackets. Warren Brazier was, among many things, a careful man. The rampant crime in Russia had generated a thriving industry for security consultants to businessmen traveling there. Brazier Industries had on retainer one of the world's best security firms, augmented by the company's own large and well-trained security staff.

Not a word was said as they descended to the lobby and climbed into the waiting Mercedes. Brazier turned to one of his Russian aides. "He knows why we're meeting?"

"Yes, sir. I made it clear."

"His reaction?"

"Noncommittal. Simply said he would be there."

"Have the funds been moving freely?"

"*Da.*"

"His position is still secure?"

"*Da.* As far as I know."

Brazier looked at him hard. " 'As far as you know?' And how far is that?"

"I am reasonably sure that—"

"I don't pay you to be reasonably sure, Misha. I pay you to be certain."

Misha coughed and glanced nervously at the other two aides in the back of the limo before replying, "I am certain, Mr. Brazier, that the deputy prime minister's position is secure."

Brazier directed a question at another staff member. And another. The Q-and-A was cut short when the limousine pulled up in front of the Radisson *Slavjanskaya,* next to the Kiev Railway Station, its western amenities making it the hotel of choice for many American business travelers.

Surrounded by the four armed men, Brazier and his small group walked past two guards at the entrance and into the imposing two-story lobby lined with restaurants and shops. An assistant manager had been awaiting Brazier's arrival. He quickly crossed the lobby and extended a nervous hand, matched by a tentative smile. "*Dobry vecher,* Mr. Brazier. Good evening. Welcome. Welcome."

They rode in silence to the eleventh floor. The door to a corner suite was open. The manager stepped aside, bowing annoyingly. The security men waited in the hall as Brazier and his aides entered the large living room and stopped in the middle of the green-carpeted floor.

Two men sat in a corner, one young, one older. A smoky haze hung over them like an aura; the younger man smoked a long black cigar, the older gentleman a cigarette. A half-dozen glasses and a silver bucket containing ice and a bottle of vodka were on a table between their chairs. A platter of *zakuski*—sliced sturgeon and fatty sausage hors d'oeuvres—appeared to be untouched. An ashtray overflowed with cigarette butts.

For a moment, it appeared that neither group would acknowledge the other. But then the older Russian stubbed out his latest cigarette and stood. "*Zdrastvuitye,* Brazier," he said, extending his arms as though about to hug his visitor.

Brazier shook hands with Platon Mikhailov, deputy minister of finance in the Commonwealth of Independent States' Congress of People's Deputies, the government that had taken the place of the former Soviet Union. Mikhailov, a lifelong Communist, had managed to sustain his power through the party's 40 percent hold on the new Congress. Yeltsin might have won the presidential election, but the Communists still controlled a majority in the legislature, as slim as it was.

"Sit. Have a chair," Mikhailov said. To his young aide, sternly: "A chair for my guest."

Platon Mikhailov was an imposing man physically, especially when compared with Brazier's diminutive stature. Approaching seventy, he'd held a variety of positions within the party throughout his life. Born in 1927, three years after the death of Lenin, he first became active as a teenager in the party's youth movement. He was a zealous Communist, happiest when playing a direct role in the brutal Cheka, Stalin's version of Ivan the Terrible's *Oprichniki,* a militia and intelligence agency answering only to its leader. Even as a teen, Mikhailov firmly believed in the Cheka's creed: "No other measures to fight counter-revolutionaries, spies, speculators, ruffians, hooligans, saboteurs and other parasites than merciless annihilation on the spot of the offence."

Unlike many of his young friends, Mikhailov pursued higher education, majoring in finance at Moscow's coveted Academy of Economics. As his educational credentials grew, so did his positions of responsibility within the party.

When Gorbachev came to power in 1985 and speeded up the process that would result in the Soviet Union's collapse, Mikhailov and fellow hard-line Communists labored to thwart attempts at *perestroika* and *glasnost.* They failed, at least on paper and at the polls. But the Communist Party held out hope that one day the nation would be returned to its former glory through a reinstated Socialist system. Platon Mikhailov believed it would.

He told his aide to wait outside. "Your people, too," he said to Brazier, who waved his aides from the room. When they were gone, Mikhailov said, "*Vodichka,* Brazier?" He pulled the bottle from the ice bucket.

"No," Brazier replied.

"Something to eat?" He gestured to the platter of *zakuski.* "Maybe you would prefer *ikra.*"

"I don't want caviar, Platon. I'm here to talk."

Mikhailov broke into a smile, exposing teeth that looked like corn on the cob. "Of course. You are well?"

Brazier ignored the pleasantry. "What is the status of the sale?" he asked, his voice low and monotone, his eyes trained on the big Russian.

Mikhailov shrugged and poured himself a drink. Brazier sat impassively and watched as Mikhailov downed half the vodka in the glass, smacked his lips, and laughed. "You don't know what you're missing," he said, finishing the drink and pouring another.

"I'm losing patience, Platon," Brazier said.

"Are you? What is the saying? Patience is a virtue. For a Russian who must deal in this new era, it is more than a virtue. It is a necessity, Brazier."

"For some. But I was led to believe you had the ability to cut through it."

The Russian filled his glass; a hand went up in a gesture of ambivalence. "It is not easy these days, you know, my friend. It was better before, huh? But then there was not so much to gain."

Brazier knew only too well what the deputy minister meant.

"I might need more from you to finalize the sale," Mikhailov said through the smoke of another cigarette. Again, a gesture of resignation with his hand. "It's not as easy as it once was, Warren. More competition for businesses being privatized by the State."

"You mean bigger payoffs being paid," Brazier said softly, narrowing his eyes against the smoke wafting in his direction.

Mikhailov laughed, and coughed. "Not only a matter of money," he said. "Favors to be dispensed. Loyalties to be remembered and rewarded. Remember, Yeltsin was an *apparatchik,* too, until he decided to love democracy and the free market." He chuckled at his comment.

Brazier had had enough. He stood and went to a floor-to-ceiling window overlooking the train station.

"I'm sure we can work it out," Mikhailov said from where he remained seated. "How is your friend, Congressman Latham?"

"He's fine," Brazier said to the window.

"Will he be able to deliver the bill, now that he will be distracted because of his nomination as secretary of state?"

Brazier slowly turned and faced Mikhailov. He was suddenly consumed with disgust for what he saw—the hulking deputy minister of finance, cigarette in one hand, glass of vodka in the other, lips parted in a crooked smile.

"It will be a shame to lose him," Mikhailov said. "Committee chairmen are so powerful in your Congress. Secretary of state? A figurehead. Am I right?"

Brazier's response was to go to the door. He turned and asked, "When will I know whether you've paved the way for the sale of Kazan Energy to Brazier Industries?"

Mikhailov had picked up a sausage from the *zakuski* platter and had taken a bite. He finished it, licked his fingers, picked up his vodka, and extended it as a toast. "To when all is resolved, Warren. To when your Congress has passed the Russian Trade and Investment Bill, and to when Kazan Energy becomes part of your family of businesses. When do you leave Moscow?"

"In the morning."

"Call me at my office. Perhaps I will have something additional to report."

Brazier left the suite and swiftly led his administrative and security entourage to the lobby and into the waiting limousines. Unlike the trip to the hotel, he occupied one limo by himself. Two of the security men were instructed to follow in another, leaving Brazier's aides, and the other two guards, to make use of the one remaining vehicle.

Brazier was delivered to the National Hotel, where he changed into bathing trunks, robe, and slippers and went to the top-floor health club. It was more crowded than he preferred—ideally, he would have the pool to himself. He ignored the four other men, dove in, and swam energetic laps until his shoulders ached.

He dried himself, put on his robe and slippers, and looked out over the Kremlin, once the symbol of Soviet power, now nothing more than a center of bureaucratic confusion. He was seething when he had left Mikhailov; the swim hadn't fully exorcised the anger from his tightly wound body.

He muttered an obscenity in Russian. What a mess reformers like Gorbachev, Yeltsin, and their cronies had made of what had once been an equally corrupt but assuredly more orderly system to navigate, especially if you knew what you were doing.

Warren Brazier had been navigating the old Communist system since 1965. He knew it well, how the bureaucrats thought and reacted, their individual weaknesses, the greed that prevailed, and especially the chains of command you had to go through to get what you wanted.

He'd suffered countless frustrations in attempting to gain an industrial foothold in the Soviet Union. His ventures there had never been as lucrative as others in different areas of the globe. But he hung on, developing his friends in high places, building his own personal list of those who'd prospered through his generosity, and who owed him.

He'd been calculating his moves in the Soviet Union with one goal: Be the individual they turned to when the inevitable happened, the collapse of the economic system and the Soviet Union itself. His prognosis had been on the money: The system and government had collapsed.

But instead of Warren Brazier being in the right place at the right time, being the one in the best position to prosper by the collapse—being first in line to snap up formerly State-owned industries at bargain-basement prices—he'd been forced to compete with Russian business interests with longer tentacles into the reformed government, some of them in the government itself.

Brazier and Deputy Minister of Finance Platon Mikhailov went back a long way, to when Brazier made his first business foray into what was then the Soviet Union. Khrushchev had been deposed by party leaders less than a year earlier, and the Ukrainian, Leonid Brezhnev, was in power. Difficult as it was, Warren Brazier had done business with the Communists for twenty years—through the Brezhnev era, and those of Andropov and Chernenko after Brezhnev died in 1982—succeeding where few other outsiders had, or could. From his perspective, it didn't matter who was in charge of the totalitarian state. Business, Soviet style, went on as usual.

But the economy was a disaster. Technology hadn't progressed much beyond the 1950s, except in space, while the West forged ahead to develop the computer age, and toward such exotic military concepts as the so-called Star Wars defense.

Through his highly publicized efforts to create profitable industries within the Soviet Union, Warren Brazier became known as America's unofficial ambassador to it. His views on U.S.-Soviet relations were sought by congressional committees, think tanks, and even presidents of the United States. His picture appeared on the covers of *Time* and *Newsweek*. Would he launch a third political party? Brazier never said yes, never said no, encouraging grassroots attempts to draft him as a candidate one day, protesting he was too busy running his company to become mired in politics on another. Observers felt he reveled in the power such ambivalence generated, and they were right. Warren Brazier's short stature was more than compensated for by an ego of gargantuan proportions.

While his staff, except for the on-duty security men in the hall outside, drank and danced to American hip-hop music in one of many Western-style discos springing up all over the city, Brazier solemnly ate dinner alone in his suite. He'd developed over the years a taste, at times even a love, for Russian food, especially Georgian fare.

But this night, his dark mood precluded anything Russian. He ordered steak well done, and a salad, and washed it down with mineral water.

He awoke the following morning with as much anger as when he'd gone to bed.

Clearly, certain changes had to be made.

CHAPTER SEVEN

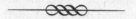

THE NEXT DAY

In Washington, D.C., there are as many jurisdictional disputes each day as there are tourists daily during cherry blossom time. The investigation of Congressman Paul Latham as nominee for secretary of state, though assumed to be a shoo-in, would not be an exception.

The FBI wanted preliminary questioning to take place at its headquarters on Pennsylvania Avenue. President Scott's chief of staff suggested that the White House would provide a more conducive setting. Latham preferred his own office. Mac Smith, as the congressman's counsel, reluctantly intervened with all the parties, and prevailed on behalf of his client.

Smith, Latham, a White House attorney, two FBI special agents, and a stenographer sat in a semicircle in Latham's office in the Rayburn House Office Building. It was eleven in the morning. The mood was relaxed. The participants exchanged quips about things in the so-called news. The two C-SPAN channels, volume off, provided silent pictures over Latham's shoulder of the House and Senate in action.

"Well, let's get to it," Latham said. "I haven't missed a vote in ten years and don't intend to now."

"I wouldn't want you to miss the vote on executive-branch appropriations," Dan Gibbs, the White House attorney, said. "I'm hoping for a raise." He didn't smile.

"Post office funding, too," Latham said. "The day of the dollar stamp is not far off."

One of the FBI agents asked the stenographer if she was ready. She confirmed that she was with a nod, then remembered and said, "Yes." He said to Latham, "You know, Congressman Latham, that this is routine."

"Of course. I assume you've already started digging into my background."

"That's right. Actually, this will probably be a lot faster than most cabinet nominee investigations. Hard to find anything controversial in your life."

"That's because I've avoided controversy. Maybe not here in the House, but certainly in my personal life."

"Let's go back a bit," the agent said. "You taught political science at U of California at Berkeley."

"Briefly," Latham said.

"Two years?"

"A few months shy of that."

"A very liberal university."

"A very open-minded and challenging university," Latham countered.

The agent turned to his colleague and asked lightly, "What did they call the university at Berkeley? The People's Republic of Berkeley?"

The second agent nodded.

Mac Smith looked at Latham for a response; his client didn't seem to be annoyed at the flippant comment.

"We managed to track down some of your students," the lead agent said.

"You're in trouble now," Smith said.

"I assume you were impressed with their educational credentials," Latham said.

"Very," said the agent. "They said you ranked among their most popular teachers."

"Glad to hear it."

"One of them said you had some pretty unorthodox theories about international relations."

"Oh? Obviously not one of my brighter students."

"She said you seemed to be sympathetic to the Soviet Union."

Latham looked at Smith and laughed. "I'm about to be called a fellow traveler." To the agent: "Don't give her name to Senator Connors. Christ, he'll call her in as a witness against me."

The questioning lasted until 11:45, when the sound of a bell from

Latham's office clock announced that a fifteen-minute floor vote had been called.

"If you want to continue this after the vote, I'll be happy to—"

"No need, Congressman," the agent said. "We're pretty much finished up here. There is one area we have to explore a little, but it can wait."

Latham, who'd gotten up and gone to his desk in search of papers relating to the vote, asked absently, "What area is that?"

The agent answered with equal casualness, "Your relationship with Warren Brazier."

Latham looked up, his brow furrowed. "Nothing to tell you about that," he said, scooping up the papers and heading for the door. "Mac, will you hang around until I get back?"

"Sure," Smith said.

Latham's chief of staff, Bob Mondrian, poked his head in the door. "Mr. Frank's on the phone."

"What does he want?"

"The vote. He says Sanders might come around to our side."

The clock's bell sounded again, indicating ten minutes left to vote. A recorded male voice reported the substance of the bill. Republican offices had their own recorded voice, which usually put a different spin on each piece of legislation up for vote.

Latham and Mondrian left the office suite. The FBI special agents closed their briefcases and said good-bye. The stenographer packed up her portable equipment and followed them out, leaving Smith and Dan Gibbs alone in Latham's office.

"Nice to hear the Bureau thinks this will be a fast investigation," Smith said. "Do you?"

Gibbs, a scholarly-looking middle-aged man with soft black hair that flopped in conflicting directions, and whose black-rimmed glasses were oversized, reclined in his chair, slung an arm over its back, and said, "Yeah, it is. Only, that doesn't necessarily translate into easy sledding with the committee. Senator Connors is no fan of Congressman Latham."

"So I hear. And read."

Gibbs got up and closed the door, took his seat, leaned toward Smith, and lowered his voice. "This question about the congressman's relationship with Warren Brazier could be problematic. I know I can raise this with you as his counsel."

"Of course. Better raised now than later. How much of a problem?"

"We're not certain. As you know, the FBI's check into his background won't amount to much. They look for obvious areas of conflict, things that might cause the president to withdraw the nomination." He laughed. "That's about as likely as the president resigning from office. But we have our own investigators dredging up everything and anything Connors and the committee's investigators might come up with—and use."

Smith grunted. "I'm sure that by the time this is over, we'll know everything we don't want to know about Congressman Latham's life, including at what age he was toilet trained and his favorite fast food. It's a brutal process."

Gibbs chewed his cheek, asked, "What do you know about the congressman's relationship with Brazier?"

Mac didn't immediately respond. He'd been around Washington long enough to know that casually sharing information with anyone, even those who presumably were in your camp, like Gibbs and the White House he represented, wasn't prudent.

So Smith did what all savvy Washingtonians did. He replied without offering anything Gibbs didn't already know.

"Warren Brazier and Paul Latham have been friends for years."

"I know that Mr. Brazier has been a big financial contributor to Latham's campaigns," Gibbs said.

"I wouldn't know about that," Smith said. "But it doesn't surprise me. I'm sure any financial help Brazier gave Paul was well within legal guidelines."

Gibbs smiled, more of a facial tic, and shrugged. "Brazier's business history in Russia is interesting. Isn't it?"

"I've found it interesting over the years. I mean, I've enjoyed reading about his adventures and successes."

"Do you know him?"

"Warren Brazier? I've met him once. A week or so ago. We shook hands."

"Congressman Latham has put through some legislation over the years that was beneficial to Brazier."

"Has he?"

This time, Gibbs's smile said something—that he realized Smith was not about to offer much. He said, "I have to get back to the White House. I've enjoyed talking to you, Mac. You have quite a reputation in this town. The congressman is lucky to have you as counsel."

"Any lawyer would do. He'll be confirmed with ease."

"I'm sure you're right." He stood and arched his back against an unseen pain. "Do me a favor?"

"If I can."

"If you come up with anything that might—well, that would give ammunition to Senator Connors and others who might not want to see the congressman confirmed—you'll let me know?" He didn't give Smith a chance to respond, adding, "I'm sure you wouldn't want to see the president embarrassed in any way."

Smith stood and shook Gibbs's hand. "I enjoyed meeting you, Dan."

"Same here. We'll be in touch." He handed Smith a business card with his White House direct line on it, and left, leaving the door to Latham's office open.

Marge Edwards entered the outer office cradling a sheaf of papers in her arms. The appointment secretary spotted Smith, dropped the papers on a desk, and stood in the doorway. "Hi, Mr. Smith. How are you?"

"Fine, Marge. Yourself?"

"Okay, I guess. Busy. Things are going nuts here with Paul up for State."

"I can imagine. How's the confirmation process seem to you to be going?"

"Proceeding at its predictable, plodding pace."

She glanced up at the clock on Latham's wall. "Oops," she said, "got to get out of here. I'm meeting Molly for lunch."

"Molly Latham?"

"Yup. I promised Paul I'd keep an eye on her now that she's a page. You know, be sort of a big sister."

"Sounds like pleasant duty."

"Always happy to help Paul. He gave me some things to give her at lunch. Books about Congress, some of his speeches." She laughed. "I think he's grooming her to become the first female president."

"The time has come."

"Want to join us for lunch?"

"Can't, but thanks. I'm meeting my wife."

"Well, another time. Great seeing you. I'm sure you'll be a familiar face around here."

"Sorry about that."

Her spirited laughter trailed behind as she bounced from the outer office, almost bumping into Latham returning from the vote. He came directly into his office, closed the door, and turned up the volume on both TV sets. A veteran Democratic representative from New York was delivering an impassioned speech from the well on wasteful defense spending. In the Senate, a controversial Republican senator from Georgia, twice divorced, spoke about the need to restore family values.

Latham pointed to C-SPAN 1's screen. "He's right, Mac. Instead of fixing what we have, the Pentagon just wants to keep developing exotic new weapons."

"That's good for you and your Silicon Valley voters, isn't it?" Smith said.

"Only if those exotic new weapons get built in my district. They left, I see."

"Yes."

"Waste of time, wasn't it? A student from twenty years ago says I was controversial. Think that'll derail my nomination?"

"I hope not. The White House lawyer, Gibbs, asked about you and Warren Brazier."

"Did he? What did he ask?"

"About campaign contributions, and legislation you've sponsored that was beneficial to Brazier."

Latham sat heavily behind his desk, slapped it, and said, "Warren Brazier is one of the greatest men this country has ever produced, Mac. He opened up the Soviet Union years before anyone else. He's a great American, and I'll be damned if I'll see his name dragged through the mud. I'd rather tell the president to find another nominee."

Smith went to a photograph on the wall of Latham and President Joe Scott together. He smiled, turned, and said, "Mind if I use this moment to offer my first piece of advice as your counsel?"

"Of course not."

"Warren Brazier is bound to come up during the hearings. You'll be pounded about him, questioned from every angle, most of it with political overtones. I suggest you tone down your defense of him. Keep your answers about your relationship with him short and factual. I know he's your friend, and has been your leading supporter for years, Paul. He's also controversial. And you can't know everything about him. Or me. Nothing to be gained by singing his praises. Keep it factual."

"Good advice, Mac. I'll heed it. I'm meeting with Warren this afternoon. He flew in from New York last night."

"Have to run, Paul. Lunch with Annabel. Talk later today?"

"What?"

"Talk later today?"

"Oh. Sure. Call me. Thanks for being here."

Mac and Annabel joined up at their favorite hangout, the Foggy Bottom Cafe in the River Inn. Over mushroom soup and Caesar salad with grilled chicken, they compared mornings.

"I really think he might buy the feather ornaments," she said, excited. "All three pieces. He didn't blink when I told him the price."

"I blink every time you mention the price," Mac said. "In fact, I flutter my eyes. How did you leave it with him?"

"He said he'd get back to me in a few days." She frowned. "I almost hate to sell those ornaments," she said. "They're among my favorites."

"Everything in your gallery is 'among your favorites,'" Smith said as a young waitress removed their soup plates. "If he meets your price, sell the feathers. Flutter your eyes. You are, after all, in business, Mrs. Smith."

"Feather *ornaments*. And I know, I know, it's good you're around to remind me I'm in business. I'd never sell anything otherwise. How did it go with Paul?"

"All right. The FBI questioned him. A White House lawyer named Gibbs sat in. Paul's friendship with Warren Brazier looms."

"Oh? How so?"

Over the next ten minutes, Mac filled her in.

"What does Paul say?" she asked.

"Gave me a speech. It was a little off-putting. Sort of a God-and-country speech, touting Brazier as being worthy of another D.C. monument. I suggested he tone it down at the hearings."

The waitress brought coffee and the dessert menu.

"Share a sour cream chocolate cake?" Mac asked.

"God, no. You go ahead. I'll have a bite."

Which, Mac knew, would result in losing more than half.

They stood in the sunshine outside the restaurant on Twenty-fifth Street, two blocks from their home. "Walk me back to the gallery?" Annabel asked.

"Sure. I'm free this afternoon. I told Paul I'd call him later."

Mac lingered at Annabel's gallery in Georgetown to examine two new pieces she'd recently purchased from a New York dealer. As he was leaving, she asked, "Sorry you got involved with Paul's confirmation?"

"No. It's a fascinating process, blatantly political but useful. At least that's the way the Founding Fathers saw it."

"I'm glad you're not sorry. I think it's great you're in the middle of something this important." She kissed his cheek, then laid another on his mouth. "See you at dinner."

"I'll be there. Sorry you weren't in the mood for sour cream chocolate cake."

"It was so good."

Mac smiled. "When will I learn to not buy that 'I'll just have a bite' routine? Enjoy the afternoon, Annie. Love you."

CHAPTER EIGHT

Marge Edwards and Molly Latham lingered over large glasses of lemonade in the Rayburn Building's spacious, bustling cafeteria. Molly, whose voluble personality held her in good stead on her high school debating team, was on a roll.

". . . and I can't believe I'll be a page in the House of Representatives. I love my roommate—she's from Mississippi and has this amazing accent—my mom wanted me to live at home, but living in the dorm is part of the experience, don't you think, Marge?"

"I know how proud your dad is of you," Marge said.

"More luck than anything," Molly said. "The Democrats are in the majority—there are only sixty-six pages—the Democrats get to appoint fifty-four of them—I'd never have made it if the Republicans were the majority. It's awesome, Marge—I'm getting paid more than a thousand dollars a month. Do you know what they used to pay pages? I mean, ages ago—three hundred dollars a month. They take three hundred from me for the room and meals—five dinners and five breakfasts—but that's not much. I'll be working in the cloakroom—the Democratic cloakroom, of course. Know what I heard? Years ago only the majority could appoint pages, and some reporters—I think it was Drew Pearson or somebody like that—maybe not—these reporters paid some pages to tell them what was going on in the majority cloakroom—wow—I mean, that's awesome—and when somebody found out about it, they changed all the rules so both parties could assign pages. . . ."

Marge listened patiently, a bemused smile on her face. Now, she laughed. Molly's enthusiasm was contagious. But there was a parallel sadness in sitting across the table from Molly Latham, whose life was all in front of her. She was sixteen years old, a junior in high school, born to a privileged family with the inherent advantages that situation creates. She was bright and pretty—golden, silky hair pulled back into an old-fashioned ponytail, face unblemished and glowing, a fit and trim figure, solid and firm.

Marge Edwards's self-image was not nearly as generous. At thirty-five, she often wondered during those dark moments alone, which seemed to have been occurring with increasing frequency, where the first thirty-five years had gone—and what was left. She hadn't married, although she'd come close a few times. At least she preferred to think marriage had been on the horizon, but had fallen through for reasons beyond her control. Men were so immature these days, she told friends, so afraid to commit and to assume responsibility.

"I can't wait to bring a message from the cloakroom to Dad on the floor. What a hoot."

"Your father is a wonderful man," Marge said.

"Hmmmm," said Molly.

"I mean, really a special man. We're very close, you know."

Molly took a long swig of her lemonade.

"It's like—well, it's almost like being man and wife, you know, working so closely together. That's what they call it"—a chuckle —"office wife."

"Uh-huh."

"You're very fortunate to have him as a father."

"I wish I saw him more. He's so busy."

"What he's doing is so important to the country."

Suddenly, Molly seemed more drawn into the conversation. "He'll be the secretary of state. In the president's cabinet."

"Yes. Unless—"

"He will be, won't he?"

"I'm sure he will. Unless something crazy happens. You never know in politics, Molly. That's one thing you learn working on the Hill."

"I guess I'd better go," Molly said, draining her cup.

"Me, too," Marge said. "Oh, here are some things from your dad. And from me." She handed Molly two packages. One was wrapped in yellow and green floral paper, and sported a large green bow. The other, which she'd hurriedly wrapped in the office before coming to lunch, was secured with brown paper and string.

Molly weighed the brown package in her hands. "It's heavy. What's in it?"

"Books, papers. Things your dad wants you to read. The other is a little present from me."

Molly unwrapped the smaller package to reveal a pretty red, white, and blue silk scarf. "It's beautiful," she said. "What's it for? It's not my birthday or anything."

Marge smiled. "Just congratulations to Congress's newest and best page."

Molly put the scarf about her neck and checked her image in the reflection from a nearby stainless-steel surface. "It's beautiful, Marge. I can wear it with my uniform—we can only wear navy blue jackets, white blouses—they let us wear slacks—or skirts—but no slits, they told us—I guess a scarf is okay."

"I'm sure it is," said Marge.

They parted in sunshine in front of the building.

"Keep a secret, Molly?"

The teen's giggle was nervous. "Sure."

"I may not be around much longer."

"Why? What do you mean?"

"I may, ah—I may take another job."

"Really?" Her eyes opened wide. "What other job?"

"It's not definite yet. *P-l-e-a-s-e,* not a word to anyone, especially your father. It would be wrong if he found out from anyone but me."

"Sure. Okay. I wish you wouldn't . . . take another job."

"Maybe I won't. But we'll stay friends, won't we?"

"Sure. Thanks for the present."

"My pleasure."

They shook hands and went their separate ways, Marge back into the building, Molly down the street in the direction of the Page Residence Hall, on the third and fourth floors of the O'Neill House Office Building, an annex to the three main House buildings. Originally the Congressional Hotel, it was purchased in 1957 and converted to office use, as well as a residence hall for pages. Girls occupied the fourth floor, boys the third.

She skirted the Cannon House Office Building, gave a Capitol policeman on patrol a big wave, entered the O'Neill Building, named for former Speaker of the House "Tip" O'Neill, gave an equally expansive greeting to the officer manning the lobby desk, and went upstairs to her room, where her roommate, Melissa, had just come from the shower and was brushing long, brunette hair in front of a mirror. Molly put the package she'd been given by Marge on her dresser and plopped on the bed.

The room was surprisingly large for a dorm. Each girl had covered her twin bed with a pretty floral spread, and had hung pictures on the wall over them, mostly of family, some of rock and movie stars.

"Hi, y'all," Melissa said, not missing a stroke with the brush.

"Hi," Molly said. "I had lunch in the Rayburn Building. Cool cafeteria. My dad always says it's a lot better than the one in Longworth. He calls that a hellhole. We'll have lunch. Not this weekend. The cafeterias are closed on weekends."

The brush kept moving. "Your daddy arrange that?" Melissa asked.

"No. Anybody can go there. But it's, like, interesting. A lot of the congressmen go there 'cause it's quick and cheap."

"You don't care about cheap, do you?"

"Sure I do."

Melissa's laugh was sardonic. "You don't have to worry about money. Your daddy's going to be secretary of state." Melissa's father owned a clothing store in Biloxi, and was active in local politics.

"Maybe he won't be," Molly said, brow furrowed.

The brush stopped and Melissa turned. "What do you mean? The president wants him."

"I don't know. Sometimes crazy things happen in politics."

The brush in motion again. "Did you see that neat guy from New York at the briefing?"

"John? He's cute."

But Molly's mind was not on the cute male page from upstate New York. Marge Edwards's words kept coming back to her—that her father might not be confirmed as secretary of state, and that Marge might be leaving for another job. What was that all about? Molly wondered. Her father wouldn't be happy losing his scheduler; he always spoke highly of Marge, sometimes too highly and too often.

The Lathams seldom argued, for which Molly was grateful. So many of her friends' parents seemed always to be bickering, and ended up divorced. Her brother, Martin, once said to her when she'd commented how well their parents got along, "It's because he's never home." Molly was overtly angry at Martin for being so flippant and disrespectful about their mother and father, and told him so. Down deep she wondered whether he might be right.

She had overheard occasional sharp words between her parents where Marge Edwards was concerned. Although Ruth Latham had never said it directly—at least not within Molly's earshot—Molly sensed that her mother suspected her husband of having an affair with Marge, a notion Molly refused even to consider. As far as she was concerned, her father, the congressman from California and soon to be the nation's secretary of state, was the most moral man in the world. The idea of him in the arms of a woman other than her mother—any woman—was anathema. Not that she was naive. She'd heard all the gossip about unfaithfulness among her friends' mothers and fathers, the occasional scandal when an elected official was caught in a compromising position, men in Washington who made their adulterous goals known, and married women at parties hosted by the Lathams who openly flirted with other women's husbands.

But not Paul Latham. Not Molly Latham's father.

"What are you doing tonight?" Melissa asked, dropping her robe and walking naked to her dresser, where she pulled out fresh underwear. Her casual nudity made Molly uncomfortable.

"I don't know. I thought I might read after dinner. My father gave me—"

"Y'all read too much," said Melissa. "We've got till ten. A few days now we'll be so tired goin' to school and runnin' all over the House floor, we'll be lucky if we can stay awake to study. What's that?" She pointed to the package wrapped in brown paper and string.

"From my father. Books and speeches. He's always after me to read more."

"Not now," Melissa said. "Come on, girl." She laughed wickedly. "Maybe we can coax John to come with us for a burger, a little dancing."

"All right," Molly said. "You really like him, huh?"

"Who?"

"John, silly. From New York."

"Oh, him. I like him well enough. I like 'em all well enough, Molly Latham. I think bein' a page in the United States Congress is goin' to be a ton a fun."

CHAPTER NINE

Senate minority whip Frank Connors was generally described as resembling an Irish pit bull with a boil, although those close to him were quick to say that his scowl and gravelly bark were considerably more menacing than his bite. Still, he was quick to snap. Once in his jaws, it was tough to shake loose unless he decided you'd finally seen things his way.

He'd just come from a Republican fund-raiser for two freshman representatives from Southern California. "Arrogant young bastards," he said to an aide as they left the Capitol Hill Club. His sentiments weren't reserved for only young House Republicans. Senator Connors found first-term representatives from both sides of the aisle to be arrogant, at best, and dumb at worst.

The aide pulled into the underground parking garage of the Russell Senate Office Building, on the north side of the Capitol, and came to a stop in Connors's reserved space. The senator set a fast pace to his office, where members of his staff awaited his arrival.

In a corner of the reception area, a bulky man with a nose of the formerly broken variety and a shadowy beard line browsed that day's copy of the *Congressional Monitor*. He glanced up as Connors burst through the door and went directly to his office, followed by his chief of staff, Dennis Mackral. Once inside, Connors asked, "Who's that out there?"

"The private investigator."

"What's his name?"

"Perrone. James Perrone."

"Is he legit?"

"According to Morris and Kellerman." Kyle Morris and Mitch Kellerman were full-time investigators on the Senate Foreign Relations Committee, the body that would hold hearings into Paul Latham's nomination as secretary of state. Connors was the ranking minority member. If the committee approved Latham's nomination, it would recommend to the Senate at large that he be confirmed.

Connors pulled a Don Lino Havana Reserve cigar from the humidor on his desk and examined it. "They say there's Cuban tobacco in these," he said, "but don't you believe it. If there was, you wouldn't catch me smoking it."

Mackral had heard the denial before. He didn't care whether banned Cuban tobacco was in the rope his boss smoked or not. That the company making them claimed the tobacco was 100 percent Honduran, and that the wrappers were from Connecticut, was good enough. What did it matter?

Connors lit the cigar with care, making sure the lighter's flame didn't touch the cigar's end. There was a time early in his political career when he smoked in public. But as his Southern California constituents led the way in the antismoking crusade—anti-everything and anything pleasurable, Connors thought—he adjusted his public posture: no smoking in public; a daily jog, especially if there was a camera to record it; plenty of pasta, vegetables, fruit, and chicken with its skin removed; and an attempt to change his approach from square-cut gray and blue suits to an occasional tan number, blue blazers over chino slacks when he felt it appropriate, and even open-neck shirts for selected photo ops.

Dennis Mackral, on the other hand, had found it necessary to become a little *less* Southern California when first coming aboard as Connors's COS, chief of staff. A year shy of forty, he'd arrived in Washington a dozen years ago as administrative assistant (same job as a COS, different title) to a California representative, a first-termer whose previous career had been in the movies. But his freshman boss was no Ronald Reagan. His being sent to Washington to represent his conservative district was considered an electoral aberration, and he was soundly defeated after one term by a conservative Republican woman, a breeder of show dogs, who convinced voters in overwhelming numbers to reject what she repeatedly called "Hollywood hedonism," which most voters didn't fully understand, but knew it sounded bad.

Mackral decided to stay in Washington after his boss packed up and headed west. He changed his California style to better conform with dark-suit D.C., although his natural coppery tan, gelled dirty-blond hair, and laid-back, beachy heritage betrayed his origins. At first, he was viewed as nothing more than a displaced Californian who'd come to town with a loser. But there was a substantive side of Dennis Mackral that eventually became known to staffers on the Hill with whom he became friends. He was hired by a House member as press secretary, was promoted to AA six months later, then joined Senator Connors's team as deputy chief of staff. Others on the staff were surprised to see the gruff, hard-nosed senator take to the boyishly handsome Mackral, increasingly relying on him to handle important legislative assignments. When the COS resigned, Connors tapped Mackral to replace him. As skeptical as other staff members had been of Mackral, they soon had to agree that he was up to the demands of being chief aide to one of the Senate's most powerful members.

"You hear from Stassi?" Connors asked from behind a sheaf of papers.

"We're set to meet at six."

"Where?"

"Judiciary conference room."

"We bringing this Perrone with us?"

"No. He's strictly unofficial, on assignment for Morris and Kellerman. Anything he comes up with is through them."

"Then why is he here?"

"I wanted you to meet him. Know what you're paying for."

"What *I'm* paying him? I thought he was getting private money."

"He is. The Yucca Valley fund. Still—"

"Bring him in," Connors said.

Perrone was even bigger than he'd appeared while seated. He wore an ill-fitting brown suit, green shirt, and yellow tie, and carried a tan raincoat over his arm.

"Say hello to Senator Frank Connors," Mackral said. They shook hands. "Have a seat," Mackral said, indicating a chair in front of the desk.

"Well, now, Mr. Perrone," Connor said from his leather chair, "Dennis says you might have uncovered some information to share with us."

Perrone shifted in his chair; his eyes were in constant motion, glancing left, right, lighting on Connors, then resuming movement again. He looked up at Mackral, who leaned against a wall, arms crossed, head cocked.

"Well, Mr. Perrone?" Connors said.

"No offense," Perrone said, "but Kellerman never did tell me what I'm being paid."

Connors looked to Mackral for the answer. The AA said, "Because you're not staff, Mr. Perrone—because you're not officially investigating Congressman Latham—it takes some time to set up the pay. But I assure you—"

Connors said, "Dennis told me a little about the direction your investigation is taking, Mr. Perrone. I'm interested. It's important to the country and the American people that such information be made public. I'm sure your fee will be worked out to your satisfaction. You have my word on that."

Perrone, relaxed in his chair, one leg slung over the other, a crooked, satisfied smile on his inelegantly handsome face, shifted position, leaned forward, and said, "I don't especially trust politicians, Senator. Any politician. Nothing personal. No offense."

Connors returned the smile: "No offense."

"What I want is some assurance that if what I'm going after pans out—you know, supports what you want—that I get paid what it's worth. I mean, I can just let it drop—or keep it quiet."

"Or get paid by the other side." Connors's voice mirrored his impatience. "What's your politics, Mr. Perrone?"

"What's that got to do with anything?"

"Dennis tells me you share my views of certain things—and people."

"If you mean I don't like liberals, you're right. I was a cop in this city for fourteen years. The liberals made it tough for us to do our job. Arrest a perp, he walks. Book a black, he's out in an hour. Judges. Politicians. Yeah, I don't like liberals."

"That means we'll get along just fine." To Mackral: "Work this out with Mr. Perrone at another time. Thanks for coming in, Mr. Perrone. It was a pleasure meeting you."

Mackral motioned Perrone from the office. He walked him into the hallway and said, "Go ahead with your investigation into the allegation you say has been made. Don't worry about money. You deliver and you'll be paid accordingly." He flashed Perrone a wide smile. "You can trust me, Jim. I'm not a politician. I just work for one." He slapped the investigator on his broad back and sent him on his way.

Mackral spent the next hour preparing a position paper for the senator. Pleased with the result, he left it on Connors's desk and exited the Russell Senate Office Building through a delivery entrance. He drove to a McDonald's in the Adams-Morgan section of the city, where he ate a Big Mac and sipped a soft drink until the person he was to meet joined him in the booth.

"Something to eat?" Mackral asked.

"No." Jules Harris, a freelance investigative reporter, took out a long, spiral-bound reporter's notebook and a pen from his tan safari jacket, and laid them on the table. "What've you got?" he asked.

"This is strictly between us," Mackral said. "We owe you from that piece you did on the senator."

The reporter picked up the pen. "Shoot."

Mackral finished the last bite of his hamburger, drank some soda, and said, *sotto voce,* "Latham's confirmation is in big-time trouble."

"I came all the way here to be told that? Warren Brazier. Right?"

"Right. But there's more."

"Oh, yeah?"

"How about a charge of sexual harassment?"

The reporter whistled, said, "You in a rush?"

"No."

"I'm hungry."

A few minutes later, a half-eaten cheeseburger in front of him, Harris said, "Proceed. My stomach's stopped growling. Mind is fed, too. Sexual harassment? Who?"

Mackral's hand went up. "First, an understanding. I want this out ASAP. Within a day."

"Hold on," said Harris, holding up his hand for emphasis. "What's the rush?"

"That's for me to know, Jules."

"I can't just go with this without *some* corroboration."

"I'll give it to you. But you've got to find an outlet within twenty-four hours."

"I'll do my best."

"That's all I can ask. We have an understanding?"

"Sure. Give it to me. Who's making the charge?"

Molly, Melissa, John from New York, and another page from Ohio went to Georgetown that evening. They would have preferred to have burgers in one of the trendy bars—J. Paul's, Houston's, Martin's, or the Grog and Tankard—but their ages precluded that. So they sat upstairs in the American Cafe and ate sandwiches and salads and drank Cokes, and talked and laughed and kidded one another. Melissa was open in her flirtation with John, although the other young male page, Peter, had also captured her attention at times.

"Aren't you ever afraid?" Peter asked Molly after another round of Cokes had been delivered.

"Afraid of what?"

"You know, being the daughter of a famous congressman. Don't you have security?"

Molly laughed as she stripped paper from a fresh straw and plunged the straw into her glass. "Congressmen don't have security," she said. "I mean, I guess some do. The Speaker, people like that. But my dad doesn't."

"But when he's secretary of state, he will," Melissa said.

"I guess he will," Molly said.

"I guess *you* will," John said.

"I hope not," Molly said.

"It'd be fun," Melissa said. "Havin' all those cute Secret Service agents around." She lightly touched John's hand on the table. "Don't you feel like dancin'?"

Molly looked at her watch. It was after nine. The weekday curfew for pages was ten, midnight on weekends. They'd signed a binding code of conduct, and were told any breach of it called for strict sanctions. "We have to get back," Molly said.

Melissa made a pouty face.

"Yeah, we have to get back," John said. "What time is the school briefing tomorrow?"

"Six forty-five," Peter said.

"That's cruel and unusual punishment," Melissa said, "having classes start that early every day. I need my beauty sleep."

John laughed, and waved for a check. "Better get used to it."

He was right.

Once school started in the attic level of the Library of Congress Jefferson Building, they'd be taking five 40-minute classes, five days a week, the curriculum accredited by the Middle States Association of Colleges and Secondary Schools. Immediately following the final class of the day, they would report to the page supervisor, where the first order of business might be filing the *Congressional Record* from the previous day's proceedings. After that, they'd be busy delivering correspondence and legislative material within the congressional complex, answering phones in the members' cloakroom and delivering those messages to them on the floor, and manning a telephone bank of incoming requests for page services. They'd be expected to be on duty until five, or until the House adjourned for the day, whichever was later, many times working far into the night. And then, back to their dorm rooms to study and to get ready for the next day. Weekends were relatively free, except for alternate Saturdays, when they were expected to attend a seminar called WISP, the Washington Interdisciplinary Studies Program.

They arrived at the O'Neill Building at five minutes before ten and were met in the lobby by one of five assistants to the dorm director. She narrowed her eyes and said, "Cutting it close, aren't you?"

Melissa made a show of looking at her watch. "It's not ten," she said sweetly.

"I'd suggest you plan your evenings a little better," said the dorm monitor. With that, she disappeared, leaving Melissa, Molly, and the two male pages alone with the security guard behind the reception desk, a heavyset black man with a wide smile, who said in a deep baritone, "Better play by the rules, ladies and gentlemen. They're taken seriously around here."

Molly and Melissa went to their room and got ready for bed. In pajamas, they sat in their beds and read, Molly the book of rules for pages, Melissa that morning's copy of *The Washington Post.*

"Look at this," Melissa said, tossing a section of the paper to Molly in which a picture of Molly's father with industrialist Warren Brazier appeared, taken a few months earlier when both were in Moscow on a trade mission led by Latham.

The photo illustrated an article reporting that Congressman Latham's long-standing personal relationship with Warren Brazier was being closely scrutinized by the Senate Foreign Relations Committee as it prepared for confirmation hearings. According to the reporter, Senate minority whip Frank Connors, chairman of the committee, was especially interested in Brazier's contributions to Latham's campaigns over the years, and legislation Latham had sponsored in the House benefitting the California businessman.

"Do you know him?" Melissa asked.

"Mr. Brazier? Sure. He's s-o-o-o rich. He sends me expensive birthday and Christmas gifts every year."

"He looks sort of mean."

"Some people say that, but he's real nice to me and Dad and the rest of the family. We don't see him much. He's always traveling. Always in Russia or some other place."

"I suppose to get that rich, you have to be tough," Melissa said. "What's the story about?"

"Oh, that the confirmation committee wants to find out whether my dad did anything wrong. You know, take illegal campaign funds from Mr. Brazier, that sort of thing."

"Did he?"

"Did he what? My father? Take illegal money from Mr. Brazier? Of course not."

"That's good. Well, quarter a seven's almost here. Night."

"Good night."

Melissa fell asleep immediately, but Molly stayed awake. For the first time, she wished her father hadn't been nominated by President Scott. She had an idea from the beginning, of course—from the moment he announced to her that he'd accepted the nomination—that it meant intense examination of him as a politician and as a man. The family, too. Like his election campaigns back home in Northern California, but magnified a thousand percent. Everything about them would come under a microscope, especially one focused by his enemies. She heard that neighbors had been questioned by the FBI. So had the principal of Molly's school; what *he* could offer was beyond her.

But as sleep slowly came, her thoughts turned more positive. It would be exciting to be the daughter of the country's secretary of state. She didn't know how her brother, Martin, felt about it because they hadn't had much contact since the nomination. Her sister, Priscilla, was even more emotionally remote than Martin, living in New York where she was public relations director for a leading steamship line.

Her final thoughts were of Marge Edwards and their lunch. Would she really leave her job as her father's appointment secretary? She hoped not. In some ways, Marge was more of a sister to her than Priscilla, and certainly a more simpatico figure in her life than Martin.

She decided to call Marge the next morning and urge her to stay with her father, at least until the confirmation process was over and Paul Latham was secretary of state. She knew her father had made enemies over the course of his career in the House of Representatives, individuals unhappy with votes he cast and legislation he championed. What he needed now were all his good, loyal friends to come forward and stand beside him. Good, loyal friends like Marge Edwards.

Paul and Ruth Latham sat side by side on a cushioned glider on a small screened porch at the rear of their Foxhall home. They were in robes and pajamas. It was after midnight. Two citronella candles cast a silent, flickering sense of peace and well-being over the small space. A neighbor's TV, played too loud, had annoyed them a half hour ago. Now, with the neighbor in bed, the chirping of crickets and the drone of cicadas were the only sounds from beyond the screens. Fireflies in the yard provided their miniature fireworks display.

"I still wish she'd decided to live here," Ruth said.

"I can understand why she wants the dorm," he said.

"I can, too. But I get nervous when I think about her on her own for the first time. Capitol Hill isn't the safest part of town."

Latham smiled and patted his wife's hand. "She'll be fine. Security at the dorm and school is heavy. Besides, if she had to get up here in time to make her six forty-five class, there'd be war in the house."

Ruth laughed softly. "Speaking of wars, Martin's due tomorrow."

"I know. I hope the chip has fallen off his shoulder."

"That's funny. The chip. He's knee-deep in wood chips every day."

"I wish he were a chip off the proverbial old block."

"Don't start on that, Paul."

"I won't. It's just that he's always so damn angry. It'll be good to see him. Heard from Priscilla?"

"She called this afternoon. She's off on another trip. Transatlantic. With a group of travel writers."

"I met with Warren this afternoon."

"Oh? A problem?"

"Yes."

Her silence said she was listening.

"I told him I was backing off on the Russian Trade and Investment Bill."

Ruth Latham had never delved too deeply into details of her husband's political activities. She was a solid campaigner for him every two years in California, and was an active participant in a variety of Washington charities, which was sincere on her part and also reflected positively on him. But the nitty-gritty of the Hill held little interest for her.

"Isn't that the bill you said a few months ago was the most important Russian trade bill in your career?"

"Yeah. I said that. And it would be. But there's something about it that's off. . . . It feels wrong. Warren's staff keeps pushing for amendments to it that—well, frankly, that would distort its original intent. He's looking for the moon in the bill—earmarked tax breaks, protection against nationalism, accelerated depreciation. Yeah. The moon."

"Was he angry?"

"He was angry before I even told him. Evidently, things aren't going well for him in Russia. He's trying to buy Kazan Energy from the Russian government."

"I've never understood that," she said. "How a government sells industries."

"Because the government doesn't own industries, for the most part, in this country. The Soviet government used to own everything. Now that it's opened up, the government is selling off its holdings to raise money, and to give credence to its new free-market economy."

"And Warren wants to buy this Russian energy company?"

"Right. If it were a fair bidding process, he wouldn't have a problem. But the people in the Yeltsin government responsible for selling its industries are on the take big-time. That's why the bill in committee is so important to Warren. He told me that if he can deliver that bill, it will grease the skids for buying Kazan Energy."

"That's awful."

"Sure it is. The Yeltsin government is—"

"I don't mean that. Wanting you—this government—to pass a bill to help him get richer sounds . . . sounds wrong, as you said."

It was a reassuring, somewhat condescending laugh he offered. "Nothing really wrong with it, Ruth, as long as it benefits this country, along with helping out an American business or industry. I admire your black-and-white view of things, but nothing gets done without compromise. When both sides benefit from a bill, it's a good deal. All the legislation I've sponsored over the years that helped Warren's business also advanced our global competitiveness, especially in Russia."

"I'm sure it has."

"Which is why I have to back off with this new legislation, unless Warren backs off, too."

"The nomination?"

"What about it?"

"Is that playing a role in your decision?"

"Sure. My relationship with Warren is looming large with Connors and his committee. Dan Gibbs, one of the president's lawyers who's handling my nomination for the White House, called just before I met with Warren. He says the president wants me to pull back on any legislation even potentially involving Warren. At least until the hearings are over."

She squeezed his hand and said, "That sounds smart to me." She kissed his cheek. "Come on, Mr. Secretary. My, that has a nice ring to it. Time for bed."

He returned the kiss, lightly, on her lips. "Not sleepy. You go on. I'll be up in a while."

He sat on the porch for another half hour before going to a dressing room separate from the master bedroom. He showered there, then went to the kitchen and brewed a half pot of strong coffee. He returned to the dressing room and put on a suit and tie, buffed his black shoes with an electric buffing machine, went to the kitchen, and left a note on the table: *Couldn't sleep, so figured might as well get an early start. Call you later. Me.* He drew a crude heart with their initials in it, and added an arrow.

He left through the front door and stood in the driveway, next to the silver Lexus that was his car; Ruth drove the white Plymouth Voyager. He looked up to their bedroom window, where his wife of thirty-one years slept soundly, at peace with herself and their life together. Somehow, in some way, he knew, his decision to accept the president's bid to become secretary of state threatened to shatter that peace. He forced the thought from his mind, got into the Lexus, and drove faster than was his custom over the empty streets of the nation's capital.

CHAPTER TEN

Bill Fadis had been a member of the Capitol police force for almost twenty years.

The force had been started in 1801 with a single night watchman, but grew rapidly over the years—exponentially after 1954, when four Puerto Rican terrorists opened fire from the gallery into the House chamber, wounding five representatives. Seventeen years later, a bomb exploded in the wee hours in a men's room of the old Senate wing, propelling the Capitol police into a highly professional law enforcement agency, incorporating state-of-the-art K-9 bomb detection capability, hostage negotiation teams, and a large contingent of plainclothes detectives.

More recently, with the increased threat of terrorist attacks on government institutions, two new units had been created—a Containment and Emergency Response Team trained by the FBI's Hostage Rescue Team, and the First Responder Unit, specially equipped to lock down the Capitol should a terrorist attack be launched.

Nothing like crisis to prompt action.

Even with the increase in manpower (currently more than thirteen hundred)—womanpower, too (almost two hundred women)—the force was spread thin, providing round-the-clock security seven days a week for the forty-block, 250-acre complex of congressional buildings. Its clients? The 435 representatives, 100 senators, and the more than 25,000 people working for the elected officials.

An unambitious, placid man, Fadis had been content to remain a uniformed officer assigned to guard building entrances. This day, he'd been on duty since midnight at the southeast entrance to the Capitol. He enjoyed the midnight shift. It was quiet at night, even tranquil without the thousands of sweaty, noisy tourists streaming in each day to see their government in action, or for some, in inaction, plus congressional staffers and members coming and going, making demands.

He was surprised to see one of those members arrive that morning.

"Congressman Latham," he said, pulling in his stomach and smiling.

"Good morning, Bill."

Fadis glanced at a clock on the wall: a little after 2 A.M. It wasn't unusual to see members of the House working late, all night at times when Congress was immersed in tricky, controversial legislation, or in times of national crisis. But things had been slow that week.

Rather than walking by, Latham paused next to Fadis. "Rainy day in the forecast," he said.

"So they say."

"You've been here a long time, haven't you?"

"Twenty years in two months, Congressman."

"A little longer than I have."

"Not by much. How's the family?"

"My daughter's a page this term."

"Oh?"

"You'll be seeing her around. Her name's Molly."

"I'll . . . be looking for her, Mr. Latham."

Latham, too, checked the wall clock. Four minutes had passed.

"Good to see you, Officer Fadis."

"Yes, sir. Have a good day."

Fadis watched Latham walk slowly in the direction of Statuary Hall, the former House chamber, refurbished for the 1976 bicentennial as a repository of two statues from each of the fifty states. During normal hours, as many as 25,000 visitors would pass through it—more this day, with rain in the forecast.

Latham thought of Shakespeare—"hush as death"—as he walked across the vast black-and-white marble floor, his steps coming back at him. The hall's quiescence was deafening. It had unique acoustics. Latham had brought each of his three children there when they were little to demonstrate how by standing in a certain place on the floor and whispering, people across the hall, also stationed in a special place, could hear the words. All three kids had been astounded and delighted.

Latham went to the south door and paused beneath the statue depicting Liberty, then turned to take in Clio, the "Muse of History," riding in a winged chariot and recording passing events in a large tablet. A gilded clock attached to the chariot had been keeping time there since 1819, the Capitol's "official" timepiece.

He drew a deep breath. The clock said two-thirty. They were to meet at three. A half hour to kill.

He spent the next twenty minutes admiring art in the Capitol's hallways. At ten minutes before three, he headed for the door that led to a small, parklike area surrounded by trees and shrubbery. On goodweather days, he and dozens of fellow House members would walk past the pocket park on their way to and from their offices when a vote had been called on the House floor.

The guard at the door, a young black man with military bearing, didn't recognize Latham and asked for his pass.

"New?" Latham said, showing him his ID.

"Yes, sir. Sorry."

"Better you do your job. Thought I'd get some air."

"Humid."

"Yes, it is. Thank you."

Latham stepped into the outside air, heavy with humidity, gray, almost green, the moon attempting to bore a hole through low, turbid clouds.

For some unexplained reason, Latham wanted a cigarette. He'd quit smoking a dozen years ago, but still had sporadic urges, usually during theater intermissions.

He sat on a small concrete bench and looked up at the illuminated twenty-foot, seven-and-a-half-ton bronze figure, the Statue of Freedom, rising into the mist from atop the Capitol dome like some ethereal figure ascending from the grave.

He stood and looked at his watch. Five past three. The urge for a cigarette was stronger. He thought of Ruth sleeping at home, unaware he'd left the house to wait in this picturesque little oasis from the strife and turmoil of Congress.

Another five minutes passed.

Angry now, he decided to wait for only another five.

Two minutes went by.

And three.

"Hello."

Latham turned in the direction from which the nearby voice came.

The discharge sound from the weapon was small and almost noiseless, a tiny *pop*.

Latham fell to his knees, his right hand involuntarily going to his right temple, where the bullet had entered. Blood ran freely down his fingers and over his hand. He pitched forward, twisting as he did so, his final living action. He landed on his back, eyes open wide, arm outstretched, more blood seeping from his partially open, crooked mouth.

A figure stepped from the shrubbery, came directly to the body, went down on one knee, and with gloved hand placed the instrument of Latham's death, a 9-mm Uzi, silencer removed, in the dead congressman's right hand, curling his sticky, red fingers around it. It took only seconds to accomplish. The figure stood, looked left and right, and disappeared into the bushes, leaving the lifeless body to be viewed only by the Statue of Freedom, looking down on it from her position on the Capitol dome, the crown of the building symbolizing the American dream, which had inspired Hawthorne to write during an 1862 visit, "the world has not many statelier or more beautiful edifices."

Paul Latham, eight-term congressman from Northern California, nominee for secretary of state, would never see it again.

CHAPTER ELEVEN

Paul Latham's body was found at five-seventeen by a member of the Patrol Division of the Capitol police's Uniform Services Bureau. He immediately notified a dispatcher in the communications room beneath the Russell Senate Office Building, who in turn passed the message on to the Contingency Emergency Response Team (CERT), housed in headquarters a block from the Hart Office Building.

"Member down," the CERT commander on duty yelled. "Congressman Latham. Let's go."

The commander and two other officers, wearing camouflage pants, white T-shirts and sneakers, pulled on camouflage shirts and bulletproof jackets and ran upstairs to the roll-call room, where a gun rack was unlocked. Each was handed an M-249 automatic weapon, capable of firing more than a thousand rounds a minute.

The watch commander joined them. "He's in the pocket park, southeast corner. He's not in succession."

An important piece of information.

Had the victim been the Speaker of the House, or the president pro tempore of the Senate—in the line of succession to the presidency—the Secret Service's CAT, or Counter Assault Team, would immediately be brought in. The Capitol police's CERT unit and the Secret Service's CAT held periodic joint drills to prepare them for such situations.

As the CERT team headed for the scene, news of Latham's death reached every division of the Capitol police. Its chief, Henry Folsom, raced to the park after issuing orders to seal off all Capitol Building entrances, and to do the same with the crime scene. As an afterthought, he ordered patrol cars to shut down the six intersections marking the perimeter of Capitol Hill. By the time he arrived at the park, it had been draped with yellow plastic tape: CRIME SCENE—DO NOT CROSS. The crime scene unit under his command was on its way. It had started to rain, as promised.

Latham had been covered with a blue blanket. Folsom reached down and slowly, gingerly folded it back to reveal the head, upper torso, right arm, and hand. He stared at Latham for what seemed to others to be a very long time. Finally, he turned to his assistant chief, Vic Lombardo. "Have the architect and sergeants-at-arms been notified?"

Lombardo lowered the cell phone from his ear. "Yes, sir. They've just gathered in the architect's office waiting for you."

Folsom sighed and pressed his lips tightly together.

As chief of the Capitol police, which he'd headed for six years after a long but undistinguished career in the FBI, he answered to the Capitol Police Board, consisting of three people—the architect of the Capitol, and the sergeants-at-arms of the House and Senate, both political appointees. Folsom really couldn't be critical of political patronage. He was the beneficiary of it, a long friendship with two powerful senators leading to his job on Capitol Hill.

As for the "architect": His name was Jack Goss. Goss was not an architect. There was a time when those holding the position possessed that credential. But that was when the job focused upon how things *looked* on Capitol Hill. Now, the architect was responsible for keeping things running, a building superintendent of sorts, charged with the technical and physical operations of the Capitol and its House and Senate office buildings, the Supreme Court and Library of Congress, even the ten thousand species of flowers and plants in the U.S. Botanic Garden. In a word, everything federal within the confines of the Hill.

Folsom carried no brief for Goss, and was disappointed when he was chosen to replace the previous architect, with whom Folsom had a better, certainly more cordial relationship. The problem, Folsom often told his wife, was that the Capitol police answered to three people who knew little if anything about law enforcement and security. At least at the FBI, you reported to pros. Folsom's first and foremost priority from the day he became chief was to continue the process of turning his force into one as capable and advanced as any other police department in Washington, of which there were many, too many as far as he was concerned.

There was—he could recite the list in his mind—the CIA's own security cops protecting Langley; the National Institutes of Health private force; D.C.'s MPD, with more than 3,500 armed cops; the FBI; 469 park police; 345 uniformed Secret Service officers; 286 Metro transit police; 159 U.S. marshals; 100 armed Federal Protective Service agents; 68 drug cops with the Drug Enforcement Agency; the Bureau of Alcohol, Tobacco and Firearms; Immigration and Naturalization; the State Department's 1,000-person force protecting Washington's vast foreign diplomatic community.

Even the Washington aqueduct boasted its own police force.

And Folsom's 1,300-strong Capitol police.

Small wonder the heads of these agencies spent half their days trying to resolve jurisdictional disputes.

Folsom said to Lombardo, "Keep everybody out of here except for the crime scene people. Everybody! No exceptions."

"Got it."

"I'll be with Goss."

"Okay."

The architect of the Capitol occupied a large, handsomely appointed office on the fourth, or attic, floor of the Capitol. Folsom, dressed in his dark blue uniform with gold buttons, the six stripes on his left sleeve and gold on his cap's visor designating his leadership rank, was immediately ushered into the office and asked to take a chair across from Goss's expansive mahogany desk. The two sergeants-at-arms and a few assistants sat in chairs to either side of Goss.

"What do we know?" Goss asked, not bothering with preliminaries.

Folsom ran it down for him. Not much to tell. Congressman Latham found at five-seventeen in the pocket park outside the southeast entrance. Possible suicide. Gun in right hand. Fatal wound to right temple.

"What's the status of the investigation?" Goss asked, hands forming a tent beneath his narrow chin. He was bald—he shaved his head each day—and wore round glasses from another era. Jack Goss was fifty years old. He had a habit of chewing on his lower lip; Folsom sometimes wondered why he didn't bite through it. His voice was unpleasantly high.

"Status? Of the investigation? We haven't even thought about that phase, Jack. We've just secured the body and the scene. Crime lab personnel are there going over everything. We've shut off the building at all entrances. Same with the intersections."

"I know about the intersections," Goss said. "The mayor called a few minutes ago. He's concerned about rush hour."

"Rush hour? That's his concern? I—"

"Hardly seems necessary to create a traffic snarl, considering it's a suicide. Where's the threat?"

Folsom told himself not to demonstrate annoyance. He said in an even voice, "We don't know if it's a suicide, Jack. We don't know much of anything at this moment. It's prudent to seal off the Capitol until we know more."

"The press?" the House sergeant-at-arms asked.

"Gathering rapidly," Folsom answered. "We're herding them into the plaza."

The Senate sergeant-at-arms said, "You've notified the FBI." Folsom would have preferred that it be put as a question.

"No," he said.

"Why not?" Goss asked.

"Premature," Folsom replied.

"What about the medical examiner?" Goss asked.

"I want the crime scene people to finish up first."

"Why?" asked Goss.

"It makes sense," Folsom said. "There's nothing to be gained calling in MPD's crime scene techs. Nothing they can do that we can't. Besides, the faster the scene is examined, the better. Less evidence to lose, or screw up."

"Washington MPD has to be called in anyway," the House sergeant-at-arms said. "It's in the code."

"Using the D.C. medical examiner is in the code," Folsom said. "Nothing about MPD."

"Disagree," the sergeant-at-arms said, holding up a piece of paper. "The MPD is authorized to help the medical examiner. That means they're part of the investigation."

"Wonderful," Folsom muttered, more to himself. "We'll be tripping over each other."

Goss's phone rang. He picked it up, listened, then slowly lowered the receiver into its cradle. "The FBI is on its way over. No need to call."

Folsom stood. "I'd better get back to the scene," he said. "Anything else?"

"Now that the FBI is involved, there is nothing else," Goss said.

Folsom returned to the park, where his people were finishing up. The rain fell harder now. The body had been covered again, this time by a sheet of plastic on top of the blanket. Folsom took another look at Latham, quicker this time. Pictures had been taken; the gun had been removed from the deceased's right hand, to be examined in the lab. If the popular congressman had killed himself, the FBI wouldn't hang around long.

But would anyone accept a suicide ruling after the Vince Foster death, investigated by the park police? Political detractors of the Clinton White House had kept the possibility of murder open, primarily through the media. The park police took a ton of criticism for having been the agency charged with the investigation, lacking homicide expertise and personnel as it did.

The Capitol police had its own homicide unit, and a good one as far as Folsom was concerned: small by MPD standards, but manned by men and women with previous city police experience.

Folsom was torn as he left the crime scene and returned to his office, on the top floor of the seven-story Capitol police headquarters, to further coordinate things. Vic Lombardo had been left in charge at the park to handle on-site coordination with the other agencies that would soon arrive.

On the one hand, he wanted the investigation of Latham's death to remain within his jurisdiction. On the other hand, there was a relief factor in having the Federal Bureau of Investigation take over.

By the time he reached his office and had settled behind his desk, he found dozens of phone messages to be returned, noted on pink slips in front of him. Jack Gross had overridden Folsom's order to block off all streets leading to the Capitol. Traffic would flow again.

A number of other decisions were made, and actions taken, in the next hour.

Latham's body was removed to the Washington MPD morgue for an autopsy.

Ruth Latham was notified of her husband's death by the Speaker of the House, who led a small contingent to the Latham home with the grim news.

A hastily called press briefing, blessed by the architect, saw Chief Folsom give a brief, factual statement of what was known to date. He declined to answer questions, saying more than once, "We have nothing more to give you at this time. We have told you everything we know."

Three members of Congress joined Folsom at the press briefing, and took the opportunity to praise the deceased member and Cabinet nominee. Their opportunistic attitude dismayed Folsom, but he reminded himself that were he an elected official, he'd probably do the same—gravitate to any microphone or reporter with a pad to say hello to the voters back home. "Man is by nature a political animal." Who'd said that? Folsom wondered. Yogi Berra? Probably not.

The president of the United States issued a terse message through his press secretary, Sandy Teller: "This is a tragedy of not only personal proportions for the family, but for the nation. We have lost a loyal, courageous, and effective representative of the American people. And I have lost a dear friend."

And Mac Smith, secluded in his study at home, poring over computer printouts on recent legal developments in Russia, got the call from Paul Latham's chief of staff, Robert Mondrian.

"I'll be there in a half hour," Smith said.

CHAPTER TWELVE

Rather than waste time looking for a parking space, Smith took a taxi to the Rayburn House Office Building. Each time he climbed into a D.C. cab—or one in New York—he thought of London and its fleet of clean, efficient vehicles driven by knowledgeable, proud drivers. At moments, he considered moving there for that reason alone.

A knot of journalists and TV cameras were on the sidewalk outside the building. A reporter recognized Smith and stepped in his path. "What's new on this, Mr. Smith?"

"I know less than you do," Smith said.

"They're keeping us outside. Hell, some of us are trying to go in to see other members."

"Excuse me," Smith said, aware that the rain, which had abated, now fell with renewed conviction.

On an ordinary day, entering a House or Senate office building involved only passing through a metal detector as found at any airport, and allowing hand luggage to go through a similar device. This morning, three Capitol police uniformed officers—there was usually only one—stopped Smith to ask what business he had there.

"I was called by Mr. Mondrian, chief of staff to Congressman Latham. I'm—I was his legal counsel. Name is Smith. Mackensie Smith."

One of the officers called the office: "Okay," he said.

Bob Mondrian was waiting, along with others on the staff. A female staffer cried quietly at her desk. Two young men huddled in a corner, discussing the tragic news.

"Hello, Mac," Mondrian said, shaking his hand. "Come on in."

They entered Latham's office, where two plainclothes investigators from the Capitol police were talking with Latham's press secretary, Harry Davis. Smith was introduced as Latham's counsel for the confirmation hearings.

The investigators, a man and a woman, each in their thirties, returned to their conversation with Davis. Smith and Mondrian listened in.

"That press conference this morning was uncalled for," the female investigator said. "Chief Folsom has been instructed to release nothing further to the press without prior clearance from the White House."

"Nothing?" Davis said. "Stonewall them? For how long?"

"Until the White House gives the go-ahead. Congressman Latham was up for secretary of state. This obviously has ramifications beyond the House."

"Sure, I understand that," said Davis. "But—"

"Look," the male investigator said, "this incident is out of our hands— out of *everyone's* hands—except for the White House. The autopsy is being performed downtown as we speak." He turned to Mondrian. "The FBI will be here shortly to start going through the office. We'll be working with them."

"How thorough a search?" Mondrian asked.

The investigators looked at each other like two children who'd been asked a silly question by an adult. "As thorough as it has to be," the male investigator said. "Right now, you and the staff will have to vacate. We're sealing this office off."

Mondrian laughed, said to the investigators, "We can't just vacate. There's a ton of work to be done here. Besides, Paul—Congressman Latham has a number of files that are classified. He's been reviewing them for his confirmation hearing."

The man said, "I understand all that, Mr. Mondrian. But we have our orders. The White House has dispatched representatives to be here when the office is searched. State Department, too, I believe."

"On whose authority?" Davis asked.

"The White House."

"This is a congressional matter, at least for the moment," Davis said.

"Let's not get into a debate on jurisdiction," said the woman. "The president has already called the Speaker and asked for an 'understanding.' The Speaker gave it to him. Look, don't make this more difficult than it has to be. Ask everyone to leave the office immediately. Nothing is to be removed by the staff except personal belongings—handbags, umbrellas, that's it."

Mondrian looked to Smith for support of his position. What he received was Mac's laconic, "They're within their rights, Bob. Where can we all gather?"

Mondrian thought for a moment. "Paul's committee office, in the Capitol."

"That's been sealed, too," said the woman investigator. She went into the large outer office and announced to the staff that they would have to leave—"Immediately!"

"Let's go," Mondrian said, coming up behind her. "Just take your purses, umbrellas. Nothing else." He returned to Latham's office, picked up the phone, and after a brief conversation announced, "The hearing room directly above us is free. We'll go there."

The male investigator said, "We'll want to be questioning each of you. Along with the FBI. I suggest you stay in that room until we contact you." Mondrian gave them the hearing-room number, and led the staff and Mac Smith to their temporary nesting place. Once there, and settled at a large conference table in front of the tiered section at which House members sat when conducting hearings, Mondrian took a pen from his jacket pocket, pulled closer a yellow lined legal pad on the table, and said, "Before they start questioning, maybe we should discuss this together. You know, get a sense of what anyone of us knows."

Glances all about, shoulders shrugged, muttered denials of knowing anything of interest.

Smith said, "I'm probably more in the dark than any of you. All Bob told me when he called was that Congressman Latham was dead, and that it was an apparent suicide." He turned to Mondrian. "A gun, you said?"

Mondrian filled Smith in, to the extent he was able, on the discovery of Latham's body and events occurring since then.

"Anyone have an inkling that Paul was depressed, anxious, *suicidal*?" Smith asked.

"He's been uptight," a young woman said. She was part of a team that answered Latham's constituent mail.

"Natural," Mondrian said. "The nomination on top of everything else he was juggling."

"Beyond that," Smith said. "Any unusual pressures on him? Any threats?"

"Threats?" Harry Davis said. "It's a suicide."

"Allegedly," Smith said. "Even if it is, there might have been some threat that drove him to take his life."

No one knew of any.

"What about you, Mac?" Mondrian asked. "You've been staying close to Paul lately."

"I spoke with him late yesterday afternoon. He sounded—well, under the gun. Even a little angry."

"About what?" Davis asked.

"I have no idea. The conversation was brief. No more than a few minutes."

The door opened. "Congressman Latham's staff?"

"Yes," Mondrian replied.

"We're FBI. Mind if we come in?"

"Please do," Mondrian said.

Four special agents of the Federal Bureau of Investigation entered the room and were introduced by the agent in charge. "We'd like to talk to each of you individually about the death of the congressman. The House clerk told us there's an adjacent empty room over there." He pointed. "We can use that."

"I have a question," one of Latham's staff said. "Why are we being questioned by the FBI? Paul—Congressman Latham—killed himself."

"We have to investigate any unusual death on the Hill, ma'am. It won't take long."

"I'm Mackensie Smith," Mac said. "I was counsel to Congressman Latham for his confirmation hearings. I assume I'm free to go."

The lead agent chewed his cheek and consulted a paper he'd taken from his briefcase. "We'd like to speak with you, too, Mr. Smith. But we can do that later today, if you'll make yourself available."

"Of course." Smith slid a business card to the agent. "Call me. I'll be at this number all afternoon."

The light on Smith's answering machine was blinking when he returned to his Foggy Bottom home. Annabel had called twice. She'd heard the news on the radio. "Where *are* you?" she said through the tiny speaker.

Smith realized he should have called her at the gallery before racing to Latham's office. He did so instantly.

"Was it suicide?" she asked.

"That's what they're saying—now. He had a gun in his right hand. The wound was to his right temple."

"Can it be?"

"Who knows? He was under a lot of stress. The FBI and Capitol police have sealed off his office. They're doing the autopsy at the MPD morgue."

"Have you talked to Ruth yet?"

"No. Dreading the call."

"Want me to make it?"

"Let's let it go until tonight. We'll make it together. I'm sure she doesn't need us intruding so soon."

"Mac."

"Yes?"

"Is there any talk of murder?"

"If there is, I haven't heard it. But after Vince Foster, I don't think anybody in this town will take suicide for granted again. They'll nail it down, and quickly, I imagine. At least I hope so."

"The president is speaking in a half hour."

"Oh? I'll turn on the TV."

"Will you be there the rest of the day?"

"Expect to be, unless something comes up. Sorry I didn't call you this morning before going to Paul's office. I'll let you know if I leave again."

The majority of other calls on his machine were from media people, requesting interviews, comments, etc. But the call that captured his attention to the extent that he returned it immediately was from Jessica Belle, former student in his class on Russian-U.S. legal systems, who'd followed Giles Broadhurst to his new position at the CIA. She answered on the first ring of the direct number she'd left.

"Thanks for getting back so fast, Professor. I—"

"Make it Mac. Okay?"

"Sure. Can we get together?"

"Of course. What about?"

"Paul Latham."

"I should have assumed. What do you hear about it?"

"Probably more than you have, or than I want to."

"What does *that* mean?"

"When can we meet?"

"I'm free right now."

"I'm into a meeting in ten minutes. Four?"

"All right. Where?"

"The Marriott at National?"

"All right."

"The bar? At four."

"I'll be there."

He called Annabel and told her where he'd be later that afternoon.

"Any idea what she wants?" Annabel asked.

"Not a clue."

"The president's on in ten minutes."

"I'll watch."

"Call after he's through."

"Shall do."

The president spoke from the White House briefing room. Joseph Scott's broad, handsome face was drawn and sad as he placed notes on the lectern, issued a flat greeting to the reporters, and said, "This is a very sad day for me personally, for the nation, and for the entire world. Congressman Paul Latham was not only a dear and trusted friend, he was one of the most able members of Congress. I nominated him to be our secretary of state because the nation and world need the sort of steady hand on the rudder he would have provided.

"I urge each of you not to speculate on the circumstances of the congressman's untimely death until more is known. This is a dreadful blow to his family. Speculation will only add to their grief. Thank you."

He walked away from a barrage of questions hurled at him.

Mac called Annabel. "Tough on the president," he said.

"Have you heard anything else?"

"No. There are calls on the machine from the press. I don't intend to return them."

"I agree. But look out the door before you leave. They'll probably track you down at home."

"Yeah. Well, I'll try to get in an hour or so on the Russian project before heading for Rosslyn."

"Okay. I'll be home early. 'Bye. Love you."

The FBI man called and asked if they could get together with Mac the following morning. They would be at the house at ten.

He tried to concentrate on the U.S.-Russian legal project, but gave up after a series of false starts.

He left the house at three-thirty, relieved to see no reporters camped outside the door. It was while passing over the Theodore Roosevelt Bridge on his way to Rosslyn, Virginia, that it struck him for the first time: Latham's appointment secretary, Marge Edwards, hadn't been at the office that morning. Was she sick? Or was she so distraught at the news that she couldn't bring herself to be there? He remembered Marge's comment about Paul asking her to keep an eye on Molly. She's probably with the daughter, he thought. Tough duty, beyond the call of appointment secretary.

The question came and went, replaced by the larger and more meaningful question of why he was meeting Jessica Belle.

CHAPTER THIRTEEN

The Washington, D.C., press corps was stretched thin that day trying to get a handle on the death of Representative Paul Latham—so many friends and colleagues to corner and question, so many places to be at the same time.

By four that afternoon, their ranks had swelled as reporters from other cities, and from national and international wire services and publications, arrived in the capital to follow up on the initial news.

Everyone who'd ever had dealings with Paul Latham, for any reason and in any capacity, was fair game. The reporters and photographers, remote TV trucks, cameramen, familiar on-air TV anchorpeople, and hundreds of support staff camped in front of the Lathams' Foxhall home, the Rayburn House Office Building, the White House, and the State and Justice departments. The home addresses of Latham's staff were ferreted out, and correspondents dispatched to them. Neighbors of the Lathams were interviewed for clues into the dead congressman's state of mind: "Notice anything unusual about him lately?" "Now that I think of it, yes. I saw him last weekend in the yard. I don't know, he had a funny look on his face."

No surprise either that a sizable press contingent sought out Warren Brazier, or anyone from his organization willing to speak to the media. The best that could be determined was that the industrialist was in Washington, probably in his office on the top two floors of an eight-story office building on New Jersey Avenue, within shouting distance of the Capitol and Union Station.

As with other administrative centers of Brazier Industries—Moscow, San Francisco, New York, Singapore, and New Delhi—a large corner office was kept empty for the company's dynamic leader, flowers changed each day, his favorite beverages and snacks on hand, personal staff poised to serve. Each office had a large, private marble bath with sauna and Jacuzzi, a small bedroom area, and a closet containing a full wardrobe.

Brazier had been there since five that morning. He received word at six from an aide, who'd been monitoring local television, that Latham's body had been found.

"Are you sure?" Brazier had responded.

"Yes, sir."

"I see. Thank you. Please inform the staff, and make it clear there is to be no comment, from anyone, to the press."

"Yes, sir."

Brazier tuned the TV in his office to CNN. His timing was good; the anchor had just begun an update on the story. He intoned over a still photo of Latham, "As reported earlier, Congressman Paul Latham of California, eight terms in the House of Representatives, highly respected chairman of the powerful House International Relations Committee, and nominated by President Scott to become secretary of state, is dead. . . . His body was discovered earlier this morning by a member of the Capitol police, who came across Representative Latham in a small park near the Capitol. According to our information, he was found with a revolver gripped in his right hand. Death resulted from a gunshot to the temple. An autopsy is being conducted by the district medical examiner.

"A source close to CNN tells us that Congressman Latham had recently been depressed over allegations of impropriety stemming from his friendship with the industrialist Warren Brazier. Our source further informs us that the Senate Foreign Relations Committee, chaired by California Senator Frank Connors, the committee that would have conducted Latham's confirmation hearing, had developed evidence of alleged wrongdoing by the deceased Congressman. We'll continue to bring you this breaking story as more information becomes available."

• • •

Now, at four in the afternoon, Brazier remained secluded in his office. He'd spent much of the day conferring with top aides, including his chief lobbyist, Tom Krouch. Krouch was a veteran Washington hand on the Hill, a switch-hitter, having worked for a number of senators and representatives, Republican and Democrat, both on their office staffs and on committees. His extensive network of congressional contacts trusted him, a lobbyist's most precious commodity. He ran Brazier Industries' lobbying effort by the book, which meant he knew how to walk that fine line between legal and illegal lobbying, crossing it only when he was confident he'd get away with it.

The other member of Brazier's senior staff with whom he spent considerable time that day was Aleksandr Patiashvili. Patiashvili, headquartered in Moscow, had flown into Washington two days earlier. He headed up the company's Russian executive corps, including the dozen or so in the Washington office whose responsibility was, among other things, to advise Krouch's lobbying group on matters of direct interest to the company's Russian projects, and to maintain liaison with various embassies in Washington representing nations of the CIS, the Commonwealth of Independent States, which had replaced the Soviet Union. As a group, they were young and well educated, with the exception of Patiashvili, who'd been with Brazier for more than twenty years.

Before joining the company, he'd been an old-line Communist, a general in the *Komitet Gosudarstvennoi Bezopasnosti,* the KGB. Many eyebrows were raised when he left that post to become a Brazier Industries' employee. You didn't just walk away from the feared and powerful Soviet intelligence agency to join an American company without the move having been blessed from high up. Speculation was that Brazier had paid handsomely, not to Patiashvili, but to leaders within the Soviet government to bring onboard someone with Patiashvili's heavy credentials.

While these meetings took place, Russian executives on the floor below assigned to Brazier's Washington office caught up on things back home with the three young men who'd accompanied Patiashvili from Moscow. They sipped tea and nibbled on an overflowing platter of *blinchiki svarenem,* the jam pancakes favored by the boss, that were flown in regularly from Russia. They commented on the news that the boss's friend, the American congressman from California, Paul Latha committed suicide that morning. But none of them knew close—more important, how interdependent—Brazier and L been. It was a Warren Brazier management technique never one else in his organization know the big picture. That, he reserved for himself.

Soon, talk among the young Russian men turned from suicide to more pleasant things. There was laughter and good-natured kidding, the latest jokes told, most of them sexual, but one of the young men in the room did not seem to be enjoying the banter. Anatoly Alekseyev, thirty-four, an employee of Brazier Industries for two years, left the room twice to make a phone call. When asked whom he was calling, he replied, "A friend. Just a friend."

Alekseyev's area of responsibility was in the energy division of the company. Brazier's joint oil-drilling venture with the French and Russians on *Yuzhno-Sakhalinsk* had been receiving most of his attention the past six months. What had started as a relatively forthright project had deteriorated into a bureaucratic morass, complicated by a falling-out between Brazier and his French partners. Adding to Alekseyev's daily burdens was the recent attempt by the company to buy Kazan Energy from the Russian government. He'd been working twelve- and fourteen-hour days, seven days a week, which cut annoyingly into his social life as a Washington bachelor. He enjoyed America's capital city, especially Georgetown and its many pubs and nightclubs, where singles gathered to perform the mating dance.

He was a handsome young man, tall and angular with thick black hair worn short, and a serious, dedicated, olive-skinned face. He'd gradually replaced the suits he'd brought with him from Moscow with Western-style clothing, which draped neatly on his slender, muscular body. He did nicely at those watering holes frequented by singles, if such success was determined by not going home alone. Upon arriving in Washington, he lived in a one-bedroom apartment in a building constructed on upper Wisconsin Avenue to provide housing for employees of what was then the new Soviet Embassy, built on the city's highest point, Mount Alto, and providing a troublingly direct line of sight into the White House. But after a year there, Alekseyev moved away from this Russian conclave to a decidedly fancier and certainly more American apartment complex on the banks of the Potomac River, in lively Georgetown. He was much happier there.

Alekseyev and the others waited to be summoned by Brazier. But at five-thirty, to their surprise, the boss's personal secretary entered the room and said, "You must be living good. He says everyone can go home except for a few people. Enjoy your evening. He wants the staff here at seven in the morning. There is to be no comment to any member of the press. Anyone who violates that will be dismissed immediately." The young execs waited until she was gone before allowing sarcastic chuckles to surface.

Alekseyev and his Washington-based colleagues went to their offices to pack up for the night. Offices were to be spotless and uncluttered overnight; Brazier was known to wander through at odd hours, leaving caustic notes for those who violated that rule, one of many.

The three newcomers, who'd flown in from Moscow with Aleksandr Patiashvili, were unsure what to do. They lingered in the hall. "We can leave, too?" one asked another.

He shrugged. "I don't know."

Their question was answered by Brazier's secretary. She came to where they stood and said, "Wait here." She poked her head in Anatoly Alekseyev's office doorway and said, "He wants you to make sure they get dinner and arrive back at the hotel without incident."

"Me?" His voice mirrored his disappointment.

"Yes, Anatoly, you. And make sure they're back here by seven."

She returned to the three young men in the hallway and repeated, in surprisingly smooth Russian, the admonition about not speaking to the press.

Alekseyev led his three charges from the building, exiting through a back entrance leading from the building's basement. Although the majority of reporters were in front, there were a half-dozen waiting at the rear doorway. They shouted questions, but Alekseyev waved them off, saying as they walked, "No comment. No comment."

His car, a two-year-old Buick Le Sabre, was parked in the outdoor lot. The four piled in, and he pulled from the lot and into the street, almost hitting a young female reporter who'd followed them. One of the three muttered a comment in Russian about her breasts, causing the man seated next to him to laugh loudly. The third man's response was different. He kept his eyes on the young woman until she was out of view. The veins in his forehead and neck swelled like snakes devouring a meal; his mouth was a tight, straight line.

The one who'd made the suggestive comment poked his serious colleague in the ribs with an elbow. "Hey, Yvgeny, don't tell me you didn't notice those big ones."

Yvgeny Fodorov forced his thin, pale face to relax, even to smile as he said, "*Da*. She has nice big ones."

CHAPTER FOURTEEN

Mac Smith showed up at the Marriott Hotel at National Airport precisely at four and went to the bar, where he ordered a white wine. A TV set was tuned to a channel providing continuous stock market quotes at the bottom of the screen, while talking heads conversed with each other above the steady stream of symbols and prices.

When Jessica Belle hadn't arrived fifteen minutes later, he considered calling her office. But as he was about to head for a phone, she came through the door with a flourish, flashed an "I'm sorry" smile, and shook his hand.

"I got hung up in traffic coming out of Langley," she explained, sitting on an adjacent stool. "I think they call it the Puzzle Palace because of the parking lots. Insane."

"Drink?" Smith asked.

"Something soft." To the bartender: "Club soda, please, and lots of lime."

"Well," Smith said after she'd been served, "what brings us together at the airport for this seminar?"

"Hope you didn't mind driving over here, Mac. I'm catching a flight in an hour. Thanks for indulging my schedule."

"Obviously more harried than mine. Settling in at the CIA?"

"No time for that. Giles and I have hit the floor running, as that dreadful cliché goes. Head is swimming."

"You sounded anxious when you called," Smith said, sipping his wine.

"Anxious to talk to you. That's for sure." She glanced up and down the bar; they could talk without being overheard, provided they did it *pianissimo.*

"I'm waiting," he said.

"Okay. First, know that I'm here with Giles's blessing."

"Why is that important?"

"Because I'm not here to debate whether the District should be given statehood. Irrelevant issues like that. I'm here, Mac—funny, I have trouble calling my former professor by his first name—I'm here because of something we've learned at Langley about Congressman Latham and Warren Brazier."

"I see." Another sip of wine, longer this time to allow time to think. "Jessica, why would you be telling *me* such a thing?"

"Two reasons, and I had to convince Giles it was important that you be rung in. First, you were one of Latham's closest friends. Second, you were his counsel for the hearings."

"But I no longer enjoy either role. He's—dead. As opposed to deceased, or passed away."

"But his reputation still lives. And there's the president's reputation."

"The president? I can't keep up with these grand leaps you're making. Let's stick to *Paul's* reputation. Something's about to besmirch it?"

"Yes. Warren Brazier."

"I'm with you so far."

"Mac, Giles and I have spent almost every waking moment since arriving at Langley poring over intelligence reports from Russia. You know we're charged with helping American industry overseas."

"Yes."

"Warren Brazier is a major player in American business development in Russia—*the* major player."

"That's not new, Jessica. Doesn't take the CIA to know that."

She smiled. "Of course it doesn't. But it does take an agency like the CIA to get beyond what the media reports about Brazier's Russian activities, and what's *really* going on there."

"Okay. What's *really* going on?"

She leaned closer to his ear. "Warren Brazier had Paul Latham in his pocket since Latham first ran for Congress. All the strings from Latham have been in Brazier's hands, and he's pulled them every inch of the way."

Smith winced, but not at what she'd said. He was due for a visit to the dentist. A sudden pain from a tooth that had been giving him trouble confirmed it.

"Jessica, let's accept that Paul Latham was influenced by Warren Brazier, maybe even to what some would consider an unreasonable level. But that's nothing new in American politics. Influence peddlers like Brazier are always on the lookout for up-and-coming political stars. They toss their weight and offer financial support to them in return for having the politicians' ear. Lots of legislation gets passed to benefit some special interest. Maybe most of it. An unpleasant reality, perhaps, but reality nonetheless."

"You're right, of course. Paul Latham wasn't the only committee chair influenced by Brazier. He's pumped money into Connie Dailey's campaigns for years." Congressman Cornelius Dailey chaired the powerful Ways and Means Committee, which had joint jurisdiction where tax breaks for businessmen like Warren Brazier were involved. But Dailey, one of Latham's closest allies in Congress, was known to follow Latham's lead on most international issues.

"Fast forward for me, Jessica," said Smith. "The president. What's this have to do with him?"

"He's known about it."

"And?"

"Still puts Latham up as secretary of state."

"Have you considered—?"

"The Russian trade bill Latham's been pushing through committee is a total sellout to Brazier."

"Have you considered that the bill might benefit this country as well as Warren Brazier? A strong market economy in Russia is good for us."

"Maybe. Maybe not. There's more."

"Oh?"

She checked her watch, finished her drink. "Have to run pretty soon. All the new airport security. No more last-minute sprint for a plane."

"Then you'd better talk fast."

"Latham was about to be charged with sexual harassment."

Smith's eyes widened, and he directed a stream of air through pursed lips. "Who's making the charge?"

"A female employee. A—" She screwed up her broad, pretty face in thought. "A Marge Edwards."

"That's nonsense."

Why hadn't Marge been at Latham's office this morning?

"Maybe," she said. "But that's a personal thing. Not important now that he won't be facing confirmation hearings."

Tell that to Ruth Latham and the kids.

"The second revelation has a lot more significance, certainly for the country. We believe Warren Brazier has been funneling large sums of money into the Communist movement in Russia."

"Why would he do that?"

"To see them come back to power. The Yeltsin government hasn't been especially cooperative with Mr. Brazier. He's trying to buy a company, Kazan Energy. You've heard of it?"

"Yes. An industrial giant."

"Brazier always had easy access to the powers that be when the Communists were in control."

"Wait a minute, Jessica. Are you saying that legislation Latham championed benefiting Brazier also benefited the Communists, not the free-market democratic leaders like Yeltsin?"

"*I'm* not saying it, Mac. That's what our intelligence indicates."

"I'm not convinced."

"You don't have to be. Brazier and the Communists are cozy with the Russian mafia."

"According to your intelligence."

"According to our intelligence. Brazier routinely uses them as security."

"Buys security from them?"

"Uses them."

"Lots of American businessmen buy security when doing business in Russia. In any of the independent states. Crime is rampant there."

"There's buying security—and then there's *hiring* Russian thugs and mobsters."

She checked her watch again. "Gotta run."

Smith smiled, then laughed. "I love this," he said. "Former student joins the CIA, calls me, meets me at the airport, and drops a series of provocative charges on the bar. Then runs for a plane. Why have you told me these things?"

"Because you might be in a position to find out more for us."

" 'For us'? For the CIA?"

"Not exactly. Look, we're on the same side, want the same thing. If Paul Latham was used by Brazier—and that's probably what happened—

at least I hope that's what happened, that he was duped—and this comes out—which it undoubtedly will—"

"If someone wants it to."

"—Latham's sterling reputation will be badly tarnished. Think of his family. President Scott's reputation will take a hit, too, by extension."

"Assuming that's true, why do you think I'm in a position to find out more about it?"

She stood and straightened her white skirt, checked her appearance in the bar mirror. "You've made lots of contacts within the Russian legal system. Latham's family could be a source. His staff." She raised her pretty blond eyebrows and cocked her head. "Just a thought. Giles is all for it. Thanks for indulging me, and sorry to run like this."

Smith stood, too, and they shook hands. "Where are you off to?" he asked.

"L.A."

"Business?"

"Of course. Thanks again. Oh, let me buy." She opened her purse, but Mac placed his hand over it. "My contribution to national security. Safe trip."

" 'Bye."

He watched her exit through the door, a bag slung over her shoulder. He couldn't help but smile. He always took particular pride in seeing former students, especially female ones, go out and conquer the world—or think they have—with a few ideas of his included in their arsenal of knowledge. Bright, scrubbed young women striding down a city street, briefcase in hand, clothing stylish yet appropriate to their careers, never failed to provide a pulse of pleasure. He sometimes wished he'd had a daughter, as well as the son who'd died.

He paid the check, went to his car, and headed home. It was during the ride, slowed by rush-hour traffic, that the impact of the conversation he'd just had hit him. He was being recruited by the CIA, through a former student, to feed that agency information, even as journalists, athletes, academics, businessmen, and even run-of-the-mill American travelers had been asked to do for decades.

Marge Edwards charging Paul Latham with sexual harassment? That had to take first and immediate priority. As Latham's counsel, he owed it to his dead client's family to ascertain the truth about the allegation he'd just heard, and to do what he could to put it to rest.

The dome of the Capitol came into view, so proudly emblazoned against the sky, the dignified, harmonious, utilitarian center of the democracy that was America. Inside, members of the House proved it was aptly named the House of Representatives, 435 American men and women representing the nation's citizens at their best, and worst.

This day tilted toward the latter category.

CHAPTER FIFTEEN

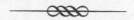

Washington's medical examiner's office and MPD's forensic laboratories were housed in a salmon-colored building on the grounds of the District's general hospital, at Nineteenth and Massachusetts Avenue, S.E. It had been a relatively quiet night in a city where the homicide rate rose as fast as the city's coffers declined. A disgrace, the nation's capital struggling to stay afloat like some Third World city, was the nonpartisan view. How to fix it was another story, one that brought out party labels and histrionic bickering—political fiddling while America's Rome burned.

But the building's quiet had been shattered that morning when Congressman Latham's body was wheeled into the building from a rear loading ramp. Unlike routine homicides, in which the body is accompanied by a couple of med techs and maybe a uniformed MPD officer, Latham's wheeled stretcher was surrounded by dozens of people, including members of the Capitol police, FBI, MPD, Secret Service, and the House of Representatives' deputy sergeant-at-arms. The parking area was clogged with press vehicles; the scene was thoroughly captured by TV cameras and still photographers. Shouted questions from reporters were ignored.

The medical examiner, Cooley Ashburn, alerted to Latham's imminent arrival, had put into motion preparations for the autopsy to be performed. Dr. Ashburn was a stooped man with sleepy eyes that seemed unusually large through his round, thick glasses. His hair was mouse colored and lifeless. The staff always said, out of his hearing, that Ashburn didn't look much more alive than the bodies over which he labored. He, of course, became aware of such comments, but dismissed them as not being worthy of reaction. There was little in the ME's life other than his job. The place of the dead was his life, you might say, his virtual home; he lived alone in a small apartment two blocks from the office. He was divorced, no children. When he smiled, about twice a year, there seemed to be pain behind it, as though he had to struggle to rearrange his facial muscles into what would pass as pleasantness.

His assistant entered Ashburn's office that morning and said, "He's downstairs."

"Prepped?" Ashburn asked as though not expecting an answer.

"In the process. I took a quick look."

"And?"

"Clean entry, right temple."

Ashburn slowly nodded. "Clean?"

"Appears that way to me."

"I'll be there in a few minutes. Who'll be observing?"

"I don't know. There's plenty of people."

The ME yawned, not bothering to cover his mouth with a hand. "Not *too* many," he said.

The assistant left, and Ashburn resumed reading a new textbook on homicide investigation. No matter what others thought of him as a person, no one questioned his dedication to his specialty, nor his constant attempt to stay abreast of the field. In time, he made his way downstairs.

Latham's body was naked, plastic bags secured over his head, hands, and feet. He was wheeled into the examining room and placed on a stainless-steel table with a lip to catch bodily fluids before they dripped to the floor. Ashburn, his assistant, and representatives from the Capitol police, FBI, and Secret Service, all wearing green surgical gowns, masks and hats, and latex gloves, stood over the body. The assistant ME carefully removed the plastic bag from Latham's head. Ashburn turned it so that the right temple was exposed, illuminated by the overhead fluorescent lights and a headband he wore containing a high-intensity light. With the light from his forehead leading the way, he slowly, carefully pushed aside hair to better uncover the entry wound. As he proceeded with his examination, he gave a running commentary into a tiny microphone pinned to his gown.

". . . entry of bullet clean, skin has closed over it—slight grease ring from bullet—circular discoloration around circumference of entry—

bruising—no sign of gross destruction of surrounding tissue—no scorching—no sign of gases undermining skin—no visual sign of powder."

He turned Latham's head to the other side, where the bullet would have exited. It had not.

"No exit wound—bullet undoubtedly in skull—X-ray confirmation needed."

He said to his assistant, "We have the weapon?"

"Yes."

"Test fired?"

"Not yet."

"Please do."

After another ten minutes of visual inspection of Latham's head and body, and an X ray of his skull, the ME announced, "I'm going in after the bullet. You might want to leave."

No one moved.

Ashburn shrugged. "Give me the saw," he said to his assistant, as though asking for the salt to be passed.

An hour later, after the bullet had been retrieved from Latham's brain—impact with bone matter on its way in had severely flattened it—and with only the FBI observer still in the examining room, Ashburn and his assistant discarded their gowns, masks, caps, and gloves and went to Ashburn's office, where they conferred for another half hour. The interested parties had increased by three, much to Ashburn's chagrin—Senator Frank Connors's administrative assistant, Dennis Mackral; Capitol Police Chief Henry Folsom; and White House attorney Dan Gibbs. What the hell can you contribute? Ashburn thought. Political vultures . . .

"Look," the ME said in a weary, reedy voice, "it's my professional opinion, based upon my visual examination of the deceased, that he did not take his own life. The weapon was fired from at least eighteen inches away, probably further."

"But you can't be certain without conducting the rest of the autopsy, can you?" Mackral said.

"The rest of the autopsy, as you put it, will shed no light on whether the shot was fired close enough for him to have inflicted the wound himself, or whether it came from a distance. The test firing of the weapon doesn't conflict with my finding." He shoved the report of the weapons test across his metal desk.

"Did he have any drugs in his system?" Mackral asked.

"We haven't gotten that far yet," Ashburn responded.

"Why would you ask that?" Dan Gibbs asked Mackral.

Senator Connors's AA shrugged. "Maybe he took some medication that depressed him."

Gibbs turned to Dr. Ashburn. "As you're aware, Doctor, there's a blackout on information concerning Congressman Latham's death, including from this office."

Ashburn nodded, and yawned.

Gibbs looked at Capitol Police Chief Folsom, Dennis Mackral, and the others in the cramped office. "That's understood by everyone?" Their lack of response said to Gibbs that they understood. But he raised it again to Mackral. "Senator Connors understands this?"

Mackral responded with a smile. "Of course. He was on the phone with the president right after Latham's body was discovered. He urged the president to buy as much time as possible—in the event it *wasn't* suicide."

An FBI agent chimed in: "We're in agreement with the president. If what you say is accurate, Dr. Ashburn, that it wasn't a suicide, then we've got the murder of a leading member of Congress to deal with."

"The problem is," said Chief Folsom, "does anyone in this room really think this can be kept under wraps for very long?"

"We can try," the representative from the Secret Service said. "At least keep it quiet for a day or two."

Gibbs said to Ashburn, "I think we're agreed, Doctor. You won't be releasing information because you don't have it all. Correct?"

"I have enough to know that—"

"Doctor, all that's being asked of you is that you say what is the truth, that the cause of the congressman's death has still not been determined with any certainty. How long will the rest of the autopsy take?"

A long, pointed sigh from Ashburn. "A day at the most."

"Two days," Gibbs said. "Because he was such an important person—hell, he was up for secretary of state—your office, Doctor, has undertaken a precise, careful, and painstaking examination of the deceased."

"Yes. I understand."

"All right," Gibbs said, patting an errant strand of hair back in place as he stood, briefcase in hand. "We have two days' grace. Dr. Ashburn, I think it would make sense for you to come outside with us and give a brief statement along the lines I've suggested."

Ashburn's expression said he was, at once, surprised and reluctant.

"Just say the autopsy of Congressman Latham is going on as you speak, and that there will not be a determination of cause of death for two days. No questions. Just say it, and get back inside."

"I'd really rather not," Ashburn said.

They left the office, Gibbs leading the way, and went to the rear loading dock, where reporters and cameras waited. The group's sudden appearance provided a surprise for the press. When Ashburn stepped forward and raised his hands, prompted by a gentle nudge from Dan Gibbs, a hush fell over the parking lot.

"The autopsy of Congressman Paul Latham has started. It will be two days before it is completed. Thank you."

Ashburn walked away from his "handlers" in the direction of the door. The press merged into a solid block of followers, tossing a stream of questions at him. Gibbs and the others took the opportunity to head for their cars. A few reporters split from the main group and pursued them. "No comment," they said, almost as a chorus. Only Dennis Mackral stopped long enough to say, "Dr. Ashburn just told you the situation. That's it."

"What's his name?" a young reporter asked.

"Ashburn. Washington medical examiner." He spelled "Ashburn" for them. "Excuse me. You're in my way."

Now, at the end of the day, Cooley Ashburn sat alone in his office. The impromptu appearance on the loading dock had unnerved him. Each time he thought of it, his heart tripped. An occasional tic in his left eye was more pronounced.

The continuation of the autopsy on Latham had been conducted by members of his staff, including the removal of all relevant organs for lab testing. Ashburn spent the rest of the day taking phone calls from a variety of people, all of them unwelcome.

The mayor called twice, congratulating him on his aplomb in handling the press, and reminding him to say nothing else.

The chief of police called three times, once to ask how he was holding up, once to receive an update on the autopsy—he was dismayed that all roads led to murder rather than suicide—and finally to warn Ashburn that he would be hounded by the press when he left the building, and to stand firm in his public silence.

Dan Gibbs called from the White House: "Nice job, Doctor. Keep it up. The president is appreciative of your discretion. There is a great deal at stake here. National security. That sort of thing."

His former wife called. She'd seen him on TV, and told him he should speak slower if he was going to be making public appearances. Hearing her voice was strangely comforting, but she hung up before he could continue the conversation.

All calls from the press—there were more than a hundred, according to the switchboard—were answered by the operators, who'd been briefed by an MPD public affairs officer to say that there would be no statement until the autopsy was completed.

Ashburn's wasn't the only phone ringing that day. Every person who might know something, anything, and be willing to share it was contacted repeatedly by the burgeoning, frustrated press corps. Rumors grew like weeds. But anyone who could provide a definitive answer kept it close to the vest.

Dennis Mackral returned to Senator Connors's office in the Russell Building and made a series of calls. He'd placed the last of them and was about to leave when another staffer answered a ringing phone, held her hand over the mouthpiece, and said to Mackral, "For you."

"Who?"

"Petrone? Perone?"

Mackral picked up the extension on his desk, waited until the female staffer had hung up, and said, "Yeah? What's up?"

"We better talk."

"Okay. But why?"

"She's gonesville, man."

"What the hell are you talking about?"

"Your Ms. Edwards. She's split."

"You sure?"

"Yeah. I'll find her, but that wasn't part of the deal. That costs more."

"The McDonald's in Adams-Morgan. Eighteenth and Columbia. A half hour."

"McDonald's? I don't do business in McDonald's. The Palm in a half hour. I got this sudden yen for lobster."

CHAPTER SIXTEEN

"Why don't they just turn the damn boat around?"

Martin Latham, dressed in jeans, a yellow T-shirt, and sandals, angrily tossed the question out from where he sat at the kitchen table. With him were his mother and younger sister, Molly. Two dozen visitors milled about in other parts of the house. Outside, clots of law-enforcement and media personnel blanketed the lawn and street.

"Because they can't," Ruth Latham said.

"Because they won't," Martin snapped.

"Pris will fly home the minute they reach port," said his mother. "The last place she wants to be at a time like this is in the middle of the North Atlantic. How are you doing, Molly?"

"All right, I guess," she said, breaking into tears as the words tumbled out. Ruth pulled up a chair and wrapped her arms about the youngest of her three children.

When Molly stopped crying, she said, "I think I'll go to my room."

"Okay, sweetie," her mother said.

Ruth and Martin Latham watched the young girl walk from the kitchen and up the stairs to the second floor.

"She was so excited about being a House page," she said.

"She still can be," Martin said. "She'll get over this."

Her son's coldness caused Ruth Latham to close her eyes against it. You just don't "get over" a parent's death in a hurry. He was so unlike every other member of the family, who were quick to hug and to praise, and to use terms of endearment, even silly ones. Not Martin.

Latham's chief of staff joined them. "Ruth. A minute?"

Ruth followed the boxlike Mondrian into the den, where the Speaker, two other members of Congress, the deputy secretary of state, and the White House counsel Gibbs stood in a corner talking. The arrival of Latham's widow caused conversation to cease. Mondrian nodded at Dan Gibbs, who excused himself from the group and accompanied the COS and Ruth to the screen porch, where she and her husband had spent their final moments together. Mondrian shut the door. Ruth and Mondrian sat on the cushioned glider. Gibbs chose a red director's chair on which Congressman Paul Latham's name had been stenciled in white. A matching chair with Ruth's name on it occupied a far corner.

"Sorry to talk business at a time like this, Ruth," Mondrian said, "but there are things that need to be covered."

"Of course. Please, don't worry about me. I'm fine. It'll take a few days before I fall apart." She tried a laugh, instead swallowed hard and wiped a tear from her cheek. "What is it?"

"First," said Mondrian, "you're going to have to identify Paul's body."

"Identify it? Why? . . . Why, Bob? Is there any doubt it's him?"

"Strictly a formality, Ruth," said Gibbs. "Required by law."

"When?"

"Tomorrow. We'll go with you," Mondrian said.

"All right. I'll brace for that. Next?"

"Paul's office has been sealed," Gibbs said. "We have representatives there during the search. The White House, I mean."

"Of course."

"The house is next."

"The house? *This* house? Why, for heaven's sake?"

"To look for anything indicating Paul was in a frame of mind that might have led to taking his own life," Gibbs said.

"I assure you there's nothing here that would bear on that."

Gibbs nodded, smiled. "I'm sure you're right, Ruth, but again, it's—"

"A formality."

"Yes."

"Why is the White House so involved?" Ruth asked, pique in her voice. "Paul was a member of Congress. He never made it to the Cabinet."

"They'll also be looking for any files Paul brought home with him from the office," said Mondrian.

"And there's the funeral," Ruth said to her lap.

"The National Cathedral," Gibbs said.

"And a special memorial service in the Capitol. Statuary Hall, most likely," Mondrian said.

"That would be nice. Paul would have . . . liked that."

"Have you heard from Mr. Brazier?" Gibbs asked.

"Warren? No. Not yet. He's probably out of the country."

"He's here in Washington," Gibbs said, hoping it didn't sound as though he was challenging her.

"Then I'm sure he'll be calling soon," Ruth said.

Gibbs and Mondrian looked at each other before Gibbs spoke. "Ruth, did Paul say anything lately about his relationship with Brazier?"

Her cocked head said she wondered why the question had been asked.

"They'd been working closely on legislation in the economic policy and trade subcommittee," said Gibbs. "There's scuttlebutt; they had a falling out over it."

This time, Ruth's laugh came through. "Scuttlebutt? In Washington, D.C.? I can't believe it."

The men laughed gently.

"I've heard rumors that Paul was murdered."

Another glance between Gibbs and Mondrian. No comment.

"I don't believe he killed himself. It wasn't Paul. You asked about Warren. The answer is no. I don't know of any rift between them."

But then the conversation she'd had with her husband the night before came back to her:

HE: "I met with Warren this afternoon."

SHE: "Oh? A problem?"

HE: "Yes. . . . I told him I was backing off on the Russian Trade and Investment Bill."

SHE: "Isn't that the bill you said a few months ago was the most important Russian trade bill in your career?"

HE: "Yeah. I said that. And it would be. But there's something about it that's . . . wrong. Warren's staff keeps pushing for amendments to it that—well, frankly, that would distort its original intent. . . ."

SHE: "Was he angry?"

HE: "He was angry before I even told him. . . ."

And Paul had told her the president wanted him to pull back on any legislation involving Warren Brazier until the conclusion of the confirmation hearings.

She made a decision on the spot not to mention that conversation. She'd been in Washington, had been around government long enough, if only as a leading congressman's wife, to have developed the inherent, reflexive sense to think before speaking to anyone in an official capacity. Paul had been fond of quoting from a song to make that point, a blues tune by the pianist and singer Mose Allison: "Your mind is on vacation, your mouth is working overtime." He even sang it on occasion when in a scampish mood at parties, and given an extra bourbon and soda.

"The president called," Ruth said.

"I know," said Gibbs. "They were good friends."

"Mutually respectful," Ruth said. "Paul really believed in Joe Scott. The day of his inauguration, Paul was happier than I've ever seen him. He really felt Joe was the right person to lead the country."

"He was right," Gibbs said.

"When will they search the house?" she asked.

"They wanted to do it today," Mondrian said. "We convinced them it would be barbaric to do that to the family."

Ruth sighed. "No more barbaric than Paul being dead. He did not commit suicide!"

"That will be determined at the autopsy, Ruth," Mondrian said.

Martin Latham opened the door and said, "Mac Smith and his wife are here."

Mac and Annabel stood at the entrance to the living room. Ruth approached them, arms outstretched.

"I'm so sorry," Annabel said, embracing her.

"A terrible shock," Mac said. "How are you holding up?"

"Best we can, Mac. Come in. There's coffee and Danish. The bar is open. Paul would have wanted me to be the perfect hostess, no matter what the circumstance. A requisite for a congressman's wife."

They followed her into the large room, where others greeted them. New arrivals streamed into the house. Ruth shut drapes against the harsh lights from TV crews outside.

Mac and Annabel had coffee. As they sipped, Mac stuck out his hand to intercept Bob Mondrian on his way across the room. "A word?" Mac said.

"Sure."

"Just the two of us?"

"Okay."

Mondrian led Mac to the porch, which was empty. Alone, door closed, Mondrian said, "Ruth's doing pretty well. Martin and Molly, too. Priscilla's on a ship, but she'll be home in a couple of days."

"Bob, I have to ask you something."

"Go ahead."

"Where's Marge Edwards?"

"Marge? I—she's home, I suppose."

"She wasn't at the office this morning."

"No, she wasn't. I never even thought about that in the confusion. Why do you ask? Is there a problem?"

"There may be. Look, Bob, I have to do something I always dislike when others do it. I was told something today about Marge by someone whose identity I can't reveal. I don't know whether it's true or not, and I'm not asking you for verification. But I'm compelled to bring it up."

"Sounds serious."

"Not as serious as Paul's death, but damned unpleasant for Ruth and the kids."

"I'm listening."

"Marge was about to level a charge of sexual harassment against Paul."

If Smith's flat statement had an impact on Latham's chief of staff, his broad face didn't reflect it. He stared at Mac with unblinking eyes.

"Were you aware of this?" Smith asked.

"No."

"No hint of it? You and Marge work closely together."

"If I knew anything about it, I would have acted immediately." He scowled. "You aren't suggesting I knew about it and did nothing, are you?"

"Of course not."

"Assuming there's any validity to it."

"Yes. There's only the assumption. But let's say there *is* truth to what I was told. Let's say Marge did intend to bring such a charge against Paul. Have you ever witnessed anything that might give credence to her claim?"

He guffawed. "Of course not. Paul is—was—the classic straight arrow. Office hanky-panky? Fanny-patting? 'Gimme a kiss' by the watercooler? Come on, Mac. Paul Latham was the consummate gentleman, maybe not always when taking on another member of Congress, or an administration, but always the gentleman in his personal life."

"Of course, that's my read, too," Smith said. "Still, I had to bring it up with you. I'd like to talk to Marge before this rumor grows legs. You assumed she was at home. Can we give her a call?"

"Sure, only . . ."

"Only what?"

"Only I think it would be inappropriate to make that call from here. Ruth. The kids."

Smith nodded. "You're right. Annabel and I will be leaving soon. I tried Marge from home a few hours ago. There was no answer. I'll try again."

"Good. Anything else?"

"No. Heard anything on the autopsy?"

"Nope. Ruth's convinced he didn't kill himself. I agree."

"If he didn't—"

"Yeah. *If he didn't.* Thanks for bringing up this Marge thing, Mac. Sorry if I reacted badly at first. It's so ludicrous, it's almost laughable."

They were unsmiling as they prepared to leave the porch.

"I'll tell you one thing," Mondrian said. "If there is any truth to what you've told me, that Marge was considering making a ridiculous charge like this against Paul, it could only be because she's so damned unstable."

"I wasn't aware of that," Smith said.

"Some day I'll fill you in. This isn't the time."

Mac and Annabel left the house at nine. He tried Marge Edwards's number several times from home, to no avail.

Annabel had held off asking her husband what he and Mondrian discussed. She knew, of course, why Mac had cornered Latham's COS; he'd told her about Jessica Belle's allegation the moment he returned home from Rosslyn. Now, she asked.

He recounted the conversation with Mondrian.

"And?" she said when he'd finished.

"I can't help but be concerned, Annie. There's no reason for Jessica to have told me about it, other than being sincerely worried about the negative impact it might have on the Scott administration. Paul dies of a gunshot wound, and Marge can't be reached. Mondrian lays on me the idea that Marge is unstable. Is that true, or is it spin control in the event Marge *was* intending to charge Paul? Yeah, I'm concerned. It would devastate Ruth."

"But now that Paul is dead," Annabel said, "there's no reason for Marge to make such a charge. Is there? I mean, if she intended it to derail his confirmation—and that's assuming she ever intended any-thing—that goal is not to be gained any longer."

"True. But maybe she wasn't intending it to spike his confirmation. Maybe she really believes she's been a victim of sexual harassment, has some noble purpose for making it public."

"You know what, Mac?"

"What?"

"Here we are talking as though Jessica was right, that Marge did in-tend to bring such a charge. *We're* giving it legs."

Smith smiled. "Exactly what I told Mondrian I wanted to avoid. And that's what we'd better try and do before it takes off at a sprint."

The last person left the Latham house at midnight. Friends had offered to stay with Ruth and her two children, but she declined. "I think we'll do better if we can just be together alone," she told those who offered. They understood, having spent the night projecting themselves into her shoes.

Martin turned on the television, leaving Ruth to sit with Molly in the young girl's bedroom. They said nothing for a while, content to sit quietly and chew on their individual thoughts. It was Molly who broke the si-lence.

"Daddy didn't kill himself, did he?"

"We'll know that in a day or so," Ruth replied. "But no, I do not think he did."

"I mean, why would he? Everything was going great." She sat up on her bed, more animated. "He was going to be secretary of state. And he knew we loved him. Didn't he?"

This time, it was Molly's turn to comfort her mother, who broke down and sobbed softly.

"Didn't he know that?" Molly repeated.

"Of course he did, Molly. And we know he didn't kill himself. Some-one—someone shot him. God."

"Who?" Molly asked.

"I don't know, Rabbit. Some evil, warped person. But they'll find out. In the meantime, we have to be as strong as Daddy would want us to be.

We have to be dignified, and celebrate the wonderful life we've had with him. And that means we all need to get our sleep."

She hugged her daughter, running her hand through her silky blond hair. "I love you," she said.

"I love you, too, Mom. I even love Martin."

They both laughed quietly. Ruth said, "Martin just has trouble accepting our love. But down deep he loves this family as much as you and I do. Good night, sweetie. It'll be a tough day tomorrow."

As Ruth Latham went to the door, she noticed a package wrapped in brown paper and string on Molly's dresser. "What's that?" she asked.

"Oh, that? Just some books Dad gave me to read."

"Well, you won't be reading much for a few days. But once you're back in the page dorm, you'll have time to read again. Night."

She closed the door to Molly's bedroom, leaned against the wall, and wrapped her arms about herself to stem the shaking.

It *had* been murder. Her husband, Paul Latham, congressman from California, lover, father, companion, had been taken from them by another human being.

A murderer.

That realization doubled her over, and sent her to the bathroom, where she fell to her knees in front of the toilet.

CHAPTER SEVENTEEN

Anatoly Alekseyev's mood hadn't improved since being designated tour guide and baby-sitter for the three young Russians who'd flown into Washington with former KGB general Aleksandr Patiashvili.

After leaving Brazier's Washington offices, he'd driven them to where they were staying, the Holiday Inn on Capitol Hill, and waited in the lobby while they freshened up. They came down and said they were in the mood for seafood, so he took them for dinner to the appropriately touristy Hogate's, on the District's southwest waterfront.

Now, it was close to midnight. Alekseyev had wanted to drop them back at the hotel after dinner, but two of them, already tipsy from vodka consumed during dinner, insisted upon going to an American disco. Anatoly pointed out that discos were no longer the rage in America, which didn't dissuade them; they were popular in Russia. He decided on Georgetown's Deja Vu, one of many popular hangouts for Washington's young professionals, and where he often ended up after a night of pub crawling.

Deja Vu was crowded, as usual, and the rock music was played loud. They found space at the bar and ordered more *vodichka*, "darling little water" in Russian.

Alekseyev had twice excused himself during dinner at Hogate's to make phone calls. And he excused himself at Deja Vu for the same se.

rejoined the three at the bar and tried to participate in their drunken conversation. It wasn't easy. The two outgoing members of the group had grown increasingly boisterous and aggressive with young women seated next to them, fueled by the seemingly unending shots of vodka they'd downed. Alekseyev was uncomfortable with their behavior, and wished he'd taken them to a bar where he wasn't known. Too late for that. Getting them to leave took center stage.

He found an ally in the third member of the trio, Yvgeny Fodorov. Fodorov was obviously one of those people for whom alcohol generated depression, perhaps even anger, certainly not expansiveness. Unlike his flamboyant friends, Yvgeny had sunk deeper into morose drunkenness, his thin, sallow face set in a perpetual scowl, corners of his mouth drawn down, eyes watery from the alcohol.

"Hey, you all right?" Anatoly asked him.

"*Nyet.* I want to leave."

Alekseyev laughed. "Good. So do I." He slapped Yvgeny on the back and said to the others, "Come on, my friends, let's go."

They agreed to leave, but only if Anatoly would join them for a final drink at the hotel. "Okay," he said. Anything to get them out of Deja Vu.

The bar at the Holiday Inn was closed, but Alekseyev knew one a block away that would be open.

"*Nyet,*" Yvgeny said as they left the lobby. "I am going to bed."

Alekseyev envied him.

Later, at the bar, a quiet, neighborhood place with swing era big-band music coming softly from a jukebox, the two young Russians, new to Washington, quieted down considerably, to Anatoly's relief. Although they continued to drink, they seemed to sober up to some extent, and talk turned to topics other than sex and drinking—*dusha a dushe,* heart-to-heart talk.

"So, what do you do for Brazier Industries?" Alekseyev asked.

"Finance," one said. "Dealing with Russian banks."

"You?" Alekseyev asked the other.

"The same. The Central Bank must do something to avoid a liquidity crisis. We're trying to influence the bankers in this direction." He snickered. "The old man, Brazier, is going nuts, huh, trying to deal with Yeltsin and his cronies?" He lowered his voice as though to pass on a confidence. "You know what? He wants to buy Sidanco."

"Oh?" said Alekseyev.

"*Da.*"

"I would have known," Anatoly said. "It produces oil. My

A loud laugh this time. "Why should you know? No one knows what the next person is doing in this company. Am I right?"

His friend agreed.

"*Da.* He wants to buy Sidanco, but the government auction—some auction—the rules mean that only Oneximbank can buy it. Some auction, huh?"

"Some auction," Alekseyev agreed. He wasn't anxious to get into a lengthy debate over auctions, or banks, or anything, for that matter. Not at that hour.

He changed the subject. "What about Yvgeny?" he asked.

The two looked at each other and laughed. "The fag?" one said.

"Weird," said the other.

"What does he do for Brazier?" Alekseyev asked.

They shrugged. One said, "I asked him on the flight. He said he worked for security. I think it was the only thing he said the whole trip."

"Security," the other said scornfully. "We have more security than anything else. They're everywhere. Like the KGB, huh? Idiots!"

"He doesn't look like a security man to me," Alekseyev said, putting money on the bar and standing. "Tomorrow at seven." He checked his watch. "Almost two. Come on, or we'll be here all night."

He walked them back to the hotel, got in his car, and drove to his apartment.

Across town, in the Holiday Inn on Capitol Hill, Yvgeny Fodorov was too busy to think of sleep.

There had been an envelope in his room when he arrived after their night out. He opened it and removed the airline ticket it contained, the note, and the five hundred dollars in American money, which he put in his wallet.

The ticket was for the Delta Shuttle from Washington's National Airport to New York's LaGuardia.

The note, written in Russian, instructed him to take the first flight the following morning, and to contact a person in Brighton Beach, Brooklyn, whose phone number was included.

The final line of the note was: *You are to stay there until contacted. Everything you need will be supplied.*

The note wasn't signed.

Fodorov paced the room. Every light burned brightly; the television was on, loud. His mind raced. So much had happened to him in such a short period of time.

• • •

Yvgeny Fodorov's mother, Vani, had stipulated in her will that she was to be cremated, and that there was to be no religious service. Instead, she asked that her closest friends gather in a favorite restaurant, and eat and drink in her memory. She earmarked a small sum from her estate to pay for this.

The party to celebrate Vani Fodorov's life was held in B. B. King Blues Club on Sadovaya-Samotyochnaya, which had opened to considerable fanfare because of the appearance of the American blues master for whom the club was named. Vani's party was attended by a few dozen men and women, who feasted on American-style ribs and cornbread, augmented by Russian *shashlik*—grilled spicy lamb—und *pelmeni*—stuffed cabbage leaves—with *vodichka,* a Russian champagne called *shampanskoye,* and later, *konyak,* brandy from Georgia.

Yvgeny, of course, was there as the grieving son, receiving words of condolence from his mother's friends and fellow writers, hearing the expressions of horror at how she died: "The *mafiya,*" they said. "Pigs! Killers!"

"And all of them writers. Killed. In one day. Why?"

Yvgeny told them he didn't have an answer. "Maybe it wasn't the *mafiya,*" he said. "Maybe it was a sick, demented individual. A nut."

His suggestion was met with a firm, "*Nyet!* How could it be one person? Four writers murdered in the same day, many miles from each other. I tell you, it was the damned *mafiya.*"

The arguments were short-lived because there was too much food and alcohol, and dancing to the infectious blues music coming through massive loudspeakers, to enjoy.

Privately, there were comments made about Yvgeny, few of them complimentary. His brooding, cold nature was well known to those at the party, if not through direct experience with him, certainly because of stories told over the years by his mother. Guests made remarks behind his back about his black suit and shirt and skinny white tie. Some at the gathering were aware of his friendship with the lower echelons of Moscow's criminal society. They, of course, were not the ones espousing to his face the theory that Vani Fodorov and three other writers had been murdered by the mafia.

The party started at four and lasted into the night. Most stayed—Vani Fodorov's celebratory party would have made her happy—but Yvgeny left at six, saying good-bye to no one. He wasn't missed.

He took a city bus to the Mezhdunarodnaya Hotel, got off, and walked along Krasnopresnenskaya-Naberezhnaya until reaching the floating casino, the Alexander Blok, permanently moored there. It was one of dozens of casinos that had sprung up in Moscow, feeding on the inflationary climate of the city and the former Soviet Union.

The gaming tables were already busy when he arrived. He walked through the main room to a door leading to a set of stairs down to a small dock area, where a half-dozen men sat at a makeshift table playing cards. They glanced up at Yvgeny as he descended the wooden stairs, but paid him no more attention than that, returning to their game.

Yvgeny lit a cigarette and leaned against a wooden railing. Below, small craft bobbed in the brown wake of excursion boats. The sky was clear and blue, marred only by fast-moving cirrus clouds high above. A gentle breeze came off the water, carrying the smell of the waterway's pollution to his nostrils.

He'd been there ten minutes—three cigarettes—when the door opened and his friend, Felix, came through it, followed by an older, heavyset man. The card players laid down their hands and watched. The older man, the second to come down the stairs, waved for them to leave, which they did immediately, and without discussion.

Felix and Yvgeny embraced, awkwardly, as men tend to do. The older man watched, heavy legs planted solidly on the weathered gray wood of the dock, a cigarette jutting from his lips in an ivory holder, giving his crude, large features an odd touch of elegance.

Felix stepped back from Yvgeny and said, "My friend, please meet Mr. Pralovich." He stepped aside for Yvgeny to shake Pralovich's large hand.

"Yvgeny Fodorov," Pralovich said, as though deciding whether he liked the sound of it. "*Da*. I know of you. From Felix. From others."

Yvgeny knew Gennady Pralovich by reputation. He was a Moscow *mafiya* boss, a *rukovodstvo*, a made man, with dozens of street gangs reporting to him through a cadre of underbosses. He lived in a mansion, was driven in an armor-plated Mercedes 500, and was fond of Fendi fur coats and Hennessy cognac at such favored bars as the Up and Down Club.

Like other mafia organizations in other countries, the Russians didn't limit their criminal schemes to street-level bullying. Their influence and power reached into the highest echelons of government, into the offices of the secretaries of the party district committees, the Central Committee, and the Council of Ministers. Pralovich, it was claimed, controlled more than a hundred Moscow business enterprises, seemingly legitimate, but firmly directed by him and his lieutenants; a small percentage, perhaps, of more than forty thousand *mafiya*-controlled businesses in Russia—an estimated half of the country's one hundred stock exchanges, 60 percent of its 2,200 banks—but lucrative enough to rank him as a leading criminal boss.

It was also said of Gennady Pralovich that when other *mafiya* bosses needed an assassin for a particularly difficult assignment, they turned to Pralovich. His small group of hitmen, many of them Chechens imported from the Caucasus to Moscow, were considered the best. They'd made a solid contribution to the dramatic rise in Moscow's premeditated murders, from a little over one hundred in 1987 to almost fifteen hundred in 1993—eight and a half murders a day, more than half of them never solved.

"Felix tells me you are a good man, Yvgeny Fodorov, a good soldier."

Yvgeny didn't know what to say.

"I know from others, too, about what you have been doing for us. Impressive. Very impressive." He pulled a cigarette pack from the pocket of the tight-fitting gray suit he wore, and offered it to Yvgeny.

"Nyet," Yvgeny said. *"Spasiba." Don't offend him by failing to say thank you.*

Pralovich said to Felix, "Go get a drink or something. Your friend here and I have something to discuss."

Yvgeny was uncomfortable seeing his friend go up the stairs and disappear through the door, leaving him alone with Gennady Pralovich. The *mafiya* boss leaned on the railing and looked out over the water, drawing deeply on his cigarette. Yvgeny lighted up, too, not sure whether by choosing his own brand, he would offend. It didn't seem to matter.

Pralovich continued to smoke in silence, increasing Yvgeny's discomfort. Then, in a voice void of emotion or inflection, he said into the breeze that had picked up, "You killed your own mother."

"I was told—"

"Yes, I know, Yvgeny Fodorov. You were told to do it. What is impressive to me is that you followed that order. Your own mother. Flesh and blood. You came from her womb."

"I want to please," said Yvgeny, wishing Pralovich would turn and face him.

"Of course you do. So do many other young men like yourself. But most would not . . ." Now, he turned slowly and smiled. "Most would not follow orders to kill their mother."

"I—"

"But you did."

"*Da.*"

"Did you love her?"

The question stunned Yvgeny. Love her? Why would he ask that?

"Did you? Love your mother, Yvgeny?"

What should the answer be? Which answer would please him?

"I am used to having my questions answered," Pralovich said.

"I loved her."

"Did you? I am glad to hear that. We should love our mothers, *da*? They give us life."

Yvgeny said nothing.

"It must have been even more difficult for you to kill her, loving her as you did."

"It was."

Pralovich now leaned his back against the railing. He looked up into the sky and smiled, drew an audible deep breath. "Today is a good day. A clear day."

"It is a clear day," Yvgeny parroted.

"Have you ever been away from the Soviet Union, Yvgeny?"

Yvgeny was surprised that Pralovich used that name for his country. It was pleasing to his ear.

"*Nyet,*" Yvgeny replied. "Never."

"Would you like to take a trip?"

"Yes."

"Are you free to leave immediately?"

"Yes."

"If I decide to choose you for this very important job, you must realize the great danger you will face."

Yvgeny's blood pulsed strong. His heart pounded.

Please, let it be me he chooses.

"We have a customer, Yvgeny, a client who pays us well. He has asked that we do him a great service. It will be difficult to satisfy him, but with the right person—"

"Yes, Mr.—Comrade Pralovich. I am ready to serve."

"Are you?"

"Yes, sir."

"But you do not know what you must do. Do you not care?"

"*Da*, I care, but I am willing to do anything."

"Yes, I suppose you are. You killed your beloved mother to prove that to us. I mustn't forget that. It was necessary to send a message from our Communist friends to the fools in power, huh? Necessary. Your mother, and others whose interests were different from our friends', wrote bad things about them. Our customers. It will happen to others, I can assure you."

Pralovich returned his attention to the water. A sightseeing boat passed, and passengers waved. Pralovich returned their greetings. Yvgeny started to, but kept his hands at his sides.

The *mafiya* boss turned and looked through Yvgeny's thick glasses into his anxious eyes. He nodded. "Yes, I think you are the one, Yvgeny Fodorov. Here." He handed Yvgeny an envelope. "In it you will find everything you need. You are to contact the person mentioned in this envelope immediately. He will provide you with other things. You leave tomorrow."

Yvgeny wasn't sure he could get the words out. "Yes, tomorrow. Where am I going?"

"America. Washington, D.C. The capital of that powerful country."

"And when I am there?"

"You will be told when it is necessary for you to know. Go now. The person mentioned in the envelope waits for you. *Dobry vecher*, Yvgeny Fodorov."

"Yes, sir. Good evening."

"Do your job well."

"I will. I will."

"One final thing."

"Yes?"

"Buy a better suit before you leave. You look like a fool in that."

By midnight, Yvgeny had purchased a more conservative suit and accessories, and had met with the man mentioned in the envelope, who gave him a passport, instructions on who to contact upon arrival in the United States, and emergency numbers to call in the event of trouble. His flight would leave from Moscow at ten in the morning, not much time for most people to pull together last-minute things. But for Yvgeny Fodorov, there was nothing to pull together.

When he met Felix for a drink at one in the morning, his small bag was packed and he was ready to go.

"What are you to do?" his friend asked.

"I don't know," Yvgeny answered truthfully. "I will be told."

"It must be very important, Yvgeny. *Very* important."

"*Da.*"

"I envy you."

"Yes."

"Good things will be yours—if all goes well." He managed to keep the resentment he felt from his voice. He'd brought Yvgeny into the gang. It should have been him, Felix, chosen for such an important assignment.

"I know."

Yvgeny then did something uncommonly gregarious for him. He raised his glass in a toast. Felix touched his rim to Yvgeny's.

"To my only friend, Felix."

"And to a safe journey for you, Yvgeny."

As Felix said it, he knew he would never see Yvgeny Fodorov again.

CHAPTER EIGHTEEN

By the time Mac and Annabel got up the next morning, an hour before their clock radio went off at seven, the Washington press corps was reporting two startling, unsettling stories.

According to "reliable sources," Congressman Paul Latham had not taken his own life. The autopsy showed that the bullet had been fired from a distance.

And, according to another reliable source, a charge of sexual harassment was to have been leveled against the congressman by a female employee, his scheduling secretary, Marge Edwards.

The latter story broke in that morning's edition of the conservative Washington *Standard,* and was reported on local TV. The article had been written by Jules Harris, a freelance journalist, who said in his piece that repeated attempts to contact Ms. Edwards had been unsuccessful.

Harris's timing had not been good. The thrust of his story was that the sexual harassment charge had been a factor in Latham's decision to take his life.

But the other story—that Latham *hadn't* killed himself—rendered the Harris article itself unreliable, despite its so-called unimpeachable source.

Over melon and berries, toast and coffee, Mac and Annabel watched the early morning news in their kitchen.

"Well," Mac said, "it's out."

"Marge Edwards, you mean?"

"Yeah. I can only imagine what Ruth is feeling."

"And it was murder."

"If the 'reliable source' is right, which I suspect he or she is. 'Suicide' wasn't in Paul's vocabulary."

Annabel shivered against a sudden internal chill. "Murder! A U.S. congressman gunned down. It had to have been a professional killing, an assassination."

"Certainly looks that way. Whoever shot Paul took the time to place the gun in his hand. Still, not a very smart assassin. Any fool knows that even the most inept medical examiner can determine whether a shot was fired close enough to have been suicide."

"Maybe he did it to cause confusion, buy some time."

"Or he decided to improvise. . . . Why do we keep saying 'he'?"

"Assassins are usually men," Annabel said.

"*That* sort of assassin, at least."

She let it pass.

"Marge Edwards. I'll try to reach her again. This story that she was going to charge Paul with sexual harassment might be just that, a story. All she has to do is deny it. That'd put an end to it."

"If she's willing to come forward. Looks like she's gone underground."

"To avoid having to comment."

"Do you think your friend Jessica Belle might be the source of this reporter's story?"

"Can't imagine why."

"She was *your* source."

"Hmmmm."

"You've been reasonably close to Paul all these years, especially recently. Who would have wanted him dead?"

"No idea. He was one of the most revered members of the House."

"Powerful, too."

"Meaning?"

"Power makes enemies."

"Sounds like something Kissinger might say."

"He probably has. Mac, this is all just now hitting me. The meaning of it."

"Me, too."

The phone rang. Mac reached for the kitchen extension.

"Hello, Jessica. Yes, I've heard. Where are you?"

"Still in L.A."

"It's three in the morning for you."

"I haven't been to bed. Anything you can tell me from that end?"

"No. Annabel and I have been watching the news. We've been to see Ruth Latham."

Mac realized he was *reporting* to Jessica.

"I'm flying back this morning. I'd like to talk to you again."

"All right. Any idea who leaked the rumor about Marge Edwards?"

She said nothing right away; time to think? he wondered.

"No. You?"

"No."

"The allegation that he was murdered hasn't been verified, has it?"

"Not as far as I know, Jessica. But it makes sense, doesn't it?"

"I don't think murder ever makes sense," she said.

"I meant that it was highly unlikely he took his own life. I'll look forward to your call."

When Smith hung up, Annabel said, "You seem angry."

"Not angry. Perplexed is more accurate."

The phone rang again. A reporter. Another called ten minutes later.

"Want me to answer while you shower?" Annabel asked.

"No. Let technology handle it. Come on, this promises to be a splendid day I'm sure we'll both rather forget."

After showering and dressing, Mac called Bob Mondrian at Latham's Rayburn Building office.

"How goes it?" he asked the COS.

Mondrian answered with an audible exhalation. "They turned the offices upside down, Mac. Walked out of here with boxes of materials."

"To be expected. Have you been in contact with Marge Edwards?"

"No answer at her apartment. She hasn't shown up here."

"That's cause for concern, isn't it?"

"Sure. I've got a couple of my people looking for her. I talked to her father in Indiana. Mother's dead. Her father says he hasn't heard from her."

"Did he have anything to say about the story?"

"No. And I didn't raise it. He said he'd have her call me if she showed up."

"The autopsy leak. I assume it's true," Mac said.

"Right. For some reason, the ME is dragging his feet in releasing the results. I heard this morning that Senator Connors is behind it."

"I heard the president is."

"I doubt that, Mac. The faster Paul's death is verified as murder, the faster this ridiculous rumor that Marge was about to charge him with sexual harassment vaporizes. Anything new on your end?"

"No. The FBI is due here at ten. Spoken with Ruth yet about the stories?"

"Yeah. She's a strong lady. She dismissed the Marge Edwards thing with 'That's nonsense.' End of comment."

"Good for her. I'd like to come down after my session with the FBI. You'll be there?"

"I expect to be, trying to put this place back in order."

"Noon. Free for lunch?"

Mondrian laughed. "Lunch? What's that? Sure. I'll order sandwiches up."

Annabel joined her husband in the den.

"The FBI's due here in an hour," he said.

"I don't have to be here, do I?"

"I don't see any reason why you should be. Unless you want to."

"I don't want to. I think I'll head for the gallery, catch up on some paperwork."

"I'm going to Paul's office at noon."

"Oh? Why?"

"Talk to Mondrian. See if I can learn more about the Marge Edwards story. Mondrian says she's still missing."

Annabel's face took on a worried look.

"I'm sure Marge has simply decided to lay low for a while, stay out of the spotlight," he said.

"I hope you're right."

Fifteen minutes later she reappeared in the den dressed to leave. They kissed. "Keep in touch," she said.

"I will."

He walked her to the door and opened it. Outside, a half-dozen media types milled about. Two uniformed MPD officers in a marked car kept an eye on them.

"Ready?" Mac asked.

"Sure."

They greeted the press and walked past them, down the street to the garage they rented from an elderly neighbor. Reporters followed.

"Any comment about the sexual harassment charge against Latham?" one asked.

"No," Mac replied. "No comment."

"He was your client."

"Right."

"They say he was murdered."

"I'd prefer to wait for the official autopsy report," Mac said.

"Mrs. Smith, have you talked to Mrs. Latham?"

Annabel ignored the question.

"What's the mood over there?" the reporter followed up.

Annabel stopped, started to express her dismay at the question, shook her head, and followed Mac into the garage. " 'What's the mood over there?' " she said disgustedly. "Joyous, of course."

"Ignore them," said Mac, opening the driver's-side door for her. "They're just doing their job."

She started the engine.

"Drive careful, Annabel," Mac said, a sudden, fleeting vision of his wife and son being hit head-on causing him to wince.

"I will. And you take care."

Mac went to the sidewalk, where the press stood in front of the open garage door. "Better get out of the way," he said. "She has trouble backing up."

The two FBI agents who questioned Mac that morning were efficient, polite, and on time. Their questions were short, well prepared, and to the point. Mac told them what he knew, which wasn't much. The only question that piqued his interest was about Marge Edwards. One of the agents said, "We've put out an all-points on Ms. Edwards, Mr. Smith. You haven't heard from her, have you?"

"No, nor would I expect to. I knew her, but only as someone working in Congressman Latham's office. His scheduling secretary. I didn't know her outside of her office capacity."

The agent jotted his reply in a notebook.

The questioning went on for another ten minutes. Satisfied Smith had nothing to offer beyond what he'd already told them, they thanked him for his time and were gone by ten-thirty.

He again tried to concentrate on research for the Russian project, but couldn't get more than ten minutes into it each time before the phone would ring.

His boss, dean of GW's law school, called "just to chat," eventually getting around to asking Mac what was *really* going on in the Latham case.

A woman from a local library called to see whether Mac would be the guest speaker at an October program. He said he'd be in Russia, but thanked her for thinking of him.

Annabel called just to see how he was.

He let Rufus out in the postage-stamp-sized fenced yard long enough for the dog to mark his favorite tree, called for a taxi, and waited in the foyer for its arrival. The phone rang. The cab pulled up. Mac locked the door behind him, waved off questions, climbed into the back of the cab, and told the driver to take him to the Rayburn Office Building.

Inside the Smith residence, the answering machine gave out Mac's message: "I can't take your call right now, but please leave your name, number, and a brief message after the tone and I'll return the call as soon as possible." He'd recently added to the message: "And please, either repeat your number, or say it slowly the first time." Callers who rattled off numbers had joined what was becoming a long list of Mackensie Smith's pet peeves.

Marge Edwards listened to Smith's outgoing message. When it was finished, she slowly, quietly hung up.

CHAPTER NINETEEN

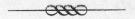

Yvgeny Fodorov had gotten to National Airport three hours before the first Delta Shuttle flight to New York. He sat stoically on a bench until a coffee shop opened, and ordered two jelly doughnuts and tea, into which he poured four sugars.

He was first in line when the flight was called, his only luggage the small carry-on he'd traveled with from Moscow. As with the flight to the United States, he felt naked without the gun. He had it with him always back home. But one of his instructions before leaving Moscow was that he was never to attempt to carry a weapon aboard any flight. There would always be another weapon, he was assured, at his various destinations.

The driver of his taxi was a black man. Yvgeny hated black people even more than Jews. Being in America was uncomfortable enough without having to be close to so many of them. There were few blacks in Russia, but too many Jews. You had to get rid of them, or at least keep them in their place, if any country was to be successful.

He showed the driver the address in Brighton Beach, and settled into the backseat.

The cabbie, one of New York's friendlier, more talkative ones, tried to engage Yvgeny in conversation, asking him where he was from—"Soviet Union"—what it was like there—"Nice, good"—and what he thought of America—"Nice, good." But that was the extent of it. Most of the tr into Brooklyn was made in silence, with Yvgeny staring out the w at the striking visual mosaic that was New York, crossing the river by bridge and proceeding into the borough of Brooklyn, down Ocean Parkway, turning off onto Coney Island Avenue until the outlines of the Cyclone roller-coaster and the rusting, abandoned steel skeleton of the parachute jump came into view. A few minutes later, they were on Brighton Beach Avenue, and soon Yvgeny felt more at home. They passed shops heralding Russian food—*kasha,* black bread, herring, sturgeon, and caviar—on signs written in Russian. People on the streets looked Russian. There were no black faces.

The cab came to a stop in front of a peeling, two-story gray building. Yvgeny leaned closer to the window and squinted through his thick glasses to read the sign above the door: BRIS AVROHOM. The driver said, "Here you are, my man," and pointed to the meter. Yvgeny dug money from the envelope in his jacket pocket and handed it to the smiling driver, who counted off the fare and handed back the change. "Welcome to the good ol' USA, my man," he said. "Glad we're not at war with you guys no more." He laughed heartily.

Yvgeny said nothing as he exited the taxi and slammed the door. The driver leaned across the front seat and said, "What's the matter, man? I didn't give you a nice ride?"

Yvgeny stared at him.

"This is America, buddy. We tip cabbies in America." He extended his hand, palm up, through the open window.

"Nyet," Yvgeny said. *"Ya nye panimahyu!"* But he *did* understand what the driver wanted. Before the collapse of the Soviet Union, tipping was rarely practiced. But with the influence of the West, that had changed.

"Da svidanye," Yvgeny said, turning away and entering the building, his curt good-bye prompting a loud and vigorous string of obscenities from the driver, ending with "You Commie bastard!"

The driver couldn't know how right he was.

Yvgeny shut the building door against the tirade and looked about the small room that he'd entered. There was a metal desk and two chairs, a long wood— bench along one wall, a four-drawer steel file cabinet, and a yellow braided rug that needed to be cleaned.

the few pictures on the wall, photographs of Russia, he al scenes of mountains and rivers taken in the good

dow.?

losed door behind the desk. Should he open it? Fodorov

wondered. His question was answered when the door was opened by someone else.

A slender man dressed in a heavy wool three-piece suit, white shirt, and narrow red tie entered the room. His hair was wet, and combed from ear to ear across a tan, pitted bald pate. He wore glasses tethered around his neck by a black cord. His mustache was a thin line across his upper lip.

Fodorov greeted him in Russian. The man returned the greeting. "You are?" he asked.

"Yvgeny Fodorov. Here."

Fodorov handed him a piece of paper included in his envelope of instructions.

The man moved his glasses lower on his nose and read the note. His expression was pained, as though the note had wounded him. He handed it back to Fodorov and said, "Come."

They went through the door and up a narrow stairway to the second floor. The man opened a door and stepped back for Yvgeny to enter.

The room into which Fodorov stepped was as plush as the downstairs had been spartan. The floor was covered with thick Oriental carpets, one on top of the other. The furniture was oversized, chairs with wide wooden arms and heavy brocade red and yellow cushions and backs. The smell of incense and the scent of fried foods hung heavy in the air.

A small kitchen was off the main room. The shadow of someone in it moved like an ethereal vision across the walls.

"Sit there," Fodorov's greeter said, pointing to one of the chairs and leaving the room.

Yvgeny tried to see who was in the kitchen, but the shadow prevailed. Then, the open doorway to the kitchen was filled by a hulking man with a huge belly, whose shaved head almost touched the top of the frame. He wore a black T-shirt, brown cardigan sweater secured by a single button, baggy black pants, and carpet slippers. A massive cross sat on his bulging stomach, secured to his thick neck by a leather thong. Large gold rings studded with diamonds on both hands caught the light, tossing their brilliance at Fodorov.

Fodorov stood, mumbled hello.

"*Zdrastvuitye,*" the man echoed in a deep, gravelly voice. He stepped into the room and extended his hand; Yvgeny's hand disappeared into it. "I am Pavel Bakst. Welcome."

"Thank you," said Fodorov.

"Sit. Some coffee? Tea? Vodka? Beer?"

Fodorov asked for tea with sugar.

Bakst disappeared into the kitchen. A minute later a tea kettle's whistle sounded. Bakst reappeared carrying a tray with tea, a sugar bowl, milk, and a plate of *vetchina,* sliced ham, a salted cheese called *suluguni,* and blini, small, traditional Russian pancakes.

Yvgeny ate eagerly while Bakst, who'd settled in a facing chair, watched, his thick lips set in an amused smile. When Yvgeny had finished, Bakst said, "So, Mr. Yvgeny Fodorov, you work for Brazier Industries."

"*Da.* But only temporary. On a special assignment."

"I see. I am told you are an associate of Gennady Pralovich in Moscow."

Fodorov wanted to agree, but was anxious not to stretch the truth. "Associate? *Nyet.* I am only a soldier."

"But he sends you on such an important assignment. He must think highly of you."

"I like to think so, Mr. Bakst."

Bakst shifted his bulk in the chair. "Well," he said, "it is our pleasure to host you until you are needed again. We will do everything to make your stay pleasant."

Yvgeny felt an inner glow. To be treated with such respect was warming. He suppressed a smile of satisfaction.

"Do you know what they call this Brighton Beach, Yvgeny?"

"*Nyet.*"

"Little Odessa. Twenty, maybe thirty thousand fellow Russians here. Like being home, huh?" He laughed.

"It feels good," Fodorov said. "I do not like America."

"Oh? You do not like the land of opportunity?"

"I do not."

"The streets are paved with gold here, Fodorov."

Yvgeny's laugh was scoffing.

"You laugh. But it is true. We do very well here. Better than in Russia."

Yvgeny's face was serious. "How can that be?" he asked.

"There is more money here to be gotten," Bakst said. "We have made nroads in America. Millions from our gasoline-tax projects erica is ripe for the taking."

nodded. "I see," he said.

"Of course, we have had to make certain business arrangements with the local Italians. They have had it all to themselves for many years. Now, they have become weak, their leaders sent away. And we are here to step in."

"One day . . ."

"One day what, Fodorov?"

"One day when Yeltsin is gone and we are again in power in Russia— when it is the Soviet Union again—there will be gold on our streets, too."

Bakst had wrapped a blini around some ham and cheese, and had just bitten into it when Yvgeny issued his proclamation. The large man laughed, coughed, and spit the food onto the rugs. He continued laughing. Fodorov felt anger, but quickly told himself not to show it. He waited until the coughing and laughing had subsided before asking, "I am sorry if I said something wrong, Mr. Bakst."

"Who are you talking about?" Bakst asked, kicking the food aside with his slipper.

"Who? I meant the Communists."

"The Communists?" He fell into another laughing and coughing fit.

Fodorov decided to say nothing.

"The Communists? An *apparatchik,* are you, Fodorov? A loyal believer."

"*Da.* Aren't you?"

"*Nyet,* Fodorov. I hold no beliefs for any political party. It does not matter who sits in the *Kreml.* They call it the Kremlin here. Americans want to go to Moscow to see the Kremlin. For what? To spend their money? To look at something that never worked? Communism. Democracy. What does it matter? It is only the *Organizatsiya* that matters, my young, idealistic friend. Only us, the *mafiya.* The Italians call it 'our thing.' It is no longer their thing. Now, it is *our* thing."

Fodorov fought himself to keep from extending the conversation. He was confused, but did not want to admit it.

In Moscow, he and his colleagues worked for the Communists, did they not? Was it not the same here? The Communists paid for his services, for the services of everyone in the organization. He'd been paid by them to kill his own mother. Not directly, of course, but he knew why he'd been instructed to do it. To send a message, the way they'd sent a message by taking away his father so many years ago for his traitorous writings, or refusing to register his mother's typewriter.

Killing his mother had been surprisingly easy. He'd hated her for what seemed to be his whole life. Still, while driving back to Moscow after leaving her lifeless body in the *dacha,* he'd suffered a wave of sadness, even self-loathing. It didn't last long. By the time he reached the city, an exaltation had consumed him, and he couldn't wait to report that he'd accomplished his mission, and to receive their praise, slaps on the back, shots of vodka to down in celebration for having taken on such a difficult assignment. That's exactly what did happen upon his return to Moscow, and he hadn't felt sadness or self-loathing again.

"It is very good tea, Mr. Bakst," Yvgeny said.

"Thank you. It is time to take you to where you will stay. Tonight, you will join us for dinner. We have some fine restaurants here, Yvgeny. Authentic. Good Russian food and drink. Music. Entertainers. Later, there will be a woman for you."

Bakst brought Fodorov downstairs to where the little man with the mustache sat at a desk. He instructed him to have someone pick Yvgeny up immediately, and to take him "to Misha's house."

"I would like to have a weapon," Yvgeny said quietly. "For protection. They would not let me bring mine."

"Of course they wouldn't, because they are smart. But you won't need protection here, my friend." He slapped Fodorov hard on the back. "We take care of each other. Go now. Rest. There is plenty to drink and eat at Misha's. Not far from here."

Fodorov stood on the sidewalk with Bakst until the car arrived. Many people passing greeted Bakst. He must be very important, Yvgeny thought. A leader. A boss.

He looked back at the sign above the front door. BRIS AVROHOM. "What is that?" he asked.

"A fine organization to welcome our Russian citizens to America, help them settle, find work, housing. We are not—how shall I say it?—we are not an official part of it. But we raise money for it. The sign is good, huh? It says we care, to the authorities at least." A laugh. "We have our own ways to welcome our fellow Russians to this country. The sign? No one tells us to take it down, so it stays up. Ah, here is your car. I will see you tonight, Fodorov. Take a nap. Nights last a very long time in Little Odessa."

The party at Rasputin, one of Brighton Beach's most popular Russian restaurants, lasted until four the next morning. A band played loud dance music, augmented during its intermissions by strolling minstrels.

The first course was served at eleven—*borscht,* containing real red beets, Yvgeny was told, as opposed to the borscht of the old Soviet Union, consisting mainly of cabbage. Crab and shrimp dishes followed, then lamb smothered in a succulent sauce of mushrooms and cranberries, accompanied by stuffed cabbage leaves and rice and potatoes and over-flowing green salads. Fodorov had never seen so much food at one sitting, and he took advantage of it, stuffing his face while attempting to engage in the spirited, raucous conversations around him.

A pretty young girl asked him to dance. He didn't want to because he didn't know how. She laughed when he told her that, and said she would teach him.

On the dance floor, she said in a giddy voice, "My father says you are a very important person from Moscow."

Fodorov wasn't sure how to respond, so he laughed. "Who is your father?" he asked, stumbling over his feet as she led him to the beat of the music.

"Bakst," she said.

"Bakst. Oh. He is your father?"

"Yes. He says you are here on an important job."

"I—I cannot talk about that," Yvgeny said.

She giggled. "Of course you can't. Now watch, follow me. It's easy."

Yvgeny kept his eyes on Bakst's daughter, Trina, all night. He liked her. She was pretty, like Sofia, but without Sofia's silly ways. Trina had called her father by his last name. Strange, thought Yvgeny. It must be the way *mafiya* bosses are referred to in America. Each time Fodorov thought of what Trina had said, that her father considered him an important person from Moscow, he was filled with pleasure he dared not exhibit.

After all, he was now a hardened, paid killer.

Hardened, paid killers did not smile.

At five in the morning, Yvgeny lay in bed with a prostitute Bakst had dispatched to Misha's house for the visitor's pleasure. He knew he was not a skilled lover, so sought to compensate by treating the short, pale, chubby girl roughly. She didn't complain, simply went through her motions as quickly as possible and left the small room.

Outside, she climbed into her Russian pimp's Cadillac. The sun was rising over Coney Island and Brighton Beach. She gently touched her breasts through the fabric of her dress, where Yvgeny had hurt her.

The pimp had told her that her final customer for the night would be an important visitor from Moscow, according to Bakst.

"How was he?" the pimp asked, lighting a cigarette and starting the engine.

"Creepy," she replied. "A faggot."

Her pimp laughed as he pulled away from the curb. "Next time we should send him a boy," he said.

"Next time," she said, "send him a dog."

CHAPTER TWENTY

Mac Smith walked into the office of former congressman Paul Latham and went directly to where Bob Mondrian sat at a computer. Mondrian held up his index finger, and went back to his task. Smith waited patiently. Finally, Mondrian stood, shook Smith's hand, and suggested they go into the congressman's office.

"Getting squared away?" Smith asked once the door was closed behind them.

"In a manner of speaking," Mondrian said. "The official ME's autopsy report is about to be announced. I got the call a few minutes ago."

"No surprises, I assume."

"No. It was murder. That's a definite. The FBI is holding a news conference in a half hour."

"Murder's no novelty in Washington," Smith said, more to himself than to the chief of staff. "But a congressman . . ."

"Presidents have fallen to the bullet," Mondrian said, settling behind Latham's desk and gesturing to a chair across from it.

Smith sat.

"Another blow to the country," Mondrian said. "Every time a leader is killed, the whole nation loses another thread in its moral fabric."

Smith looked across the desk at Bob Mondrian. He was aware of the high regard in which Latham had held his COS. Mondrian, besides being a skilled and effective staffer, was a keen student of history. Latham had once told Smith, "Sometimes I feel downright inferior to Bob. I love history, but he really *knows* it. Quotes Thucydides all the time. Considers him the greatest of all the historians. Spends his vacations traveling to major historical sites. He'd make a hell of a professor, if he wasn't such a good pol."

Smith asked Mondrian, "Any leads that you know of?"

Mondrian shook his head. What he then said gave credence to his reputation. "I spent a few weeks this summer in Albania, Mac. On a CODEL."

"CODEL?"

"Congressional Delegation trip. Never got close to Corfu, though, where the Peloponnesian War took place between Athens and Sparta. It settled the question of who would dominate Greece. Once Athens lost its navy, it was no contest." Mondrian smiled. "Don't mean to ramble."

"Feel free."

"The minute I heard about Paul's death, all I could think of was what Pericles said about leaders being killed."

"What did Pericles say? My history's not up to yours."

" 'Trees, though they are cut and lopped, grow up again quickly, but if men are destroyed, it is not easy to replace them.' "

"As true now as back then, before the coming of Christ," Smith said.

"Maybe even more so now," Mondrian said gruffly.

"The FBI interviewed me this morning," Smith said.

"Right. You said they would be. Painless?"

"Relatively. They've put out an all-points on Marge Edwards."

"So I understand. Her father called here this morning."

"And?"

"He was upset. He now knows about the story that Marge was poised to charge Paul with sexual ·harassment. Some local press out there are bugging him for a statement. And he was visited last night by a guy billing himself as a private detective."

"Who's this detective working for?"

A shrug from Mondrian. "I didn't ask. Her father said his name was Petrone. Something like that."

"Uh huh. Any word on who'll fill Paul's seat?"

"The leadership wants Ruth to push for it."

"Oh?"

"She won't, of course. A great congressman's wife, but basically apolitical."

Smith smiled. "That might be one of her most endearing attributes."

Mondrian raised his eyebrows, then allowed a half smile to surface. "Not a fan of the political process, Mac?"

"Depends upon who's doing what in that process. Bob, when I told you at Paul's house about the Marge Edwards rumor, you dismissed it, then said that if it were true, it was because she's so—how did you put it?—because she's so 'damned unstable.' Care to elaborate on that?"

Mondrian chewed his cheek, sat back, and rubbed his eyes. He came forward again and ran his hand through his thinning hair. "What I'd rather do, Mac, is wait to see if she was, in fact, going to charge Paul. No sense telling Marge Edwards tales out of school unless necessary."

"You already have," Smith said, slightly annoyed at Mondrian's sudden concern for her reputation. "You've told me she's unstable. I'd like to have some examples of what leads you to that conclusion."

Mondrian sighed. "I understand what you're saying, Mac. But I also know that with Paul's murder, you don't have an official reason for staying involved. As I understand it, your only role was as Paul's counsel at his confirmation hearings."

Smith didn't allow the comment to nettle him. He replied, "That's right. But I feel a continuing obligation to Paul's family. That's not hard to understand, is it?"

Mondrian shook his head. "No, it's not. Forgive me. I've been under the gun."

Smith acknowledged that he understood; no forgiveness necessary, despite the overly apt expression. He also knew that Mondrian was not about to offer more about Marge Edwards. He stood. "Thanks for your time, Bob."

"Lunch? I'll order the sandwiches."

"No, thanks. By the way, how about giving me Marge's father's number?"

Mondrian thought for a second, then said, "Sure. I have it outside. Anything else I can do for you?"

"I don't think so. Not for the moment anyhow."

"Amazing," Mondrian said as he walked Smith to the outer offices. "It's only been a day since Paul was murdered, and all the focus is back on politics. Who'll run for his seat? Who will the president nominate now for State? Who will the leadership put up for Paul's chairmanship of International Relations?"

"Just business as usual, D.C. style," Smith said, accepting the slip of paper from Mondrian on which Marge Edwards's father's number was written.

"Just a word of caution, Mac," Mondrian said.

"Yes?"

"I'd think twice about contacting the father."

"Why?"

"He didn't sound—I don't know—maybe he's old, losing it. Just a thought."

Just a thought, like his off-hand comment about Marge's stability was "just a thought."

"Thanks, Bob. Stay in touch."

Smith meant—with reality.

CHAPTER TWENTY-ONE

Congressman Paul Latham's funeral service was held at night in the National Cathedral, where former secretary of state Jake Baumann's death had been officially mourned. His body would be flown to California for burial.

The day after the funeral, a tribute to him was held in the Capitol's Statuary Hall. A succession of congressmen and senators offered words of praise and sadness, and directed their condolences to Ruth Latham and her three children, who sat erect and proud in the front row. Priscilla had flown in from London, arriving just in time for the National Cathedral service.

When it was over, the Latham family formed a receiving line of sorts, and greeted the hundreds of friends and colleagues who'd shown up, Mac and Annabel Smith among them.

"They were touching and fitting tributes," Smith said to Ruth Latham.

"Paul would have been proud," she replied, dry-eyed.

Smith shook Martin's hand. The only Latham son, hair tied in a long ponytail, wearing one of his father's suit jackets over a T-shirt, chino pants, and black sneakers, thanked Mac for coming.

"Your father was a good friend," Smith said. "And a good man."

"Your tennis partner."

"Among other things."

As they spoke, Annabel chatted briefly with Priscilla Latham. She hadn't seen Priscilla in at least two years, and was struck by the young woman's radiant beauty. She carried her nicely cut English suit and simple silk blouse with grace; she spoke with parallel aplomb.

". . . I suppose the hardest part, Mrs. Smith, is knowing my father was murdered. That happens to other families, inner-city families, poor families."

"I'm sure they'll find the person responsible soon," Annabel said, continuing to hold Priscilla's hand.

"I hope so. We could use some closure."

Smith had moved on to Molly Latham. He wasn't sure what to say to the sixteen-year-old, whose expression told him she was trying to balance a desire to appear composed with the need to bawl her brains out.

"As sad as all this is, Molly," Smith said, "I find myself celebrating all the years your father was my friend. Hard to do sometimes, but it's the way he would want it. At least that's the way I choose to view it."

She nodded and forced a small smile. "He always said such nice things about you and Mrs. Smith."

"That's good to hear."

"I remember when he and Mom came back from your wedding." She glanced at Annabel. "I remember he said you were the best-looking couple in Washington, except for him and Mom."

Smith laughed, squeezed her hand, and moved to the next person in line. Molly introduced her: "This is my roommate in the page dorm, Melissa Marshall."

"Pleased to meet you," Smith said, noticing that Annabel was now in front of Molly.

"Mah pleasure," Melissa said.

Smith turned and asked Molly, "When will you be getting back to being a page?"

She shrugged.

Melissa answered for her, "As soon as possible, Mr. Smith. Ah certainly do miss her."

The Smiths left the Capitol and stood in the sunshine, as far from the hundreds of press people as possible. Security was heavy. The Lathams had twenty-four-hour-a-day MPD escort. Capitol police seemed to be everywhere. FBI agents, trying to be unnoticed, were obvious in their attempt.

"Lovely day."

"As far as the weather goes," Annabel said.

"They seem to be holding up quite well."

"The collapse will come later. What time is your flight?"

"Four. Out of National."

"Still sure you want to go?"

"Yes. I've been chafing ever since Bob Mondrian told me I basically didn't have any business asking questions about Marge Edwards. When I called her father, he came off to me as a rational, intelligent man. Mondrian said he was losing it, as he put it. Why?"

"Maybe that's the way the father came off to *him*."

"Possibly. His name is Jim. The father. I didn't intend to go out to Indiana to see him. But when he said the last time Marge called him, she said that if she were ever in trouble in Washington she'd call me, I figured I owed her this."

"You no longer think she's simply gone underground to get away from the glare?"

"Still a possibility, Annie. But I have this gut feeling that—"

"Which you tend to trust more than I trust mine, women's intuition aside."

"I have this feeling that Marge Edwards is in trouble beyond simply claiming her boss sexually harassed her. If that's even true."

Annabel said, "Go to Indiana and talk to . . . Jim, is it? I just hope you're wrong."

CHAPTER TWENTY-TWO

Jim Edwards picked him up at the Indianapolis Airport. He was not what Smith expected him to be.

For some reason, since his conversation with Bob Mondrian, and during the flight from Washington, Smith had conjured a vision of an old, crusty Indiana farmer.

Instead, he was greeted by a handsome, youthful gentleman dressed in sport coat and tie. He had a full head of bushy brown hair, with some gray at the temples. Mac judged him to be in his mid-fifties—maybe a few years older than that, considering lines in his ruddy face. His smile was wide and genuine, his handshake firm.

They drove to Edwards's home in his red Jeep Grand Cherokee. His home wasn't far from the airport, a well-kept small tract house with a manicured lawn and pretty white front porch. As they approached, Edwards slowed down and pointed to a TV satellite van and four or five people leaning against it.

"The press caught up with you, I see," said Smith.

"Yes. I don't know how people in the public eye stand it, the constant scrutiny, the interference in your life."

"It's a negative perk," Smith said. "Goes with being a public figure."

They pulled into the driveway. Smith, carrying his small overnight bag, walked with Edwards across the lawn and to the porch. The reporters cut them off before they had a chance to go up the four steps.

"Any word from your daughter?" Edwards was asked.

"No," he responded. "No word."

"Who are you?" a reporter asked Smith.

Smith smiled against the questioner's bluntness. "Mackensie Smith."

Another reporter said, "Congressman Latham's lawyer."

"Former counsel," Smith corrected.

"Why are you here, Mr. Smith?"

"Just visiting," Mac said. To Edwards: "Can we?"

They stepped up onto the porch. Edwards opened the screen door, used his key to unlock the inner door, and ushered Smith inside.

They stood in the living room, a square space with sheets on the chairs and couch. "I keep the furniture covered, Mr. Smith, because of the dogs and cats."

Smith looked about. "My dog would be all over a guest," he said.

"So would mine, if I let them. I keep them in a small apartment over the garage when guests are coming. The cats are probably frightened. One of them will venture out in a while. Please. Sit." He whipped the sheet from the couch. "Can I get you something? You haven't had dinner, have you?"

"Peanuts and a Coke on the flight," Mac said. "That's what seems to pass for a 'snack' these days with the airlines. But I'm not hungry. I'll eat later at the hotel."

"I made a reservation for you at the Holiday Inn. Only a few miles away. The invitation to stay here is still open. It's just me and the animals these days."

"Thanks, but I don't want to intrude. A cup of coffee would be fine, if it's no trouble."

"Never any trouble with instant coffee, Mr. Smith."

Smith, a self-acknowledged coffee snob, said, "Any tea?"

"Sure. Only be a minute."

Smith used Edwards's absence to stroll and to take in the living room. Mondrian had said Edwards's wife was dead; a dozen pictures of a woman, obviously her, helped to preserve the memories for her widower.

There were also pictures of Marge; as a small child cuddling a puppy, at high school graduation, on prom night, and a more recent one taken in front of the Capitol Building. She looked happy in all of them.

Smith had just picked up a book from a table—surprised to find a collection of short stories by Arturo Vivante that had appeared in *The New Yorker;* Smith also had a copy, which rested in a section of a bookcase reserved for favorite works—when Edwards reappeared with tea and a small plate of vanilla cookies.

"Perhaps you'd prefer a drink. Liquor, I mean," Edwards said.

"No, thank you. Tea is fine."

"You don't mind if I do? It's that time."

"Sure. Go ahead," Smith said.

They passed the next few minutes talking about Vivante's book and others. Edwards said he and his deceased wife, Sue, had always been ravenous readers despite jobs that were distinctly not literary. Sue Edwards had worked as a secretary at a small manufacturing plant. Jim was employed as a maintenance supervisor at a rental car's Indianapolis office.

Smith finished his tea and addressed his reason for being there. "Jim," he said, "Paul Latham was a dear friend of mine. His family, too, has always been close. As you know, a rumor surfaced that Marge was considering—I suppose that's the accurate way to put it—she was considering bringing a sexual harassment charge against Latham, which conceivably could have caused a serious problem with his confirmation hearings as secretary of state."

Edwards, who sipped from a glass, said nothing, simply nodded as Mac made his points.

Smith continued. "Then, of course, as you know, Congressman Latham was murdered."

"That's definite?" Edwards asked. "It wasn't suicide?"

"No. The autopsy confirms it was murder. It was on the news."

Edwards sounded defensive. "I don't watch much of the news. Everything's so grim these days. I prefer to read."

"I can certainly understand that," Smith said. "Naturally, with Paul Latham dead, the question of whether Marge was, indeed, intending to bring the charge changes considerably. A question for you, Jim. Did she ever indicate, in any way, that Paul Latham had demonstrated sexual, romantic interest in her?"

Edwards thought before responding. "No," he said. "Never. The gentlemen from the FBI asked about that, too."

"They interviewed you?"

"Yes. A man and a woman from the Indianapolis office. They were very nice. Very polite."

"That's always been my experience. Unless, of course, you give them a hard time."

"I would never do that," Edwards said.

"I'm sure you wouldn't," Smith said. "How much has Marge discussed with you about her job as Latham's scheduling secretary?"

"Not much." He drank. "Sure I can't tempt you?"

Smith shook his head. "What did she say when she *did* discuss it? Her job, that is."

"Oh, I don't know. She complained a lot about how hard it was. But she liked the congressman. Liked him very much, the way I heard it."

"What about her colleagues in the office? She like them, too?"

"Oh, yes. Well, there is a chap—name is, ah, Bob—"

"Bob Mondrian, Latham's chief of staff."

"Yes, that's right. It seems Marge and this Bob didn't get along all that well."

"Any reason for it?"

"Not that she ever said. I gather he's a bit of a dictator."

"The pressure in those jobs is intense," Smith offered. "Anything else Marge might have said about the people she works with?"

Edwards shook his head. "I'm ready for a refill," he said.

"I will join you," Mac said. "Scotch, bourbon? With water?"

"Either one."

"Bourbon. Light."

Glasses in their hands, Smith continued.

"Do you have any idea, Jim, where Marge might be?"

"No."

"Other family she might have gone to? Close friends?"

"I've talked with other family members as recently as this afternoon. They haven't heard from her."

"Has she disappeared like this before?"

"Not that I recall. No, never. Oh, we fall out of touch from time to time, but—"

"For how long at a stretch?"

"A month, sometimes. About a month. She's real busy in Washington. Nice city. I've visited her a few times since she moved there."

"She's a pretty, vivacious young woman. An active social life, I imagine."

"Marge always had lots of beaus. Real popular in high school and college." It was a small, rueful laugh. "She's like most women her age, I suppose. Hears the biological clock ticking and wonders why she isn't married and doesn't have kids. She came close a few times."

"Really?"

"Funny, asking before about whether she had any problems with people she works with . . . The maddest I've ever seen her—I mean, since she became an adult; lots of temper tantrums in high school, like most teenagers—was when she was going out with the congressman's son."

"Martin Latham?"

"That's right. She was really in love with him, I can tell you. Called every other night to tell me how happy she was. I thought I was about to have a son-in-law."

"What happened?" Smith asked.

"It broke up. Martin left Washington and went someplace to become a woodworker, I think. Some craft like that. Marge wanted to go with him, but he wanted to go alone. She was very hurt, very angry."

"I see." Smith tried to recall whether Paul Latham had ever mentioned to him that Martin was dating Marge Edwards. He hadn't. Interesting pairing, Smith thought. Martin had to be eight or ten years younger than Marge.

"I wasn't aware they'd dated."

"She was never quite the same after that episode in her life," Jim Edwards said. "There was a bitterness that crept in. Not overt. Not a big deal. But I could tell whenever we spoke."

Smith had been waiting ever since his arrival at Jim Edwards's house for the right moment to bring up Mondrian's contention. Was there ever such a right time? This was as good a time as any, he decided. Jim Edwards was a nice man, open and candid. Unlikely he would take offense at such a question.

So Smith asked, "As Marge's father, you obviously know her as well as or better than anyone else. Would you consider her unstable?"

The question caused Edwards to pause. He squeezed his eyes shut as though forcing the right answer to emerge through his mouth. He opened his eyes, inhaled, let the air out, and said, "I suppose you could say that. No, let me clarify it. Marge has always been high-strung. Very much like her mother was. Emotional. Feelings always on the surface. She's capable of flying off the handle, even when it isn't in her best interests. But so are a lot of people. Is that a definition of unstable? Maybe it is. I'll leave it up to you."

Smith said, "I'm really not in a position to judge your daughter, Jim, nor would I want to be. I'm here because I care about her, and want to know where she is so that I might be able to help her."

"That's what she said, you know. She said if she ever got in trouble in Washington, she'd want to talk to you. And I appreciate you coming all the way out to Indiana. May I ask you a question?"

"Sure."

"Do you think something terrible has happened to Marge?"

"I—"

"I've tried not to worry. I prefer to think she's just gone away for a few days because of this damned stupid rumor about the congressman and her. She's a big girl, all grown up. Still, I do worry. I guess you never stop being a father."

Smith thought of his son. Sometimes you do stop, because you're forced to.

"No, you never do, Jim. I'm glad I made this trip. I wasn't sure why I wanted to come, couldn't come up with a tangible reason for it. But I'm glad I did. To answer your question: No, I don't think anything terrible has happened to Marge. Probably exactly what you said. She got away for a few days, and will probably be calling in any day to say she's okay and to put to rest the rumor. By the way, I understand a private detective visited you, asking about Marge."

"That's right. A big fellow named Petrone."

"Did he say why he was looking for her?"

"No. Well, he said he knew her. Was a friend."

"A private detective. He didn't say he was here on behalf of a client?"

"No. I have his card."

Edwards dug it out from a pile of papers on a small desk in the corner, and handed it to Smith.

"James Perrone."

"Yes. Perrone. Not Petrone."

"Mind if I take this with me?"

"Not at all. I don't intend to call him if Marge gets in touch."

Edwards offered another drink, but Smith said he was tired and wanted to get to the hotel.

"Have you there in no time," Edwards said. "You're flying back tomorrow?"

"Yes."

"I'd drive you to the airport but I have to be at work."

"A cab will do just fine. But thanks for thinking of it."

They stood up to leave and the phone rang. Edwards looked at Smith with a questioning expression.

"Go ahead," Smith said. "I'm in no rush."

"Hello? Yes, he's right here, Mrs. Smith. Just a moment." He handed the phone to his guest.

"Hello, Annabel. Anything wrong?"

"No. But I'm glad I caught you. Marge Edwards just called."

Smith glanced at Edwards, who was in the process of taking their glasses to the kitchen.

"Where is she?" Mac asked quietly.

"I don't know. She wanted to speak with you. I started to tell her where you were, but she said she'd call again and hung up."

"At least she's alive. How did she sound?"

"Too brief a conversation to tell. How's it going there?"

"Good. Ironic, huh?"

"What's ironic?"

"I come to Indiana, and she calls me in Washington."

"Life's a series of ironies."

"I know, I know. And most of them I could do without. How are you?"

"Fine. The press has decamped from in front of the house. They fly out with you? How's Mr. Edwards?"

"Nice guy. He'll be happy to hear about the call. He's driving me to the hotel. I'll call later from there."

"Okay. And—oh, yes. Love you, Mac."

Smith sensed Edwards had entered the room and stood just behind him.

"Me, too," he said, returning the phone to its cradle.

Smith told Jim Edwards about the call from Marge as they drove to the hotel.

He could hear the man literally breathe easier.

"That's a relief," Edwards said. "I wish she'd called me."

"I'm sure she will. Sometimes when you're under pressure, you don't want to bring your family in on it until it's over." He didn't know whether that was true or not, but it seemed the thing to say.

They shook hands at the entrance to the Holiday Inn.

"Thanks for all your Hoosier hospitality, Jim."

"No. Thank you for caring so much about my daughter. You'll let me know when you talk to her?"

"Count on it."

CHAPTER TWENTY-THREE

Smith had a light dinner in the Holiday Inn's coffee shop, and spent the next few hours reading a book he'd brought with him, *How Russia Became a Market Economy,* published by the Brookings Institution. He checked in with Annabel before turning in for the night. Marge Edwards had not called again.

The next morning, he took the first flight to Washington, and had the taxi drop him in Georgetown at Annabel's gallery.

After a serious embrace, she said, "I really missed you. You were gone weeks, not overnight."

"Glad to be back. I swung by here because I'm not sure what to do with the knowledge that Marge Edwards is alive and presumably well."

"I was thinking the same thing. Maybe you should report her attempt to reach you."

"I suppose I should. Still, I didn't speak with her. We have no idea where she is. No, I think it can wait till I actually talk to her."

"It's your call. Tell me more about Jim Edwards."

Smith gave her a thumbnail sketch of his time with the father.

"So, he confirmed that his daughter might be termed unstable at times," Annabel said.

"Not in so many words, Annie. But he didn't paint her as a rock of emotional stability."

He handed her the card given Edwards by the private investigator, James Perrone, and explained why he had it.

"Hmmmm. Based here in Washington," Annabel said, noting a suite number at an address on New Jersey Avenue.

"Yeah. He told Edwards he knew Marge. I wonder if he did, or if he went out to Indianapolis for a client."

"Who would that client be?" she asked. "Has Paul's staff, maybe Bob Mondrian, hired him?"

Mac shrugged. "I might drop in on Mr. Perrone."

Her eyebrows arched. "Why?"

"To follow up in every possible way on Marge's disappearance. As long as this sexual harassment rumor floats out there, I think I owe it to Ruth and the kids. Spoken with Ruth?"

"Yes. She sounded okay."

"Well, looks like nothing is new here," he said, gesturing within the gallery. "Mind if I take the car?"

"Nope." She handed him the keys; he knew the garage she used.

He drove home and unpacked. Mac Smith was as meticulous at unpacking as he was at packing. That applied to his briefcase, too. His first action upon returning home each evening was to empty it, put things away, and repack for the next day. Obsessive-compulsive? Certainly about his briefcase and luggage; he wore the badge proudly. He walked Rufus, had a bowl of soup, locked up, and headed for New Jersey Avenue.

He'd considered calling ahead to Perrone's office, but opted instead simply to drop in on the PI. He didn't know what he was seeking from Perrone. Knowing why someone might have hired a private investigator to find Marge Edwards would be interesting, but to what use? He wasn't even sure why he was continuing this quest to find her. He could easily rationalize it—and had done so to Annabel more successfully than he had to himself—by his concern for Paul Latham's reputation in death. The family. Bad enough to have lost a husband and father, but even worse to have a cloud of sleaze hanging over the loss. Like finding evidence of infidelity in a dead husband's desk drawers at the office.

By the time Smith parked, and entered the building on New Jersey Avenue, he no longer grappled with motivation. You could spend your life questioning why you wanted to do something, and end up never doing it.

The sign on the door read J. PERRONE, PRIVATE INVESTIGATIONS. There was a button to push, and a squawk box to the right of the handle. Smith pushed the button. A distorted female voice said, "Yes?"

"I'm here to see Mr. Perrone. Mackensie Smith."

"Do you have an appointment?"

"No. I'm—I was Congressman Latham's legal counsel."

A prolonged pause.

A buzz sounded. Smith opened the door and stepped inside a small, cramped reception area. A receptionist sat behind a desk. "Mr. Smith?" she said.

"Yes. Is Mr. Perrone in?"

"Yes, but he's in conference."

A fancy way to say he's busy, Smith thought. Or does not want to see me.

"If you'd like to make an appointment, Mr. Smith, I'll be happy to do that."

"Actually," Smith said, "I'm only looking for a few minutes of Mr. Perrone's time. I'm not here as a potential client. It has to do with Congressman Latham's murder"—the word came out hard—"and the disappearance of Ms. Marjorie Edwards."

Smith sensed as he spoke that his words were being piped into Perrone's private office. It didn't take long for that to be confirmed. The door opened and Perrone came through it, an unlighted cigar jutting from his mouth, a brace of red and yellow suspenders holding up his pants. He wore a mustard-colored shirt and wide black-and-white tie. The investigator was no fashion plate.

"Mr. Smith?" he said.

"Yes. I take it you're Jim Perrone."

"Right." They shook hands.

"Sorry to barge in like this, but I thought I might get lucky."

Perrone smiled. "If seeing me is good luck, Smith, your luck's running bad. Come on in."

"I don't want to disturb your . . . conference."

"It's over."

He stepped back to allow Smith to enter.

It was a pleasantly furnished and decorated office, nothing Raymond Chandler would have created for his hard-boiled, lean-and-mean, honor-driven private eye, Philip Marlowe. There was a softness to the pastel walls, thick wall-to-wall rose-colored carpeting, and mauve drapes. A woman's touch, Mac thought.

"Sit down, Mr. Smith," said Perrone. He took a high-back leather chair behind a teak desk on which there were few papers or files. The office was a lot neater than the man. "You were Latham's lawyer, huh?"

"That's right." No need to qualify, Smith decided.

"And you're wondering where Marge Edwards went."

"Right again." He'd heard every word from the reception area.

"So, why are you here talking to me?"

"Because you've been looking for her, too."

Perrone's hand went to his heart. "I have?" he said with exaggerated surprise.

"According to Marge Edwards's father, Jim. Indianapolis?"

Perrone lighted his cigar. "You don't mind, huh?"

"Not at all." The suit was due for the cleaners anyway, Smith told himself.

"Jim Edwards told me that you claimed to be Marge's friend. Or at least knew her."

Perrone nodded.

"How did that come about?"

"What do you mean?"

"How did you become friends with her?"

Perrone dismissed the question with a smoky wave of the cigar.

Smith knew he would have to justify his questions if he hoped to receive any useful answers. He said, "Because Marge Edwards can't be contacted, the rumor that she claims to have been sexually harassed by Paul Latham stays alive. I care about the Latham family, and want to put a stake through the rumor's heart. I thought you might help me."

"Maybe I would," Perrone said. "Tell me why I should."

"A sense of decency. You say you know Marge. Maybe you can tell me—"

"*You* say I know her."

"*You* told her father you know her."

"I met her a couple of times."

"She ever tell you that Congressman Latham harassed her? Sexually, that is."

Perrone nodded, drew smoke.

"She did?"

"Yeah."

"When?"

"I don't know. A month, two months ago."

"Where did she tell you?"

Perrone stood and stretched.

Smith asked, "Why did she tell *you*?"

"Where? When? Why? What is this, the Inquisition?"

"You've heard of that."

"Yeah, I—look, Smith, thanks for stopping in. If you want to hire me to find Marge Edwards, the fee is two-fifty a day and expenses. Interested?"

"Is that what your other client is paying you?"

"Have a nice day, Smith."

Smith stood. "You, too, Perrone. Good of you to see me on such short notice."

Mac got into his car and drove home. His brief encounter with James Perrone had angered him. At the same time, he found the exchange to have been of interest, perhaps even useful. He didn't believe for a minute that Marge Edwards had claimed to Perrone that Paul Latham had sexually harassed her. And he seriously doubted they even knew each other, although he had nothing upon which to base that belief. Marge and Perrone would have had little in common, nothing to cause her to open up to a PI, if he was a PI.

Unless—unless it was money, that great social leveler.

He picked up the phone in his den office.

"You have reached the offices of Anthony Buffolino," said a woman via the answering machine. "We are unable to take your call right now. Please leave your name, number, and a message if you wish and we will return your call as soon as possible. Thank you."

"This is Mackensie Smith," Mac said, "calling at—"

"Mac?"

"Tony? Don't interrupt. I was talking to the machine."

"Yeah. That time of the month. Everybody wanting to get paid. Great gadget, the answering machine. You get to answer—or not answer. Some calls I pick up, some I don't. You, I pick up for even before you call. If you know what I mean."

Mac Smith and Tony Buffolino (with an *O*) went back a long way together. Buffolino had been a Washington MPD detective, and a good one. His fifteen-year record was clean; a desk drawer was filled with citations of merit and letters of appreciation from local politicians and citizens groups.

Then, after taking three bullets in his right leg, two in the thigh and one in the knee, in a shootout during a bank robbery, he was retired on full pay.

But retirement wasn't on Buffolino's agenda. Despite the objections of his second wife, and the gibes of fellow officers who only dreamed of being retired at full salary, he undertook extensive physical rehabilitation, passed the physical, and was reinstated as part of a special task force formed to combat Washington's burgeoning drug trade.

In retrospect, it was the wrong decision.

A year after joining the D.C. drug task force, one of his children from his first marriage developed leukemia, and the medical bills mounted, soared, until he made a fateful move that would forever change his life. He crossed the line between cop and criminal to cut a one-time deal with a notorious Washington-based Colombian drug dealer named Garcia. He would take Garcia's dirty money only once, he rationalized, and simply turn it all over to his first wife so she could pay the doctors and labs and hospitals. Just a one-shot indiscretion.

Once was all that was needed for the MPD to set up a sting, with Garcia's cooperation in return for leniency on a previous arrest. It occurred in a Watergate suite, and Tony Buffolino, with an *O*, was marched through the lobby in cuffs, forever disgraced, the fifteen years of heroic service, all the citations and awards nothing more than a measure of how far he had fallen.

Enter eminent Washington criminal attorney Mackensie Smith, through an intermediary for whom Smith had considerable respect. As abhorrent as drugs were to Mac, there was, at once, a mitigating set of feelings he developed for Buffolino. The cop had been stupid in seeking money from a drug dealer. He'd broken the code and dishonored himself. At the same time, having used a vicious drug dealer like Garcia to nail an otherwise good cop was anathema to Smith. And there was Buffolino's motivation. Not to get rich or to live the high life. Separated, and eventually divorced from his second wife, he lived in an industrial area of Baltimore in a hovel he called an apartment, and drove a faded red 1978 Cadillac with a cracked white landau roof and white leather interior grimy from age and too many greasy cheeseburgers and spilled sodas.

Smith interceded with the MPD and local prosecutors and cut a deal for Buffolino: no criminal prosecution, but a dishonorable discharge from the force, loss of pension and other rights, and a public confession of wrongdoing.

It was a good deal for Tony. But although he accepted its terms, he viewed Smith as having sold him down the river, and treated him that way. Until one day, Smith needed the services of a private investigator, thought of Buffolino, who'd set up shop in Baltimore as a private eye, called him, and they got together.

The friendship they forged from that moment certainly wasn't based upon common interests. They moved in vastly different circles. But there was a shared respect, Tony for the great trial attorney-turned-learned-professor-of-law, Mac for the gritty resolve of the private investigator whose street smarts and sometimes skewed view of life made him the most effective private eye Smith had ever known.

Buffolino married again, to a supportive and understanding woman named Alicia. Mac and Annabel often said Alicia had "tamed" Tony, which was true to an extent. That she'd managed to accomplish the feat without taking from him his spirit, or charming rough edges, was a tribute to her skill at wielding a whip, and a feather.

"I was going to give you a call, Mac, about this Latham case I've been reading about."

"I beat you to it, Tony. How's things?"

"Tip-top, Mac. I'm taking the high road these days. No more peeping in motel windows to nail a roving husband for some wife who's probably in some other motel down the road. Strictly business investigations these days."

"Glad to hear it," Smith said, remembering that Tony was screening calls to avoid creditors. "How's Alicia?"

"Good. Sometimes you get lucky. Drives me up the wall now and then, but she's a woman. And a good driver, if you get my meaning."

Smith smiled, asked, "What do you know about a colleague named James Perrone?"

"Colleague? Not even in the same league as me."

"But you do know him?"

"Yeah. A lowlife. Wears funny clothes, always has his big hand out for a payoff."

Wears funny clothes? Smith thought. Buffolino did not exactly define *haute couture*, although Alicia had managed to spruce him up a bit.

"A clean record?" Smith asked.

"I guess so. Nobody yanked his license I know of. Hey, Mac, you aren't thinking of hiring that *schmuck*, are you? What'd I do to lose your business?"

Smith laughed. Alicia, who was Jewish, had obviously substituted a little Yiddish for Tony's usual Italian slang. "No, Tony, I'm not looking to hire Perrone. I just want to know more about him."

"Having to do with the Latham murder, I suppose."

"Yes."

"You need me, Mac?"

"I could use you to come up with hard information on Perrone. Maybe even to keep an eye on him for the next few days. But since you're now taking the high road, as you put it, I suppose that would be out of the question."

"Yeah, it's not what I've been doing lately. Still, for you, I'd make an exception. I am busy. Up to my neck, you might say. But just for a few days? Shadow him? Yeah, I'll do it. My rates went up, I should inform you. Inflation."

"Of course. Can you get on it right away?"

"I'll make a point of it. How's the gorgeous redhead?"

"Annabel's very well, thank you. She often asks for you."

"Yeah, well, give her a big kiss for me. You'll be around?"

"Yes."

"You'll hear from me."

CHAPTER TWENTY-FOUR

President Joseph Scott's press secretary, Sanford Teller, fielded a question about Paul Latham at the daily White House press briefing:

"Some sources are saying the president knew when he nominated his friend Congressman Latham for secretary of state that the sexual harassment charge by a female employee was about to be leveled. Any truth to that?"

Teller, aptly named for a spokesman, showed his anger in his pale blue eyes. He cast them over the reporters in the briefing room and said, "Those so-called sources give your profession a bad name. The rumor that a female employee of Congressman Latham was going to bring such a charge is just that, a rumor. As for the president, I can tell you that as a close friend of Congressman Latham, he's pretty upset—no, amend that—he's pretty damn mad about the rumor. Those on the Hill who seek political gain from perpetuating this slander against Congressman Latham are not only prolonging his family's lingering grief, they're feeding the public's already negative perception of politics. Until and unless the young lady in question comes forth, that question's off the table here. Next? Helen?"

Mac Smith switched from C-SPAN to CNN, then to MSNBC, and finally turned off the set. Good for the president, he thought. Maybe if more people displayed outrage about rumors, they would diminish.

Senator Frank Connors, the Senate minority whip, had also watched the White House briefing. With him in his Russell Senate Office Building suite were his AA, Dennis Mackral, and Republican Congressman Mario Stassi, the ranking member on what used to be Paul Latham's House International Relations Committee and its subcommittee on International Operations and Human Rights.

Connors said over Teller's voice, "Since when does the president's press secretary get to spout his personal opinions? I'd fire the son of a bitch if he did that to me."

"It reflects the president's views, Frank," Stassi said.

"That comment of his was pointed at me," said Connors, lighting a cigar. He looked at Mackral. "Am I right?"

"I'd say so," Mackral replied. "The statement we issued yesterday was pretty blunt."

"I wish you'd run it past me before it went out," Stassi said. "The majority leaders are pressing for Jessup to take Latham's committee chair. Bad enough we're the minority without causing undue antagonism with the other side."

"We're still looking for her," Mackral said.

"Why?" Stassi asked, not attempting to disguise his annoyance. "Latham's dead. There's not going to be any confirmation hearings. This sexual harassment thing should have been dropped the minute he died."

"Dropped where?" Connors asked, his tone belligerent. "In my lap? We're taking enough heat about it without folding our tent and slinking away. You just heard Teller—the president—hell, they're out to paint us as irresponsible rumormongers. They've turned it into their advantage—the heartless Republicans, spreading false accusations to derail a great nominee for State. I think it's more important than ever to find Marge Edwards and get her to confirm the story."

"*Get* her to?" Stassi said. "You have to *get* her to confirm it?"

"You know what I mean, Mario. Put her in front of a camera to tell everybody it happened. Latham played grab-ass with her. Then she says that now that the poor man is dead, there's no need for her to go any further with it. Let him rest in peace. But at least confirm it, for Christ's sake."

"And you have no idea where she is?"

"We're working on it."

Mackral walked Stassi to the hallway. Stassi stopped, turned, looked hard at Mackral, and said, "I think this stinks, Dennis. It has all the aroma of a phony setup. We're taking a lot of heat on the House side.

Paul Latham was a leader. And he was one of us. If I were you, I'd push your boss to drop the whole thing before it really backfires."

Mackral shrugged, said, "You know Frank, Mario. He won't budge. Frankly, I agree with you. But there's not a lot I can do, although I'll keep trying."

"Yeah, do that," Stassi said. "You know what the first polls say? What my voters back home say? They don't give a damn about some missing, neurotic woman claiming Paul Latham kissed her or whatever. They *do* care that somebody murdered him."

"Of course," Mackral said.

"Level with me, Dennis. How did Marge Edwards get to you and Frank, tell you that Paul harassed her?"

"I'm not at liberty to say at the moment," Mackral responded. "But it was through a reliable source."

Stassi guffawed.

Mackral shot him a California smile. "Trust me, Mario. The source was good."

"I'm sure it was. And nobody cares, except Frank Connors. Look, Dennis, I butted heads with Paul every day. He ran the committee with an iron hand in a velvet glove. Do it his way or no way. Cross him, you kissed off your own constituent needs. But he was a hell of a man. A good and decent man. He would have made an excellent secretary of state. Sure, I would have gone along with the minority and tried to keep Scott from getting what he wanted. Not that I could have done much. Confirmations are a Senate prerogative. I would have made some speeches on the floor about his cozy relationship with Warren Brazier. Hell, as you know, the offensive against Paul's confirmation was all scripted by our leadership. But this sexual charge. It's scummy, Dennis. Ranks right up there with Dick Morris on the slime meter."

As he spoke, Stassi became red in the face. He started to say something else, abandoned it, and walked away.

Mackral started back to the office, changed his mind, left the building, and went to a phone booth two blocks away. Perrone took the call. "What's up?" he asked.

"We need to talk."

"Come on over."

"No. You know the rules. The Monocle. A half hour."

"You know, Mackral, you're taking up one hell of a lot of my time. Time's money, they say. All I've got to sell is time."

"Just be there, huh? There'll be enough money to pay for your god-damn time."

The Monocle, on D Street, N.E., between First and Second streets, just north of Capitol Hill, was within a few blocks of both the Capitol and the Supreme Court. Its location had made it a favorite hangout for years of staffers from both institutions, especially Senate aides. Slightly south of the Capitol was another venerable watering hole, Bullfeathers, which appealed more, for no apparent reason, to staffers from the House.

Mackral was there within minutes. Although he seldom frequented the Monocle, he was recognized as he entered by some people at the bar. After returning their greetings—slaps on the back, squeezes of the arm, and quick one-liners—he headed for a table at the rear of the room adjacent to the bar. He ordered a Diet Coke and waited, his eyes on the door.

He saw a man enter a few minutes later, obviously no staffer, but paid no further attention to him. Tony Buffolino took a seat at the ten-stool bar, sat back, and surveyed the room. "Nice place you got here," he said to the bartender, a chain-smoking older gentleman wearing a red-and-white-striped shirt, red tie, and suspenders.

The bartender introduced himself in a southern accent as Robert. He looked over half-glasses and asked Buffolino what he wanted to drink.

"A beer. Rolling Rock."

Tony sipped his beer and waited for Perrone to arrive. He'd followed him from Perrone's office building on New Jersey Avenue to the Mono-cle's parking lot, parked his silver Ford Taurus at the opposite end (things had improved since his rusty red Cadillac days, including his level of taste), and used other vehicles for cover on his way to the bar's door. What was Perrone doing out there? he wondered. Had he changed his mind and taken off? Did he become aware he was being followed?

All around him at the bar, the conversation was politics. Nothing but politics. Political jokes. Political insight. Political BS, he thought. And enough cigars to call it a Te-Amo convention.

He was poised to go outside in search of Perrone when the bulky PI came through the door. Buffolino turned so that his face wasn't visible. He and Perrone didn't know each other well, but they had met on a few occasions. Perrone lumbered by him and joined a man at a nearby table.

o shifted position so that he could keep an eye on them without himself.

Buffolino's perspective, the two men knew each other but

weren't especially friendly. A visible tension manifested itself in rigid body language. If he hadn't been afraid of being recognized by Perrone, he might have considered taking a table closer to them. But that was out of the question. Besides, from the way they were speaking to each other, it seemed to Buffolino that they were trying to keep their words private. An intrusion into their space might cause them to leave.

So he continued to sit at the bar, nursing his beer and wishing he'd learned to read lips.

Perrone and Mackral conferred for twenty minutes. Buffolino was on his second beer when Mackral left the table and headed for the front door. A young man seated next to Buffolino grabbed Mackral's arm. "Hey, Dennis, how goes it?"

"Okay," Mackral replied, a little angrily, from Buffolino's perception. This was a guy who'd just had an unpleasant conversation and was anxious to get out of there.

The bar patron insisted upon telling Mackral a joke. He listened patiently, smiled—this guy's either an actor or a displaced California beach bum, Buffolino decided—said good-bye, and was out the door.

"Dennis," Buffolino said under his breath, noting the name on a cocktail napkin.

He returned his attention to the table, where Perrone was in the process of placing an order with a waiter. Buffolino wondered whether he should follow this Dennis, but ruled it out. Mac Smith had been specific: Follow Perrone.

Perrone had ordered a shrimp cocktail, steak, fries, and a side order of pasta.

" 'Nother beer?" Robert, the bartender, asked in a deep baritone.

"Yeah. And some snacks. Peanuts, maybe?"

It took Perrone an hour to finish his meal. A third beer for Buffolino. He noticed that Perrone hadn't paid when he left the table. Dennis must have picked up the tab.

Buffolino again turned so Perrone wouldn't get a clear look at his face. The minute Perrone was out the door, Buffolino dropped money on the bar and stood. "Thanks, Robert," he said.

The bartender nodded, drawled, "Y'all come back."

"You should be on the radio," Buffolino said, smiling and waving as he left.

He fell in behind Perrone, headed across the city in the direction of the Theodore Roosevelt Bridge. Traffic was heavy, the going slow. When he was a cop, Buffolino took pride in his driving ability when following someone, knowing how far he could hang back to avoid being noticed without losing his target.

Perrone, driving a sand-colored, almost new Dodge sedan, took them over the bridge into Virginia. He continued through the small cities on that side of the Potomac until turning at Route 66 West, which he stayed with until joining the Dulles Toll Road, settling into a steady sixty miles per hour. Buffolino adjusted his cruise control to remain a comfortable distance behind.

Eventually, Perrone left the highway at Exit 9, which Buffolino noticed put them on Sully Road. Five traffic lights later, Perrone turned left onto Waxpool Road; they were in the town of Ashburn. Buffolino followed Perrone to a residential street called Rising Sun Terrace, which wound through a development of single-family homes and town houses, creating the sort of typical planned community popular in Virginia and the greater Washington area.

Perrone pulled into a driveway. Buffolino stopped a block away. Perrone got out of his car, went to the front door of a town house, and rang the bell. A woman answered. Perrone and the woman talked for a minute. It appeared to Buffolino they were arguing. Then, Perrone entered the town house, and the door closed.

Buffolino waited a few minutes before slowly driving past the house. He noted the number on the door and the cross streets before coming around the block and resuming his watchful position.

He was aware that another woman had been peering at him through her front window. He didn't need someone calling the police, or the enclave's private security force to report a stranger in a car, so he drove away, toward a sales office he'd noticed when entering the complex.

He parked, bounded up the steps, and entered the model home, where a middle-aged woman sat behind a desk piled high with brochures.

"May I help you?" she asked pleasantly.

"I hope so," he said, slipping into his best Detective Columbo hesitant imitation. "I've been thinking of buying something here in the development—I like it here. I work only a couple of miles away, but—"

"I'd be happy to show you some vacant models," the woman said, standing.

"Well, actually, I've already looked at one that appeals to me."

"You have? Who showed it to you?"

"The owner."

"Ah, a current resident."

"Yeah. Number eleven-eleven."

"Eleven-eleven? I didn't know Ms. Craig was thinking of selling. She's only been here a year."

"Something about a new job someplace. Out of the state. Ms. Craig . . ." He slapped the side of his head. "I never can remember her first name."

"Maureen."

"Of course. Maureen Craig. Sometimes I think I'm losing it, you know?"

"Yes, I do. My mother has Alzheimer's. It's such a terrible disease. Physically, she's fine. But mentally . . ." She squeezed her eyes shut and shuddered.

"Yeah, I know what you mean. Thanks a lot."

The woman opened her eyes and asked, "What did you want? We don't get involved in private sales by current residents."

Buffolino shrugged. "I guess I just wanted to get a feel for the community. Overall, you know. It's nice here, huh?"

"Very nice. Peaceful. Good people. Very few children or animals."

Not like the Congress, Buffolino thought.

He thanked her again and left, hoping she wouldn't pick up the phone and call Maureen Craig, whoever she was. He found a different spot from where he could observe the car in the driveway of 1111, thankful Perrone hadn't left while he was conning the sales agent. Now that he was back in position, he wished Perrone would get going. He was hungry; a search of the glove compartment confirmed he'd finished the last of the candy bars he kept in it as emergency rations.

Forty-five minutes later, Perrone came through the front door, down the steps and got into his car. He carried a manila envelope. The woman hadn't come to the door with him, as far as Buffolino could see. Perrone retraced his route back to Washington, where he pulled into the underground parking garage of the apartment building in which he lived.

No sense hanging out here, Buffolino decided. He went to his office and called.

"Something to report?" Smith asked.

"Maybe. I just left Perrone at home. Been with him most of the day. He spent time in that bar on the Hill, the Monocle."

"Pleasant place. Did you meet Robert?"

"The bartender? Yeah."

"Fascinating man," Smith said. "He's been there over twenty years. Seen it all."

"I bet he has. I've seen half of it. So anyway, Mac, Perrone sits with a guy at a table. They're together maybe twenty minutes. Then this guy leaves, and Perrone stays almost an hour pigging out. Steak. Pasta. The works. This other guy evidently paid 'cause Perrone didn't."

"Good friend to have. Do you know who Perrone met with?"

"Just the name Dennis. Some guy called him that at the bar."

"Dennis?" Smith ran the name through his memory. He came up with only one, Dennis Lambert, a respected senior staffer on the Hill with whom Smith had been friends for a number of years. "What did he look like, Tony?"

"Like Troy Donahue."

"Who?"

"The actor. A California type. Blond hair all slicked back, big-time tan. A salon, I figure, considering the weather here."

Dennis Mackral. Senator Frank Connors's administrative assistant.

"Catch anything they said?" Smith asked.

"No. I followed Perrone after he finished his meal. Took me all the way out into Virginia. Ashburn. Know it?"

"I've heard of it. That's pretty far. What did he do there?"

"Visited somebody named Maureen Craig."

"Know anything about her?"

"No. Here's her address."

"You've been busy, Tony."

"I got to be, Mac. Like I told you, I'm shoehorning this assignment in for you."

"And I appreciate it. Can you spend another day on Perrone's back?"

"Sure."

"And I know you'll keep good track of your hours."

"Course I will. But you get the professional discount."

"Still an extra two percent if in cash?"

"Better. Three."

CHAPTER TWENTY-FIVE

The minute Smith hung up, he called Jim Edwards in Indianapolis. No answer. Smith checked his watch. Marge's father was probably still at work.

Next, he called Ruth Latham.

"Everybody holding up all right?" Smith asked.

"Yes, although we'll feel a lot better when Paul's murderer has been brought in. Have you heard anything new on that front?"

"Afraid not."

"Marge Edwards?"

Smith sighed. "Still don't know where she is."

Should he tell her that Marge had tried to call him? He couldn't come up with a compelling reason to do it, so he let his statement stand.

"How are the kids?"

"Good. Martin has decided to stay around a bit longer. That pleases me. Pris had to get back to her job in New York, which I understand."

"And that vivacious teenager of yours?"

Ruth laughed. "Molly is doing just great. I'm taking her back to the page dorm this afternoon. She agrees with me that the sooner we all get back to living normal lives, at least to the extent that's possible with Paul gone, the better off we'll be. Some will say it's irreverent. I don't."

"A grown-up philosophy."

"Mac, there's something I learned recently from Molly that I thought you might want to know."

"What's that?"

"Just before Paul was killed, Molly had lunch with Marge Edwards."

"I know," Mac said. "I spoke with Marge as she was leaving Paul's office for that lunch."

"Molly told me that when they parted on the street, Marge said she might be leaving the office."

"Really? She'd promised Paul she'd keep an eye on Molly. No hint of thinking of leaving. Did she say why?"

"Something about another job. Molly was upset when she heard it. Ever since the rumor surfaced about Marge's intention to accuse Paul, Molly's reaction has been disbelief. She really liked Marge. Never bought it that Marge would even consider such a thing. I suppose that's why Marge's offhand comment about possibly leaving didn't register with her until now."

"Interesting, Ruth."

"Is it?"

"Yes."

"Why?"

"Oh, nothing major. I've been doing some checking of my own into Marge's whereabouts."

"You have?"

"Yup. I want to see this vague smear on Paul's character stamped out. As quickly as possible."

"So do I. Thanks, Mac, for so many things."

"Please give the family my best. *Our* best."

"Get together soon?" she asked.

"Whenever you're up to it."

He called Virginia Information and asked for the number in Ashburn of Maureen Craig. It was unlisted.

Smith called Buffolino at his office. Alicia answered. After preliminary pleasantries—she was fine, Tony was driving her batty; they were thinking of going to Italy, or going bankrupt—she put him on the phone.

"Any chance of getting hold of this Maureen Craig's number?" Smith asked. "It's unlisted."

Buffolino gave forth with a satisfied laugh. "I'm way ahead of you, my lawyer friend." He reeled off the number, which Smith wrote down on a pad. "Anything else I can do for you?"

"You've done quite enough, my detective friend. Good hearing Alicia's voice again. She says you're driving her batty."

"Yeah, I know. But what can you expect?"

"She's a woman," Smith said, wincing as he did.

"You got it, man. *Ciao.*"

Annabel arrived home as Smith was about to try Jim Edwards again.

"What's new?" she asked after kicking off her shoes and settling on the small couch in the den.

He filled her in on what the day had offered so far.

"Tony's amazing," she said.

"He's good, that's for sure. Now I want to find out whether Marge ever mentioned a Maureen Craig to her father."

He tried Edwards's number again.

"Just walked through the door," Edwards said, slightly out of breath. "Did you have a good trip home?"

"Fine, thank you. A question. Did Marge ever mention to you a woman by the name of Maureen Craig?"

"Maureen?"

Judging from his tone, he knew who she was.

"Why do you ask about her?"

"It seems that the private detective who visited you, James Perrone, knows Ms. Craig. I'm trying to establish a link between her and your daughter—if one exists."

Smith waited.

"Jim?"

"Yes, I'm here. Surprised, that's all."

"Why?"

"I haven't heard Maureen's name for a very long time. I think about her, though."

"Oh? What's her relationship with you?"

"Maureen is my stepdaughter from my wife's first marriage."

"I see," Mac said. "Were Marge and Maureen Craig close?"

"Closer than *I* was to Maureen. Had nothing but trouble with her. Headstrong and arrogant. No, I had little use for her, aside from respecting her as my wife's daughter. I tried to be a good stepfather, but stepparenting is tough and she didn't make it easy."

"When's the last time you spoke with her?"

"Oh, hard to say. Ten years? Twelve?"

"That's a long time," Smith said. "What about Marge? Has she stayed in touch with Maureen?"

"I believe so. Marge never talked much about it, but she did mention a few times—last time she was here, as a matter of fact—that she'd seen Maureen. Had dinner with her, something like that."

"Do you think there's any chance that Marge is staying with her stepsister?"

"I wouldn't know."

"Think you could call Maureen and ask if she's seen Marge?"

"I'd rather not. Would you?"

"I'll consider it. Anything else you can tell me, Jim, about Maureen? Did she go to college? Does she work? Is she married?"

"She went to college. Somewhere in New York."

"But she ended up in the Washington area. A job? A boyfriend or husband?"

"I just don't know, Mac. Wish I could be more helpful."

"You've been very helpful, Jim. Can we keep this conversation between us, at least for the moment?"

"Sure."

"The press still camped at your door?"

"No. They've left. Bigger and better fish to fry."

"Not better. But I'm glad they're gone."

"I take it Marge hasn't tried to call you again."

"No, she hasn't."

"I want you to know, Mac, that I haven't mentioned to a soul that she did try to reach you."

"I appreciate that. Well, Jim, I'll let you pour yourself a drink and have some dinner. I'll keep in touch."

Annabel, who'd been listening, said after the conversation concluded, "What now?"

"I thought you'd help me decide that, Annie."

"The man this character Perrone met was Dennis Mackral?"

"According to Tony. No, strike that. I came to that conclusion based upon Tony's description of him. If it was Mackral, that raises the question of why he'd be meeting with a private detective, whose assignment seems to be to find Marge Edwards."

"Senator Connors has never kept it a secret that he was against Paul becoming secretary of state," said Annabel.

"He's never been subtle about it," Smith said. "Possible, I suppose—and troubling—that Connors's office—Mackral—might have wanted Marge Edwards to testify at his hearings that Paul had sexually harassed her."

"Yes. Troubling to even contemplate."

"But Paul's dead. Why bother now?"

"Maybe it's a case of not being able to stop the snowball once it heads downhill. Or not wanting to," said Annabel.

"Ummm. Or maybe that bullheaded Senator Connors wants to smear the administration, and Paul Latham, dead or alive."

"This rumor that Marge Edwards was going to charge Paul with sexual harassment was reported by a single reporter, this—what was his name?"

"Harris. Something Harris."

"Jules Harris. He breaks the story, basing it on the usual so-called reliable source. Everybody else picks up on it. Paul is murdered. Marge disappears. Now, Paul's enemy in the Senate, Connors—his top aide—is working with a private detective to try and find Marge. Why?"

"Your analysis was as good as any," Smith said. "Or mine."

"Who was Harris's source? Marge Edwards herself?"

"If so, why has she run? Guilt? Embarrassment?"

"Dennis Mackral, on Senator Frank Connors's behalf—he might have leaked it to Harris to derail the confirmation."

"What do you suggest I do next?" Smith asked.

"See if Marge Edwards is staying with Maureen Craig."

"My guess is she's not. Perrone was there. If she's with her stepsister, he wouldn't have gone out to Indianapolis looking for her. By the way, Ruth says Marge told Molly just before Paul's murder that Marge told her that she was thinking of leaving Paul's office."

"She give a reason?"

"Another job. Very vague."

"It seems to me the next step is to find out more about Maureen Craig, and then approach her, see what she knows about Marge's whereabouts."

"Tony can help."

"Who's paying his bill?" Annabel asked.

"I am."

"Big spender."

"I'm getting the professional discount."

"Tony Buffolino. With an *O*. What a guy."

"In the meantime," Smith said, "I've got to get back to the Russian project. It's slipping away from me."

"The trip there is getting closer."

"I know. Bring something in for dinner?"

"I'll call. Chinese?"

"Sounds good."

Smith worked into the night, breaking only for the dinner delivered to the door. His wife secluded herself in the bedroom with a fat novel she'd started, but had put aside.

The phone rang at ten.

"Hello, Jessica. I was waiting for you to call."

"Why?"

"Because you said we'd talk again after you got back from Los Angeles."

"Right. Can we talk?"

"I'm listening."

"Not on the phone. Meet you for a drink?"

"Out of the question. Breakfast? You an early riser?"

"Not when I can help it. Sure, breakfast will be fine. Where?"

"Bread and Chocolate, on Twentieth? Seven-thirty?"

"Too busy."

"Too public, you mean?"

"Uh-huh. Washington Harbor? Bagels on me. Seven-thirty in front of Tony and Joe's?"

"Okay."

Annabel appeared in the doorway. "Who was that?"

"Jessica Belle. I'm having breakfast with her."

"Where?"

"Washington Harbor. Bagels. Her treat."

"On the promenade?"

"Yes. All very hush-hush. She's picked up the true CIA spirit."

"Any idea what she wants to talk to you about this time?"

"Not a clue. Let's catch the news."

Paul Latham's murder occupied a sizable portion of that evening's newscast—two minutes amid five-second sound bites. The FBI was in charge of the ongoing investigation; all statements would come from the Bureau. There were no leads.

The Marge Edwards story was still alive but received brief mention—only that Latham's alleged accuser was still missing.

But then the news anchor wrapped up the story with "Mackensie Smith, formerly a prominent Washington criminal lawyer, more recently a law professor at GW, and counsel to Paul Latham, returned today from meeting with the missing Marge Edwards's father at his Indianapolis home. Smith had no comment on his trip."

"I'll be damned," Smith said, leaning forward in his chair and slapping his hands on his thighs. "No comment? Nobody asked me anything. What kind of journalism is that?"

The phone rang.

"Hello," Annabel said. Smith waved his hands. "No, he's not here. Who's calling? I don't know. Yes, I expect him back tonight. Yes, of course. I'll give him the message."

The caller was the producer of the newscast they'd just watched.

The phone rang again. Annabel took another message from a reporter. And another.

"Go to the tape," Smith said, pointing to the answering machine.

A flashing light probed the drapes over the front window. They went to it and looked outside. A TV news truck was parked in front of the house.

They looked quizzically at each other.

"What did Jack Paar say," Smith asked. "They can't hurt you under the covers?"

"My sentiments exactly," Annabel said, turning off the television set. "The bedroom phone gets shut off, too."

"I like the way you think, Annie."

She grinned.

CHAPTER TWENTY-SIX

Molly Latham's return to the page dorm was harder than she'd anticipated.

Her mother drove her there as the other pages were gathering for dinner. The welcome was overwhelming, causing her to break into tears with each hug and expression of sympathy.

Her roommate, Melissa, gushed at having Molly back. "Mah, how I missed you, girl," she said. "Not the same without you. Come on, dinner's served. At least that's what they call it."

"I want to walk my mom to the car," Molly said. "Back in a minute."

"You okay, Rabbit?" Ruth Latham asked as they stood on the sidewalk in front of the O'Neill House Office Building.

"I think so. Gee, they're great, huh?"

"Yes, they are. They seem to really care. Well, you go on back in and I'll head home."

"Mom."

"What?"

"Are *you* okay?"

Ruth wiped a tear from her cheek. "I'm fine, sweetie. As long as I have you, Pris, and Martin, I'll always be fine. Go on, now. Get to dinner. Call me tonight before you go to bed."

After dinner in the page dining room, Molly and Melissa went upstairs.

"It must be tough losin' your daddy like that," Melissa said.

Molly had braced for such reminders of her loss, even when raised by the well-meaning. But her roommate's sincere and certainly accurate comment released her tears again.

Melissa came to where Molly sat, bent over, and hugged her. "Maybe Ah shouldn't have said that."

"No, no," Molly said, wiping her cheeks with the back of her hand. "It's okay. It'll be this way for a while, I know, and then it won't be. How've you been?"

"Wiped out. They run us ragged. That school's rougher than anything back home, I can say. But bein' on the floor is fun, in the cloakroom, deliverin' messages to the most powerful people in the country. I'm glad Ah'm here."

Molly smiled. She liked Melissa despite their overt differences in background and style, and felt warm and comfortable being back with her. Since dinner, she'd experienced a sense of positive anticipation at getting into the swing of things, actually working as a page in the House of Representatives, where her father had served with distinction for so many years.

"How's John?" Molly asked.

"Heavenly," Melissa said, "although boys from New York sure are different than boys from back home. They talk funny, they walk funny, and they do everything else funny, too."

Molly smiled and nodded. The more Melissa talked, the more Molly liked her.

Eventually, the girls stopped chatting and slipped into their evening activities. Melissa complained about the amount of homework facing her—"How much can one girl's brain absorb?"—but turned to it, leaving Molly to take a look at some of Melissa's textbooks, the ones she wasn't using at the moment. She glanced over often at her roommate, whose back was to her as she sat hunched over her desk, an occasional grunt of despair from her lips.

At ten, Molly announced she was going to call her mother from one of the pay phones. As she padded down the hallway in bare feet, a dorm counselor stopped her. "You had a call late this afternoon, Molly," she said.

"Who?"

"A woman. Sorry I didn't tell you right away." She handed Molly a pink telephone message slip. Notations on it indicated the call was for Molly Latham, had been received at 4:30 P.M., that the caller did not leave a number at which she could be reached, and that she would call again.

All of which was irrelevant to Molly compared with the name of the caller written on the paper.

Marge.

CHAPTER TWENTY-SEVEN

A chilly mist slapped Mac Smith's face as he left the house early the next morning to meet with Jessica Belle.

He'd slept fitfully, getting up twice to pace the house, thoughts spawned in the twilight of waking fleeing his mind no matter how he tried to capture them for further evaluation.

Annabel woke once, and came to where her husband sat behind the desk in the den, a pencil's eraser tapping out an impatient paradiddle on a yellow legal pad.

"What's keeping you awake? As if I had to ask."

"Maybe it's not what you think," he said.

"Oh?"

"I've been so totally focused on Marge Edwards and her alleged charge that Paul's murder itself has taken a backseat. But not tonight. The obvious fact that he was assassinated is keeping me up. If he'd been killed by a street criminal, a disgruntled constituent, an escapee from a mental institution, spurned lover, even a member of his own family, it would make some perverted sense. But an *assassination*? If you rule out personal or impersonal personal motives for shooting him, you're left with only politics as a possible reason. Cold-blooded. Calculating. On Capitol Hill, Annie!"

"It's a chilling realization, isn't it? Worthy of insomnia."

"I'm proving that tonight, Annabel. Ruling out other possible suspects, it leaves someone who viewed Paul Latham as a big enough political problem to warrant being killed."

"Maybe it wasn't politics. Maybe it was business."

"Paul wasn't a businessman. He had investments. We even shared investment ideas from time to time. But not business in the usual sense."

"What about Warren Brazier?" Annabel said.

Mac sat forward at the desk. "He's at the top of the list of people keeping me awake. But I can't come up with any rational reason he'd want Paul dead. Paul was his protégé in Congress, maybe too much so, if some people are to be believed. He worked closely with Brazier on opening up the Soviet Union, forging alliances there that undoubtedly played a role in bringing down Communism and opening up a free, more or less democratic market."

"Did he profit financially from his ties to Brazier?"

"I'm sure he didn't, unless you consider retaining his seat in Congress to be 'profiting.' "

"It is, you know."

"Sure. And I'm fully aware we can never know everything about a person, even those close to us. But no, Annabel, Paul Latham was not the sort of man—not the sort of elected official—who would sell out to a businessman like Brazier. To anyone."

"No argument from me. What about someone determined that Paul not become secretary of state?"

"A possibility. But a pretty dramatic way to block a nomination." Smith narrowed his eyes. "The same person, maybe, who floated the sexual harassment rumor?"

"Who was?"

"My money's on Senator Connors."

"Or his aide."

"One and the same, wouldn't you say?"

"Not necessarily. He wouldn't be the first congressional staffer to take matters into his own hands. Step over the line to help his boss. Protect the chief from direct knowledge of a nasty act."

Smith grunted. "I'm going back to bed."

"One more question. Do you think Paul's family is in any danger?"

"No. Why would they be? If we're right in assuming Paul was killed for political or business reasons, the family wouldn't be brought into it."

"Unless they know something they shouldn't."

"Something that Paul knew?"

"Yes."

Smith yawned, stretched, looked at the clock on the wall. "Five o'clock. Maybe I should just stay up. Bagels with Jessica is at seven-thirty."

"Come back to bed, Smith. I like to feel you next to me."

"An offer I can't refuse."

The TV remote truck was gone when Smith left the house and went to where he and Annabel garaged their car. Had the weather been better, he would have walked to Georgetown, not very far from Foggy Bottom. But the mist was a precursor to steady rain, the radio weatherman had promised as Smith shaved. No matter how often such meteorological promises were broken, Smith tended to heed them.

He retrieved the car, drove to the revitalized Georgetown waterfront, parked on Thirty-first Street, and checked his watch. He was fifteen minutes early. Carrying a small black pop-up umbrella, he got out of the car and entered the complex of expensive high-rise condominiums, beneath which a variety of shops and restaurants offered their wares and services to the thousands of visitors, locals and tourists, who enjoyed the views across the Potomac of the Kennedy Center to the south, and the Key Bridge to the north, leading into the busy Virginia city of Rosslyn.

The area was deserted at that hour, except for an occasional jogger detouring down the steps and running along the promenade until emerging again on K Street. The mist was thicker at Washington Harbor; fog, in fact, spreading an eerie charm along the waterfront.

Jessica Belle stood at the railing separating the promenade from the Potomac. Smith saw her through the haze and started in her direction. As he approached, a second person, who'd been behind her, stepped into Smith's line of vision. A few steps closer revealed that it was Jessica's boss at the CIA, Giles Broadhurst.

"Hello," Smith said.

"Hi, Mac," said Jessica.

"Hope we didn't get you up too early," Broadhurst added, smiling and shaking Smith's hand. He and Jessica wore what appeared to be matching tan trench coats, collars up.

"You didn't." Smith looked around. "Is this where you usually hold power breakfasts?"

Broadhurst laughed, a little too energetically for Smith's taste.

"It's a nice, quiet spot to meet," Jessica said.

"Quiet—and damp," said Smith. It had started to rain. Smith opened his umbrella.

"Let's go over there," Broadhurst suggested, indicating an overhang in front of the string of restaurants.

"Better?" Broadhurst asked.

"I suppose so. Look, Jessica," Smith said, "I'm here because you asked me to be, just as I met with you last time—under dryer circumstances. I asked you then why you told me—with your apparent encouragement, Giles—a number of things: that Paul Latham was unduly beholden to Warren Brazier, that Latham was pushing through a massive Russian trade bill to benefit Brazier, and that Brazier was funneling money to the Communists in Russia to help them return to power. Right?"

"That's right," Jessica said.

"Okay," Smith said. "I also think you said that what was important to you was the damage this could do to the president's reputation."

"Right again," said Jessica.

"Well, here I am, assuming there's something *else* you want to tell me."

Broadhurst ran his fingertips over a faint blond mustache on his upper lip. "First, Mac, let me say how appreciative we are of your cooperation and help."

"I have no idea what you're talking about," Smith said. "I feel like old Admiral Stockdale during those vice-presidential debates—who am I, and why am I here? Meeting in the fog and rain early in the morning. Secrets being whispered. That's your game, not mine."

Broadhurst's hand went up, meaning that he understood, but wanted to explain.

But Smith pressed on. "I met with Jessica the last time because she said it had something to do with my friend Paul Latham. And it did. You were the first one to tell me about the sexual harassment charge. Which leads me to a question, Jessica. Were you the reporter's source for that story?"

"No," she said.

"Where did you hear it?"

"Mac," Broadhurst said, "it really doesn't matter where we hear such things. The agency is like a sponge, soaking up thousands of pieces of information every day. Gathering it isn't difficult. Evaluating it is."

"I think we should get to the reason I asked you to meet me again," Jessica said to Smith. To Broadhurst: "Agree?"

A nod from Broadhurst. "Mac, to be right up front with you, we're here this morning to ask for your help."

"Jessica asked for my help the last time," Smith said. "She asked me to drip a few more drops of information about Paul onto your sponge. I don't have any to offer."

"This time, Mac, we have more information to offer *you*," said Broadhurst.

"To what end?" Smith asked.

"To see whether you'd be willing to do something with this new information on our behalf."

"That depends," Smith said.

"On?" Broadhurst asked.

"On whether there's a reason for me to do it. I'm a law professor. My involvement came about only because a close friend, Paul Latham, had been nominated for secretary of state and asked me to be his counsel during confirmation hearings. The only reason I ended up speaking with you was because Jessica was one of my students. When she asked that we get together, I immediately agreed. But when I left the bar, Jessica, and was driving home, I felt I was being used."

"Oh, Mac, that isn't true," she said, touching his arm. "I just thought— *we* thought because you were so close to Congressman Latham, you might pick up on something useful to help clear his name."

"Maybe even to get to the bottom of who killed him," Broadhurst added.

"Used?" she said. "The last thing I would ever do is try to use someone like you, Mac."

"I accept that. So why am I being asked to do something for the CIA?"

"For Paul Latham," Broadhurst said. "For the country."

Smith pinched off an expletive before it was audible.

Broadhurst continued: "It was never my intention when I took this job to get involved in anything but helping American industry flourish globally. I came over from ITC with that as my mission, one with which I fervently agree. But Congressman Latham's murder immediately put me in a position I couldn't foresee."

"How?" Smith asked.

"How? Warren Brazier."

"More about his allegedly pumping money into the Russian Communists?"

Broadhurst and Belle looked at each other. It was Jessica who spoke. "No," she said. "This time it's about murder. Paul Latham's murder."

"Why you?" Smith asked. "Why the CIA? Paul's murder is an FBI matter."

"It is," said Broadhurst. "But that's just a bureaucratic necessity. One agency, one voice. It doesn't mean other agencies, including ours, aren't involved. Sharing information. Feeding what we all know into a central source."

Smith looked across the empty plaza. He couldn't help but smile as he said, "I don't mean to be critical, but the three of us standing here in the rain, the two of you in trench coats with collars turned up, me holding a black umbrella, is more conspicuous than if we were having coffee in the lobby of the Four Seasons."

Broadhurst laughed, said, "You're right, Mac. We're new to this."

"Forget I said it," Smith said, "and let's get on with this meeting. What's the new information you claim has bearing upon Paul's murder?"

"Intelligence from Russia," Broadhurst said. "Concerning Brazier."

"I'm listening," Smith said.

"First, Mac," Broadhurst said, "I need to know whether you're willing to do something with the information."

"What is the information? Once I know that, I'll decide whether to 'do something with it,' as you put it."

Another set of glances between Jessica and her boss.

Smith waited.

Broadhurst spoke. "What we ask of you, Mac, is to take the information to Brazier. Tell him you came into possession of it through your close personal and professional relationship with Latham."

"And why would I do that? More to the point, what is it intended to accomplish?"

"Prompt Brazier to take some action that will help prove what we are alleging."

"And what is that?"

"That he ordered Congressman Latham to be eliminated."

Warren Brazier had stayed in his Washington office overnight. He'd managed to delay questioning by the FBI on the Latham murder until this morning. The special agents were due at nine.

He'd slept only two hours, spending most of the night poring over financial reports received that day via a secure fax line from his Moscow office.

Now, at 8:45, dressed in a pearl-gray suit, white shirt, midnight-blue tie, and black wingtip shoes, all from favorite London custom clothing shops, he walked into the conference room, where three members of his Russian staff awaited his arrival.

"Good morning, sir," Anatoly Alekseyev said, standing quickly along with his two fellow executives.

"Good morning," Brazier said, sitting in his chair at the head of the table and opening a file folder he'd carried with him. "These figures. I'm not happy with them."

The three younger men said nothing.

"It is not my intention to see everything I've worked for in the Soviet Union come to this!" He slammed his fist on the table, remarkably without moving the rest of his body.

"Mr. Brazier," Alekseyev said, "you're quite right. But the numbers are misleading when you factor in the Sidanco negotiations."

If Brazier was surprised, dismayed, or angry that his young Russian executive was aware of what had been, to date, a secret undertaking, he did not demonstrate it. Instead, he ignored the comment and turned to another project that was, in his judgment, a new example of ineptitude on the part of his staff.

Alekseyev and his two colleagues sat glumly, taking their boss's verbal blows without expression. Brazier ended with "I'm replacing the three of you at this office. You'll return to Moscow. There will be lesser jobs for you there."

"Mr. Brazier," Alekseyev said, "if I might say something."

Brazier's personal assistant knocked.

"In!" Brazier said.

She opened the door and said the visitors for his nine o'clock appointment had arrived, and were waiting in his office.

"Thank you," Brazier said, closing the file folder and leaving the room without another word.

The Bureau had assigned two of its most senior special agents to interview Brazier that morning, Matthew Miller and Kenneth Wahlstrom, both from a division formed after the collapse of the Soviet Union to deal with the new challenges presented by that dissolution.

Brazier's greeting of them was abrupt. He sat behind his desk and said, "I trust this won't take long. I have meetings scheduled all day."

The agents had dealt with difficult individuals long enough not to be put off by such behavior. Miller said, his face void of expression, "We're here to ask questions of you in the matter of Congressman Paul Latham's murder. You're free to have counsel present, if you wish."

"I don't need any lawyers here," Brazier shot back. "Ask your questions. Let's not waste time with needless preliminaries."

Again, Miller ignored it. "Where were you, Mr. Brazier, the morning Congressman Latham was shot?"

Brazier met the special agent's steady, unblinking stare. "Here," he said. "In my office."

"At that early hour?"

"I don't keep bureaucrat's hours," Brazier said. "Next?"

"Was anyone here with you?"

"No."

"There's no one to verify your statement?"

"My word is good enough." Brazier made the checking of his Rolex a conspicuous action.

The two agents had decided before confronting Brazier to allow Miller to do the questioning, and for Wahlstrom to make notes, not only of Brazier's responses, but to characterize his demeanor.

The picture Wahlstrom presented externally was as noncommittal as his partner's. Inside, he seethed with dislike for this cocky, arrogant little man whose power stemmed only from money. Unlike Miller, who tended to shrug off such people, Wahlstrom actively disliked them to the extent that he felt the excessive, even obscene wealth of industrial leaders—garnered on the backs of working people, whose relatively meager salaries were increasingly considered impediments to their leaders' bottom line—was the greatest threat the nation faced. Of course, he seldom expressed those sentiments. The Bureau tended not to react favorably to special agents with mildly socialist-sounding views.

"When was the last time you saw Congressman Latham, Mr. Brazier?"

Brazier's shrug was barely discernible.

"I'll repeat the question," Miller said.

"I saw him that afternoon."

"*That* afternoon? You mean the previous afternoon."

"I mean the afternoon of the day before he died."

"What time was that?"

"Late. Four o'clock, maybe. Four-thirty."

"You don't keep records of your meetings, especially with members of Congress?"

Brazier narrowed his eyes.

"Sir?"

"We were friends. I don't keep records of getting together with friends."

"Where did you and Congressman Latham meet?"

"His office."

"A social visit?"

"It was to discuss a few things."

"And what were they?"

"I don't think that's of concern to anyone but Paul Latham and me."

"The FBI is officially charged with investigating the murder of Congressman Latham," said Miller. "What things did you and the congressman discuss?"

"I really don't recall."

Agent Wahlstrom thought back to his pre-Bureau days, when he was a police officer in Los Angeles. Anyone displaying Brazier's swagger during questioning might have been made more cooperative with a fist to the face. He wanted to go over the desk at the contemptuous industrialist, his impatience magnified by what he and Miller had been told prior to coming to interview Brazier. Warren Brazier had become a prime suspect in Congressman Latham's murder. If Brazier had been behind it, Wahlstrom looked forward to playing a part in nailing it down. But as frustrating as it was, he knew he'd have to wait for that satisfaction. He wrote on his pad that Brazier did not recall what had been discussed during his last meeting with Latham.

"No idea?" Miller followed up. "Not even one thing that came up during your meeting?"

"No. It was a social call. Idle conversation. Sports. Movies. Family."

"Family? Did you talk about your family? His?"

"Both."

"Did the congressman seem upset about anything that afternoon?"

"No. He was in good spirits."

"Did anything he said indicate that he intended to be in that pocket park at such an early hour the next morning?"

"No." Another overt look at his watch.

"Did he indicate to you during that social call, or during any previous meetings, that there might have been someone with enough of a grudge against him to contemplate killing him?"

"Of course not."

"Why do you say 'of course not'? A man in his position of leadership would naturally make enemies."

"I wasn't one of them."

Brazier's response piqued the interest of both agents, but they said nothing to indicate it.

"You and Congressman Latham worked together closely over the years, didn't you? On legislation regarding your business interests in Russia?"

"You don't 'work closely' with a congressman. You help a congressman think through a piece of legislation, provide him and his staff with needed, helpful facts, point out the potential impact of legislation."

Miller dismissed Brazier's capsule education on congressional lobbying, and asked his next question: "Did you have an argument with Congressman Latham during that last social visit?"

"No."

A buzzer sounded. Brazier pushed a button on a compact intercom unit on his desk. His assistant's voice said, "You're running late for your next meeting, sir."

"Thank you," Brazier said. He removed his finger from the button and said to the special agents, "You'll have to wrap this up. As you can see, I have nothing to offer, except to again extend my condolences to Congressman Latham's fine and grieving family."

He stood. The interview was over, as far as he was concerned.

Neither agent left his seat. Wahlstrom continued writing as Miller asked, "Have you been in touch with the congressman's family?"

"Of course," Brazier said.

The agents knew he hadn't. Ruth Latham had informed other agents who'd interviewed her late the previous afternoon that she was disappointed at Brazier's lack of communication with her.

Miller pressed on. "Where, when, and how did you learn of Congressman Latham's death?"

"Sorry, but I must leave . . . gentlemen."

Special Agent Wahlstrom broke his silence. "How long will you be in your next meeting?" he asked.

"I don't know."

"We'll wait," Wahlstrom said.

"If you wish," Brazier said, going to the door and gesturing for them to follow. "You can wait in the reception area. You might be there awhile. A few days, perhaps."

The agents stepped into the hallway. Brazier said, "Good day." With that, he set off at a quick pace, turned a corner, and was gone.

Wahlstrom swore under his breath.

Miller smiled, placed his hand on his colleague's shoulder, and said, "Just goes to show money doesn't buy class. Or honesty. Let's get out of here."

At two that afternoon, Dr. Giles Broadhurst, head of the CIA's new division to foster American business competitiveness abroad, attended a meeting at FBI headquarters, in the J. Edgar Hoover Building on Pennsylvania Avenue between Ninth and Tenth streets, N.W. Its ironic location, two blocks south of the Martin Luther King Memorial Library, wasn't lost on Broadhurst. Hoover had tried to bring King down, yet the monuments to both shared that small parcel of land. If it was any consolation to Dr. King, his building was clearly superior in architecture—to say nothing of public sentiment—to the controversial former FBI chief's memorial. It was sometimes termed Washington's major contribution to the new design "Brutalism."

The meeting took place in a windowless office. With Broadhurst in the room was the Bureau's special agent in charge of the Latham case, Gerry Lakely.

"How did it go?" Lakely asked.

"Good," Broadhurst replied.

"He'll do it?"

"I think so. No commitment from him this morning, but my guess is he will. He's a careful, prudent man. Lawyer, you know. Professor."

"What questions did he ask?"

"Oh, why we were asking him. Why you and your people didn't simply confront Brazier with the information yourselves."

"And you said?"

"I said what we'd agreed I'd say. That his close relationship with Latham, professional and personal, made it more likely Brazier would buy what he was saying—and offering."

"Good."

"A question."

"Yes?"

"Why *are* you taking this approach, using him?"

Lakely, whose reputation within the Bureau was that of a cold, methodical agent with the ability to create elaborate scenarios in which to trap suspects, rubbed his hands together as though they were cold. He thought for a moment before replying, "If we actually had the evidence against Brazier, we'd take it to him. But since we don't physically have possession of it—although I'm sure we will in due time—we don't want this agency, or yours for that matter, to be out there swinging in the breeze. Better someone without official connection to either body. Don't you agree?"

"Of course. No progress on locating Ms. Edwards?"

"None. But there will be. Any problem with your assistant, Ms. Belle?"

"No. Should there be?"

"Only because she brought Smith into the picture. Her teacher, pedagogue, and preceptor, man to look up to. No problem that might cause her to balk? Maybe tip him off to what we're doing?"

"No. No problem."

"Good. Then I think this should move along smoothly. Thanks, Giles."

"Happy to help, although I'll be glad to get back to what I was hired for—boost American business abroad."

"I think you're doing precisely that, Giles. Let's face it. Warren Brazier, and the way he does business overseas, doesn't do anyone any good. Let me know when Smith gets back to you."

At three that afternoon, Warren Brazier's secretary took a phone call.

"My name is Mackensie Smith. I was counsel to former congressman Paul Latham."

"Yes, Mr. Smith. How may I help you?"

"I would like to make an appointment to see Mr. Brazier at his earliest convenience."

"I see. May I ask what it's in reference to?"

"Well, that's hard to explain on the phone. You might simply tell Mr. Brazier that I've come into possession of certain information regarding Congressman Latham that I know will be of great interest to him."

Smith waited while she wrote down every word.

"How can we get back to you, Mr. Smith?"

Mac gave her his number.

"I'm sure Mr. Brazier will return your call shortly. Thank you, Mr. Smith."

"I'm sure he will. Thank *you*."

CHAPTER TWENTY-EIGHT

Anatoly Alekseyev's attempts to arrange a meeting with Warren Brazier had been a resounding failure. Once he accepted the reality that Brazier would not allow him to plead personally to stay in Washington, he sent him a long, detailed memo pointing to contributions he'd made to the company's success, his loyalty to the firm's goals and its leader, and reasons why a sudden transfer back to Russia would pose a personal hardship for him. The latter reason for remaining in Washington was weak, he knew. Brazier never made personnel decisions based upon individual needs, which Alekseyev understood from a management perspective. Still, he felt he had to pull out all the stops.

There hadn't been any response from Brazier to the memorandum, nor did the young executive hold out much hope there would be. He and his two colleagues had been instructed by Human Resources to be prepared to depart within four days. The thought of leaving a city and lifestyle he'd grown to love was anathema.

This day, after starting the process of cleaning out his desk, and having made a few calls to friends in search of another job that would keep him in Washington, he left the office at four. He didn't want to stop in at any of his regular Georgetown haunts because he wasn't in the mood for idle chat. Instead, he chose the Hotel Washington, where he sat alone in the Sky Terrace Lounge, nursing vodkas on the rocks and contemplating his situation. He'd been to the hotel's rooftop before, once with friends to observe the city's Fourth of July celebrations; its panoramic views of Washington were unrivaled.

Feeling the effects of the vodka, but not drunk, Alekseyev retrieved his car from a parking garage and headed for his apartment complex, stopping on the way at Jaimalito's to take out two orders of enchiladas.

By the time he walked into his apartment, a pervasive sense of desperation had set in, fueled, to some extent, by the alcohol. He sensed he had to do something, and do it fast.

But what *could* he do?

Finding a new job would take weeks, perhaps months. He hadn't saved any money to sustain him through a prolonged search. Too, there was the fear that Brazier would put out unfavorable references about him. Or worse. The man was capable of that, Alekseyev knew. A brilliant businessman—and a ruthless one, with little or no regard for people.

"Hello," he called out, shutting the door behind him and putting the shopping bag of food on a nearby table. "Marge?"

Marge Edwards, dressed in a bathrobe and slippers, emerged from the bedroom. Her disheveled hair and puffy eyes said she'd been sleeping.

"Hi," she said in a husky voice.

"Hi," he said. "Any calls?"

"No. I don't think so. I was sleeping."

Alekseyev checked the answering machine. No tiny red blinking light.

He tossed his jacket on a chair and brought the take-out dinners into the kitchen. She followed. "Anything new with Brazier?"

"No." He removed the aluminum-foil dishes from the brown shopping bag and pulled two plates from a cupboard. "Wine?" he asked.

"I'll get it. White?"

"Yes."

They sat at the kitchen table. Alekseyev's disposition was not gregarious. He ate in silence, chewing aimlessly, drinking his Pouilly-Fuissé without tasting it.

Marge Edwards respected his mood, and silence. She knew what a blow Warren Brazier had dealt her lover. And she was not oblivious to what Brazier's decision might mean to her, at least in the short haul.

She refilled their glasses.

"I don't know what to do," Alekseyev said.

"Nothing from him?"

"No. Just Human Resources. Pack up and be gone in four days."

She covered his hand on the table with hers. "You don't have to go back to Moscow," she said. "Quit. Tell Warren Brazier to stuff it."

"And live on what? If he fired me, I could collect from the unemployment insurance. If I resign, I have nothing. And there is my status in this country."

"You have your dignity, Anatoly. You'll be able to find another job and stay here, if you work at it."

His face was drawn, sad, as he said, "The man is insane, Marge. To blame me and the others for his bad deals in Russia . . . it is wrong. Unfair. I have always done good work. I have been so damn loyal, even though I know things about him and his company that would put him in jail."

Up until being told he was being sent back to Russia—*exiled* there— Alekseyev had told Marge little about the inner workings of Brazier Industries. Nor had she confided in him what she knew about her boss, Congressman Paul Latham, and his dealings with Warren Brazier. They tended to leave work at their offices each evening, content to revel in the newfound pleasures each gave the other. What had begun as a one-night sexual fling had quickly developed into a deeper, more caring union.

They kept their relationship low-key. Their being romantically involved—sharing pillow talk—would be viewed negatively by their employers. Once, and only once had Marge casually mentioned to Latham that she'd been seeing someone who worked for Brazier Industries: "A nice guy, pleasant to have dinner with once in a while. A little strange at times. Nothing serious." Latham didn't press for further details.

But by then it had become serious. Marge Edwards, daughter of Jim and Sue Edwards of Indiana, and Anatoly Alekseyev, born, raised, and educated in the Soviet Union, now enjoying the rewards of working for a multinational company, had found each other, and had even begun to talk of spending their lives together.

She cleaned up the kitchen while Anatoly changed into his pajamas and slippers. They sat side by side on the couch and watched a television sitcom, the only laughter in the room the show's laugh track.

When the program was almost over, Alekseyev clicked off the set with the remote control, turned, and looked into her eyes. "Marge," he said, "we have to take steps now. Even if I was not being sent home, you could not stay hidden here forever. What sort of life is this? You stay in these four walls day and night, afraid to go out, to walk in the sun, drink a cup of coffee in a café."

"Are you trying to get rid of me?" she asked, lightening her tone to indicate she was being playful.

He took her seriously. "You know that is not true."

"Anatoly, you know why I'm here. I'm afraid to face the world because of what's happened. I want to leave. I want to walk in the sun and sip that coffee in a café. But you know what certain people will want of me."

He slapped his hands to the sides of his head and stood. "Marge, this silly thing about sexual harassment means nothing. Stand tall, tell them it is not true. You make such a statement and walk away. It is over. What are you so afraid of? Of telling the truth?"

"It's not that simple," she said, an edge to her voice.

"Why? Is there someone who can say that it happened? Is there someone who can prove it?"

"No. I mean, there is something that can be twisted to make it look as though it's true."

She'd never before mentioned such a "thing" in their conversations. He frowned while waiting for her to continue. When she didn't, he asked, "What are you talking about?"

She swallowed hard. "A diary," she said.

"A diary? Whose diary?"

"Mine."

The word stung him. He went to the kitchen and poured himself a glass of vodka, then returned to where Marge continued to sit, her lips pressed together, eyes focused on the rug's geometric pattern.

"You kept a diary about how Latham made sexual advances to you?"

"Yes. No, it was not that. It was not a diary of facts."

"Then what was it?" he asked angrily.

"It was . . ." She wept softly. "It was my fantasy."

Alekseyev glared at her, his focused dark eyes mirroring what he was feeling. "Fantasy?" he repeated. "What fantasy could you have?"

She turned from his hard stare, pressed her knuckles to her mouth. "Anatoly," she said quietly, "I was in love with Paul Latham."

He muttered in Russian.

She faced him. "I was in love with him from the first day I went to work in his office. This man represented everything I wanted from life. I met his wife and children, and I won't deny the envy I felt for them. I saw how he treated them, with love and respect. Not like so many men I've been involved with. Paul was gentle and kind, like a father to me."

"And you were in love with your father?" A Russian curse came from him.

"No, Anatoly. I wasn't in love with Paul Latham because he was like a father to me. I was in love with him as a man. God, how I wanted to change places with his wife, be there at home for him after a difficult day in Congress, counsel and soothe him, proud to be on his arm at parties and political functions. Love him. Is that so difficult to understand?"

"And you wrote down these feelings? These fantasies?"

"Yes. Almost every night. Just a word sometimes. Other nights, many pages."

Alekseyev poured another drink.

"Would you get me one, too?" she said.

He did, reluctantly, spilling some as he handed it to her because his hand shook.

"Where is this diary?" he asked.

"Someplace safe."

"Where?"

"I can't tell you."

"Why? I thought we cared for each other."

She forced a smile onto her quivering lips. "I thought we loved each other."

"How can you love me, Marge. You love him. A dead man."

"God!" She stood, hands held up in frustration as she crossed the room. "Can't you understand what I mean when I say I *loved* Paul Latham? Is there something in the Russian mentality that makes it impossible to accept a love based upon fantasy and wishing? Yearning for something better?" She spun around to face him. "I fell in love with my science teacher in junior high school, Anatoly. I had a crush on my college psych professor. Haven't you ever fantasized about a woman you couldn't have?"

"*Nyet!*"

His use of Russian startled her. They'd spoken only English to each other since meeting.

"Then you aren't human," she said.

That charge further angered him.

She came to where he stood and placed her hands on his arms, spoke softly to him: "Please try to understand, Anatoly."

The deep breaths he'd drawn had been calming. He stepped back and said, "I am trying to understand, Marge. But how can you expect me to—

what?—to stand by you if you tell me only some of the story? This diary of your false love for him."

"Not false, Anatoly."

"False. Fantasy. Whatever. You share just so much of it with me, yet do not trust me to know where the diary is. To see it so that I can help you."

Her pause seemed an eternity.

"I just want to help," he repeated.

"Let's sit down." She went to the couch. He joined her.

"One of my diaries ended up with my stepsister," she said.

"Stepsister?"

"My mother's daughter. From her first marriage."

"How did she get the diary?"

"Does it matter?"

"I think it matters. Did you give it to her, Marge?"

"No. Of course not. She and I were not friendly. We didn't speak for years. Then, one day, she called me. She'd moved to this area, and thought it was time for us to get together. We shared the same mother, she said, and should try to honor our blood tie.

"I agreed, and we started seeing each other, a few lunches, dinner, then weekends together, usually at her house in Ashburn. That's in Virginia."

"And you gave her this diary?"

She shook her head. "No. But I showed it to her one weekend. Silly, I know, but we'd become very close in a short period of time. I told her about it because . . . girl kind of talk. Do you understand?"

"Girl talk?"

"Something girls do when they're together." She smiled. "I told her about my fantasy of being married to Paul. She . . . Well, we had a good laugh over it."

"And then what happened?"

"I left the diary at her house by mistake. Completely forgot about it for a few days. We were so busy at the office, major legislation being prepared, everyone wanting some of Paul's time." A small laugh. "No time for fantasizing."

"Call her and tell her to give it back."

"I did."

"And?"

"She said she didn't have it."

"How could she say that?"

"She said it disappeared."

"Impossible."

"I asked if I could come help her look. She said she was too busy for that and hung up. Each time I call, she refuses to talk to me."

"I could go there and demand she give it to me."

"Anatoly, I'm sure she means what she says. She doesn't have it. Someone else has it, the same someone who's using it to back up the claim that I was sexually harassed by Paul Latham."

"Who?"

"I don't know. Someone she gave it to. Someone she sold it to. What does it matter?"

He poured another drink in the kitchen, saying when he returned, "If the diary is nothing more than what you say is fantasy, then it does not prove that Congressman Latham made advances to you."

"Of course," she said. "But how do you think I'll look, writing a schoolgirl diary about my crush on my boss, one of the leading members of Congress? I was explicit at times about my sexual fantasies. I'll be disgraced."

"And if the diary is released, even without you? You'll be disgraced also. Your name."

She pulled her knees up to her chin and wrapped her arms about them. He looked at her. "So, Marge, what will you do?"

"I don't know." Then, almost inaudibly, "There's more."

"What did you say?"

"I said there's more."

"Tell me."

She twisted and looked into his earnest olive face and soft brown eyes. "There is another diary, Anatoly. A second diary. A report, actually. A very important one."

CHAPTER TWENTY-NINE

"Mr. Brazier will see you now, Mr. Smith."

He followed the secretary down a hallway to Brazier's private office. Although the morning was cool—the city's unrelenting summer heat was fast becoming an unpleasant memory—the air-conditioning blasted frigid air into the office. Mac Smith decided as he stepped through the door that Warren Brazier either had an out-of-whack internal body thermostat, or cranked up the AC to freeze unwelcome visitors.

"Mr. Smith, how nice to see you." Brazier, in shirtsleeves and tie, came from behind his desk, smiling broadly, hand extended. Smith shook it. "Sit down, sit down. Coffee? Tea?"

"Nothing, thank you. I've had my caffeine ration for the morning." More accurately, he didn't trust anyone else's hand at coffee.

When both were seated, Brazier said, "I'm intrigued at your reason for being here, Mr. Smith. Let me refer to my notes of our brief phone conversation. You said—and I think I took it down verbatim—'I have information to share with you that I think you'll be vitally interested in.' " He looked up, eyebrows arched. "Accurate?"

"Yes."

"You also said, and I quote, 'I think you should hear what I have to say before the information goes to other people.' Right again?"

"Right again," Smith said, smiling.

Brazier pushed aside the paper, extended his hands palms up, and said, "I'm listening with great interest."

• • •

Smith had spent two hours that morning going over in his mind the "script" suggested to him by Giles Broadhurst and Jessica Belle. After they'd given him a thumbnail sketch of what they hoped to accomplish, and he'd agreed to listen, they left the soggy Washington Harbor complex for the warmth and dryness of a nearby luncheonette. Over cups of remarkably bad coffee, Broadhurst went into more detail on the mission they hoped Smith would undertake for them.

Instead of going home after the meeting, Smith stopped by Annabel's gallery.

"How did your clandestine meeting go?" she asked.

Smith grinned. "I feel like a character in an Eric Ambler novel. Almost comical, if the ramifications weren't so dire."

"What did Jessica want?"

"It wasn't just her. Her boss, Giles Broadhurst, was there, too."

"What does that mean?"

"It means Jessica just acted as the go-between," Smith replied. "Broadhurst wants me to take on an assignment for him."

"For the CIA."

"For the CIA. And the FBI."

"The heavy-hitting alphabet soups. What do they want you to do, Mac?"

"It could help get to the bottom of Paul's murder, Annabel."

"Oh? How?"

"If what I do is successful, it might flush out Paul's killer."

"Why the CIA? It's an FBI case."

"Because the information they're acting upon came through Broadhurst and his people. They're cooperating. Rare, indeed."

"Mac."

"What?"

"You haven't told me what it is they want you to do."

"Oh. Right. It's not terribly difficult. Not a big deal."

"Why do I have the feeling you don't want to tell me?"

"I can't imagine . . . why you'd feel that way. Interesting, how Broadhurst's division of the CIA came up with what they have."

"Mac!"

"They want me to . . ."

It took him ten minutes to explain the scheme set forth by Broadhurst and Belle. When he was finished, Annabel's furrowed brow and tight lips spoke volumes about what she thought.

"That's it," he said. "That's what they want me to do."

"And you agreed to do it."

"Yes."

"I am not happy, Mac."

"Funny how I sensed that right away."

"Do you realize what you're getting into?"

"I think so. I deliver this message to Brazier, and walk away. If he reacts the way Broadhurst hopes he will, he might provide the proof they need that he was behind Paul's murder. If he doesn't, I did my part and can forget about it."

"Mac."

"I wish you wouldn't say my name with that tone, Annie. It sets my teeth on edge."

"I'd like to set something else on edge."

"Like what?"

"Your head."

"Are we about to have an argument?"

"No, Mac. We are not about to have an argument. We are about to have a *war!*"

"Why?"

"Because what you've agreed to do is dangerous. What if Brazier *was* behind Paul's murder? You confront him, claiming you were given information by Paul that points to Brazier as a crook, a traitor to his own country, and a menace to society. What do you think he does then?"

"I have no idea what he'll do."

"He'll have you killed, too."

"Oh, Annie, that's stretching things."

"No, it's not. Have you stopped to think that this scheme—I love the word—this *farchadat* scheme—this crazy idea has been cooked up by the Central Intelligence Agency? They go around trying to kill Castro by poisoning his cigars. The northern Iraq fiasco. Running drugs. Crazy mind-control experiments. They tell you there's information enough to implicate Brazier in a number of criminal acts, but they also tell you they don't have 'physical possession' of it." Her tone was derisive.

"Yet."

"Yet. Maybe they don't have a thing."

"They say someone close to Paul and Brazier documented all of Brazier's illegal acts."

"Sell *that* to a jury."

"There's more. The CIA has been delving into Brazier's Russian operations for years, way back before the breakup of the Soviet Union. According to Broadhurst, they've amassed a huge file on his wrongdoings."

"Good for them. Mac, don't do it. Call Jessica and say you've thought it over and have decided not to become involved."

"Tell her my wife doesn't approve?"

"What's wrong with that?"

"Nothing. Look, ever since Paul was killed, my life has been on hold and will stay that way until his murder is solved. If I can do something to speed up that process, I want to do it. Make sense?"

"Sure it does. But to put yourself out front like this, be the messenger for the CIA? That's asking too much of anyone."

"I want to play a role in finding Paul's killer, Annie."

Her face and voice softened. "I know how important that is to you, Mac. And I'm also aware that I have a role to play, too, to support you in it. Just as you supported me when I went undercover to recover that Caravaggio masterpiece. You weren't happy when I did that, but you understood, and stood by me."

"Yes, I did. And I'd do it again."

"I love you, Mackensie Smith, more than anything in this world. I don't want to see a single hair on your head injured. You—"

"I don't have as many hairs as I used to have to worry about. Was that what you were about to say?"

Her laugh was cathartic.

They talked for another half hour. He left the gallery, secure in her support for what he was about to do, and more madly in love with her than ever.

Now, the following morning, he was about to put into play what he'd been asked to do by Broadhurst and Belle.

"Mr. Brazier," Smith said, "you're aware, I'm sure, that I was very close to Paul Latham, personally and professionally."

"Yes, I am, Mr. Smith."

"Our relationship went back many years."

"How many years?"

He's taking the offensive, Smith thought. Brazier's arrogance wasn't surprising, or off-putting. Smith had dealt with enough rich, powerful, contumelious men to understand it was their style to attempt to turn things around, to bully others into submission.

"Paul shared a great deal with me, Mr. Brazier," Smith said, ignoring his question.

Brazier held up his left arm and studied his Rolex for longer than it took to tell the time.

"And he was open with me regarding some of his dealings with you."

"Cold, Mr. Smith?"

It took Smith a second to realize Brazier was referring to the air-conditioning. "Not at all," he said. "I'm quite comfortable in here with you."

Brazier's expression was blank. He sat back and formed a tent with his hands beneath his chin.

"You go back a long way with Paul Latham, too. Lots of legislation that benefited you, lots of deals in the Soviet Union and Russia."

"Are you looking to be my biographer, Mr. Smith?"

"You've been known to hire some people whose résumés aren't what might be called mainstream."

No reaction.

"Security people, they're called."

A stare.

"And then there's your involvement in Russian politics."

"I don't get involved in politics," Brazier said. "In Russia or anywhere else."

"As I understand it, Mr. Brazier, things were better for you when the Communists were in power."

"Things are good for me now."

"That's not what I hear."

Brazier abruptly stood, went to a window behind the desk, and sat on its deep sill. He folded his arms across his chest, lowered his head, and looked at Smith from that perspective.

Smith met his gaze and said nothing.

"Paul often spoke of you, Mr. Smith, and always with the highest praise."

"The feeling was entirely mutual."

"You were a big-time attorney in this town, Mr. Smith. Darrow, Nizer, and Bennett rolled into one."

"You put me in good company."

"Obviously, you didn't achieve your success by being imprecise."

"A lack of precision was useful at times."

"But this isn't one of them."

"You'd like me to be precise about what Paul told me and gave to me about you."

"I like people who pick up on cues. I don't mean to be rude, but I do have other commitments."

"Of course."

It took no more than ten minutes for Smith to deliver to Brazier the information provided by Broadhurst and Belle. Brazier didn't interrupt, his face painted with indifference. When Smith concluded his remarks, Brazier said, "How much do they pay you to teach law, Mr. Smith?"

"GW is generous with me, Mr. Brazier."

"Not as much as when you were burning up the courtroom."

"Too much of that was blood money," Smith said. "I'm content to be out of that fire."

"I've always paid men of your caliber generously," Brazier said. "You come with pristine references."

"From a dead friend. I'm not here looking for a job, Mr. Brazier."

"Well, perhaps we can meet again."

"Whenever you wish. You'll think about what I've said this morning?"

Brazier grinned. "Oh, yes, Mr. Smith. I'll give it considerable thought. Thank you for stopping by. My secretary will show you out."

As Smith passed through the reception area on his way to the elevator—he was tempted to blow on his hands—he noticed a handsome young man sitting in a chair. He looked vaguely familiar to Mac, but he didn't know why.

Smith got in his car and breathed a sigh of relief, and satisfaction. He'd played many roles in the courtroom, but none like this. He was glad he'd done it, and at once was glad it was over.

Solving the assassination of Paul Latham was not his responsibility, he knew. But by having contributed something to the process, perhaps a closure of sorts had been accomplished. He now felt free to resume his life, especially the challenge of completing his analysis of differences between the American justice system and its counterpart in Russia, and coming up with ideas in advance of his trip to Russia as to how the Russian system could be improved.

This sudden, newfound sense of liberty consumed him as he drove to

Foggy Bottom, so much so that he never noticed the two men in the car that followed him home.

The chair in which Smith had sat in Warren Brazier's office was now occupied by Marge Edwards's lover, Anatoly Alekseyev. Brazier granted him a half hour. When it was over, Alekseyev, stifling a smile, shook his boss's hand and quickly departed the building. Once outside, he allowed the smile to erupt, and he stabbed a fist into the air, the way athletes do when winning.

His exuberance was short-lived, however, lasting only long enough for him to return to his apartment.

"Hello?" he called once inside. "Marge?"

There was no response, but a note was on the dining room table:

> Dear Anatoly:
> Getting everything off my chest to you was cleansing, therapeutic. Now that you know what really caused me to run and to hide—and I will never be able to thank you enough for being my protector during this awful period—I've developed the backbone to do something about it, to take action. I'm going to meet with Bob Mondrian and hash everything out. Then, I'll see to it that the report on Brazier Industries is placed in the right hands. I don't want to involve you any further because you have your own problems with Brazier. Maybe if I finally do the right thing, I'll be better able to help you stay here in Washington. I want that because I don't want to lose you. I will call and keep in touch. I love you (one day I'll learn to say it in Russian). Marge.

Brazier summoned his chief of Russian personnel, Aleksandr Patiashvili, to his office. A minute later, Patiashvili returned to his own office, where he placed a call to Brighton Beach, Brooklyn. Pavel Bakst answered. They spoke in Russian.

"Hello, Alek," Bakst said.

"Hello, Pavel. All is well?"

"Very well," the Russian mob boss replied. "You?"

"Problems."

"Oh?"

"The young man we sent, Fodorov. He is with you?"

"No, but close by. A strange one, Alek. A real *zhopachnik*, huh?"

Patiashvili wasn't interested in Yvgeny Fodorov's sexual orientation. "He wants him here in Washington this afternoon."

They both understood who "he" was. Brazier. The boss of bosses.

"All right. I'll put him on a plane myself. If I can wake him. He's a lazy *zhopachnik*. Better to be with you than me. *Ciao*, Alek."

CHAPTER THIRTY

Washington-area McDonald's were busy that day.

Dennis Mackral sat in a booth at the Adams-Morgan fast-food outlet with James Perrone. The private investigator ate a Big Mac as if it were an *hors d'oeuvre* and sipped a giant soda. Mackral had nothing in front of him; he was too angry to ingest anything but air.

"I'm telling you straight out, Perrone, we won't pay a penny more for this joke you call a diary. In fact, we ought to get back what we've already given you."

"Don't push me," Perrone responded, chewing.

"Don't push you? The senator and I read the diary from cover to cover. It's nothing you represented it to be. Nothing! Just the schoolgirl fantasies of Marge Edwards. It doesn't prove a damn thing."

"That's not my problem."

"The hell it isn't. You told me—and I stuck my neck out with the senator—you told me that you knew this woman who had a diary belonging to a friend who worked for Latham, and that the same diary documented his sexual overtures to her over a period of years."

"That's what *she* told *me*," Perrone said, wiping ketchup from his mouth with a small yellow paper napkin.

"I thought you looked at the diary."

"I did. She showed it to me. I didn't read the whole thing, but it had a lot of sexual stuff in it about Latham."

"Her sexual *fantasies*. That's all they were. Christ, the diary paints Latham as a saint."

Perrone shrugged. "What you do with it is your business. All I promised was to deliver it to you. I did. And you owe me money."

"No, we don't." Mackral held up his right index finger to reinforce his statement.

Perrone grabbed the finger and pressed it back, hard. "You owe me money," the investigator repeated. He released the finger. "You think this was easy, cozying up to this Craig broad?"

"You *bought* the diary from her."

"Yeah, but how do you think I even knew the damn thing existed? I had to get close."

"How much of the money have you paid her?"

"All of it."

"All of it?"

"How come you keep repeating what I say?"

"I thought you were paying her in installments."

"That's how I started. But when you put the screws on me to see the diary, I pressed her. She wouldn't budge. She's as tight when it comes to a buck as she is ugly. She wanted the rest of the ten, so I gave it to her."

"Ten thousand dollars. For nothing. My job's on the line."

"Why? You said the money came from a private fund."

Mackral leaned across the table. "A private fund that can't afford losing ten thousand dollars. We have to account for that money to . . . them."

"Twenty thousand, Dennis."

"No. We've given you, what? Six?"

"Which means you owe me four."

"Forget it."

Perrone hunched his shoulders, as though getting ready for a physical act. "Dennis," he said, "either you pay me the four grand you owe me, and do it fast, or there'll be some people, like people in *press* people, who'll enjoy knowing you and your politico boss paid money out of a secret slush fund to buy a diary smearing Congressman Paul Latham so he wouldn't become secretary of state. Understand?"

Perrone left the restaurant.

A defeated Dennis Mackral sat back in the booth, less tan than a half hour before.

•   •   •

Molly Latham and a group of fellow pages ate takeout from the McDonald's on Capitol Hill. Dressed in their uniforms, they sat on the grass in a park on Constitution Avenue, comparing notes about their classes that morning.

Molly was happy to be back. There were sudden, unpredictable moments of sadness, especially when someone mentioned her father during a floor speech, or when a member of the House made a special fuss over her. She wanted to be treated like everyone else, and hoped it wouldn't be long before that was the case.

Molly and her new friends eventually turned to what had become their favorite pastime when together, evaluating members of the House they served each day.

"Does Mr. Schumer ever stop talking?" Melissa asked.

"He's okay," said John. "At least he doesn't go off the deep end like Mr. Dornan used to. Mr. Traficant's the one cracks me up. He even dresses funny. Those ties."

"Beam me up, Mr. Speaker," they said in unison, laughing as they mouthed Traficant's favorite phrase.

"The one who scares me is Mr. Solomon. What a temper," another member of the group offered. "He blew up at me because I didn't get a message from the cloakroom to him fast enough."

"He's not as mean as Bonior or DeLay" was another opinion, voiced between bites of sandwiches.

"Mr. Dreier's so cute," said Melissa. "Wish Ah were older."

"You notice the women members are the nicest?" John asked.

"No, they're not," someone said.

"They are," John said, defending his observation. "Ms. Kelly and Jackson Lee and Waters? They're terrific."

"I like Ms. Molinari" was tossed into the conversation. "But I guess I like Republicans better anyway."

"Maybe we ought to write a book when this session is done," John said. "You know, take a poll and rate everybody in the House."

"Who's your favorite so far, Molly?" John asked, immediately wishing he hadn't. Would she feel compelled to name her father?

"They've all been okay," she replied. "Mr. Jessup's been real nice. He's going to take over my dad's chairmanship of International Relations."

"Ah like him, too," said Melissa.

Everyone else agreed.

"We'd better get back," Molly said, getting up from the grass and brushing crumbs from her skirt.

"That's a pretty scarf," another female page said.

Molly touched it. Marge Edwards had given it to her the last time they saw each other. *Where is she?* Molly wondered as she led the group back into the Capitol.

Molly was assigned that afternoon to the Democratic coatroom, her favorite posting. She'd spent the morning after classes running dozens of small American flags up and down the flagpole outside the building. Members liked giving the flags to visiting constituents, proudly proclaiming that each had flown over the nation's Capitol.

The coatroom provided more challenge, and was certainly more interesting. The phones seemed never to stop ringing, especially when there was a debate on the floor of sufficient interest to entice a large number of members to it. This was one of those afternoons; the session promised to go well into the night.

In addition, Molly noticed on the day's schedule of events that the International Relations Committee's subcommittee on Economic Policy and Trade had scheduled a meeting at seven that night. Must be an important issue being discussed, she surmised, to be slated at the last minute, and to start that late.

A rush of memories of her father engulfed her. He loved his committee chairmanships more than the House of Representatives itself, often saying it was in committee where the truly important legislation was shaped and drafted. He was fond of quoting Woodrow Wilson on the subject: "Congress in session is Congress on public exhibition, whilst Congress in committee rooms is Congress at work."

That thought triggered another—the package Marge Edwards had given her containing books and papers her father wanted her to read.

Ruth had visited the Capitol that morning, her first appearance there since the moving memorial tribute to her husband in Statuary Hall. She'd stopped in at Paul's office to collect personal items packed by Bob Mondrian and other staffers, said hello to House colleagues with whom Paul had been especially close, and swung by the page room to leave for Molly the package Paul had asked Marge Edwards to deliver to her. Knowing her mother was coming to the Capitol, Molly had called first thing to remind her to bring the materials.

Thinking about her father, and his desire that she read what he considered important, brought a lump to her throat. With a solitary tear running down her cheek, she gulped water from a fountain and headed for the page room.

The McDonald's at National Airport did a brisk business, too.

Yvgeny Fodorov got off the Delta Shuttle and went directly into the restaurant, ordering two bacon cheeseburgers, a large fries, and a chocolate milk shake. He'd been told to wait there until someone from Brazier Industries' security staff picked him up. He had time for an apple pie and another shake before his driver appeared, tapping him on the shoulder and greeting him in Russian.

Fodorov was driven directly from the airport to the company's Washington offices, where he was told to wait in an empty room next to Aleksandr Patiashvili's office. He was edgy, couldn't sit still.

His stay in Brighton Beach had been confusing.

On the one hand, he was treated with respect by most members of the Russian mob. But he was also aware of the scorn some demonstrated toward him. One in particular, about Fodorov's age, had nettled him, laughing when he saw him undressed, and once even calling him a *zhopachnik*, a fag. Fodorov considered killing him. Perhaps if he'd stayed in Brooklyn longer, he might have acted upon the impulse. And enjoyed it.

He'd found killing to be pleasurable since shooting his mother. That had been his first act of murder, but not his last. Shortly after murdering her, he'd been ordered to kill a Moscow drug dealer who'd held out on money. Remarkable, Fodorov thought as he shot the man in the head in front of his apartment building and slowly walked away, how exciting it was to plan a murder, stalk the victim, and complete the act, especially when you did it professionally, under orders, and were congratulated afterward.

He seriously considered shooting Sofia and some of her friends. But by then he'd decided that murdering for profit and praise was the only worthwhile reason for doing it. Killing those around him simply because they annoyed him rendered the act frivolous. He now viewed himself as having an occupation, a profession: Yvgeny Fodorov, professional assassin, killer for hire, cold and calculating, feared by those who deserved to die, respected by those who employed him.

He didn't know why he'd been summoned back to Washington.

The first time, it had been to kill that congressman, Latham.

How easy that had been.

Fodorov didn't know who arranged for Latham to be at the tiny park at such an odd hour, but he'd shown up, on time, alone and vulnerable. No guards. No security. What kind of country was this to allow elected officials to wander anywhere, day and night? It wouldn't have happened in the old Soviet Union.

Placing the weapon in the dead congressman's hand had been a spur-of-the-moment decision. Fodorov wasn't even sure why he'd done it, and after being sternly criticized, he wished he hadn't. It just made sense to him at the time. What did it matter? he rationalized. He was told the weapon wasn't traceable. In doing it, he delayed the official finding of murder, which gave him extra time to leave the city. What had been the harm?

But he hadn't voiced those arguments when Patiashvili chastised him: "You do what you're told, Fodorov, only what you're told, and do it the way you are told."

Fodorov had agreed, sullenly. He'd been smarting at Patiashvili's harsh words ever since.

It was almost five o'clock when Brazier Industries' head of Russian personnel summoned Fodorov to his office. Patiashvili pulled a revolver from his desk drawer and slid it across the desk to Fodorov. "Put it in here." Next to cross the desk was a slim leather briefcase.

Fodorov weighed the weapon in his hand, then opened the briefcase and slid the semiautomatic in with papers already inside.

"Thank you," Fodorov said. "What do you wish me to do?"

Fifteen minutes later, Fodorov left the building and hailed a taxi.

"Yes, sir?" the Arab driver said.

Fodorov handed him a slip of paper with an address in Georgetown written on it, sat back, lighted a cigarette, and looked through the window at the workers of Washington, D.C., on their way home after doing the nation's business.

A small smile crossed his thin lips. His work was just beginning.

Robert Mondrian met in what had been Latham's office with Jack Emerson, staff director to the House International Relations Committee, soon to be chaired by Spencer Jessup, Democrat from North Carolina. The purpose for getting together was the scheduled meeting of the committee.

"You say Brazier himself is coming?" Mondrian said.

"According to the list Brazier Industries sent over. Twelve names, one of them Brazier's."

"Twelve? It's not a hearing, Jack. It's a meeting to hash over some of the amendments. Who's on the list?"

"A bunch of his staff. Economic and banking types, I guess. There's more than a hundred amendments to the bill, Bob. Stassi wants to tack on hearings into crime in Russia. I suppose Brazier feels he needs this many people with knowledge in the areas addressed by the amendments."

"Yeah, I understand that," said Mondrian. "But why is Brazier coming along? He hasn't shown his face around here before."

"Maybe to massage Jessup. You know, he lost his angel when Paul died. Wants to cozy up to the new chairman."

Mondrian resented Emerson's characterization of his former boss but let it slide.

"Look, Bob," Emerson said, chewing on a pencil's eraser, "there's a chance of gutting this legislation before it comes out of committee. Jessup doesn't stand behind it the way Paul did. Businesses in Paul's district had a lot to gain from it. Spence's district is barely impacted."

"Maybe Paul wasn't as solidly behind it as you think," Mondrian said.

Emerson looked at him quizzically. "Explain?"

Mondrian shrugged. "Just that Paul wasn't in Brazier's camp to the extent too many people believed he was."

A staffer knocked, opened the door, and said, "Bob, a call for you."

"Get a name. I'll call back."

Her response was to motion for him to join her in the outer office.

"Sorry," Mondrian said to Emerson.

"Bob," Sue said when they were outside. "It's a woman. She says she has to talk to you."

"Who is she?"

"She wouldn't give her name."

"Tell her to—"

"She says it's a matter of life or death."

Mondrian laughed involuntarily. "Is it, now?"

He went to his desk, picked up the receiver, and punched the lighted button. "Bob Mondrian."

"Bob. It's Marge."

He sat up straight and cupped the mouthpiece with his hand. "Marge? Where are you?"

"I have to see you."

"Yeah. Sure. Where the hell did you go?"

"That's not important. Are you free now?"

"No. Meetings. I have people here."

"When?"

Mondrian looked around the office. The committee meeting was at seven. He wouldn't be there because only committee staff was involved. Others in the office would be gone by six. He'd see to it that they were.

"Here?" he said softly. "Seven-thirty? Eight?"

"The office?"

"Yeah."

She exhaled loudly into her mouthpiece, audibly sending sound into Mondrian's ear.

"Okay? You still have your pass? Yeah, you do. I've never rescinded it."

"Okay," she said. "Seven-thirty. You'll be alone?"

"Yes. I know what you want, Marge."

"I'm sure you do. All I want to do is talk about it with you."

"Seven-thirty."

"I'll be there. Make sure we're alone. Okay?"

"Okay."

Mondrian returned to where Jack Emerson waited.

"Problem?" Emerson asked.

"Everything's a problem," Mondrian replied. "Where were we?"

The moment Marge Edwards hung up on Mondrian, she called Anatoly, reaching him at home.

"Where are you?" he asked.

"That's not important," she said. "It's where I'm going to be that matters." She told him of her scheduled meeting that evening with Bob Mondrian.

"What do you hope to accomplish?" he asked.

"I'm not really sure, Anatoly. But if I can get him to come forward with me, corroborate what I know, I'll have that much more credibility."

There was silence on the other end.

"Anatoly?"

"Yes. I'm here. It sounds good, Marge. You will let me know what happens?"

"Of course. I love you, Anatoly."

"And I—I love you, too."

The click in her ear said the conversation was over.

And maybe more.

CHAPTER THIRTY-ONE

Since the murder of Paul Latham, Mac and Annabel Smith's routine had been anything but that. Which was why they decided on the phone late that afternoon to meet for drinks in pleasant surroundings, and to indulge themselves with an early dinner at their favorite Washington steakhouse, Ruth's Chris, on Connecticut Avenue, N.W. The Smiths ate little red meat, but when the mood struck, they wanted the real thing.

They started their evening at the Hay-Adams Hotel, settling into comfortable stuffed chairs in the handsome John Hay Room. They toasted each other with perfect martinis, straight up, and reveled in the soothing refrains of a pianist.

"I could use a week here," Annabel said.

"A week anywhere but Washington," Smith said.

He'd filled her in earlier on his meeting with Warren Brazier.

"How did he react when you told him Paul had confided in you about Brazier's illegal activities? Money laundering? Contract killings? I'm surprised he didn't shoot you on the spot. And grateful he didn't."

Smith shrugged. "He suggested I come to work for him."

"And?"

"I told him I was gainfully employed, happily. Arrogant bastard."

"Is this the end of it, then?" she asked in the genteel surroundings of the richly appointed room.

"Of my involvement? Absolutely."

"Have you heard from Jessica Belle or her boss?"

"No."

"So you don't know whether confronting Brazier accomplished anything."

"That's right, although it's a little early for results—if there are any. I'm still wondering whether I should drive out to Ashburn to see Marge Edwards's stepsister."

"For what purpose?"

"Just to follow up on what Tony uncovered."

"The fact that this private investigator Perrone met with her doesn't mean anything, at least on the surface. I thought your involvement was over."

Smith laughed, took her hand. "I guess I forgot. I actually was able to focus this afternoon on the Russian project. It felt good."

"Glad to hear it. Which reminds me, I'd better start thinking about what to pack for Moscow."

"Maybe we'd better pack guns first," he said. "The crime problem there is staggering, from everything I read."

"But we'll be safe, won't we?"

"Of course, provided we follow sensible security precautions. Let's not worry about it." They finished their drinks with yet another toast. "Hungry?" Smith asked.

"Famished."

"I think I'll check the machine before we head out."

"Expecting an important call?"

"No. Just like to keep in touch." He went to the hotel lobby in search of a pay phone.

Annabel's smile said many things. Her husband was hardly finished with Paul Latham's murder. But who could blame him for wanting to follow through? Once he'd made the decision to inject himself into the case, it was a natural tendency to want to keep tabs on progress, if only out of curiosity. Or to help make progress.

"Any calls?" she asked when he returned.

"Marge Edwards," he said, sitting.

Annabel sat up a little straighter. "Did she say where she was?"

"No. Said she'd call again tonight."

"How did she sound?"

"Breathless. Anxious."

"Want to call off dinner, go home in case she does call again?"

Smith thought about it.

"Red meat isn't good for us anyway," Annabel said bravely.

"Yes, it is, in moderation. Besides, nobody seems to know what really is good or bad for us. Next thing we know they'll be selling cholesterol pills to get the levels up. Come on. I'm famished."

Annabel had mixed emotions about going through with their plans. On the one hand, it had been a while since they'd gone out to dinner together, just the two of them. She loved the restaurant and its homey atmosphere. And, she was hungry.

On the other hand, she knew Mac would be distracted by Marge Edwards's latest attempt to reach him.

"You're concerned I'll be distracted at dinner," he said.

"We haven't been married long enough to read each other's minds," Annabel said.

"But you were thinking that."

"Yes."

He grinned. "My mind is only on a rare fillet, Annabel, shared with an even rarer woman."

"Who is it?" Alekseyev asked, going to his apartment door in response to a knock.

"Fodorov. From Brazier."

Alekseyev peered through the security peephole and recognized the distorted face of the creepy young man he'd taken to dinner a few nights ago.

"What do you want?" Alekseyev asked through the closed door.

"Mr. Brazier wants for me to give to you a message. It is a very important message."

"So, tell me."

Fodorov said nothing.

Alekseyev reconsidered his response toward Fodorov. Better to be polite and cooperative with someone sent by Brazier. He was hardly in a position to be surly with the boss's emissary.

Alekseyev had barely managed to save his job in Washington with Brazier Industries. He did it by telling its leader he knew of a report that could prove extremely damaging to the company, and to Warren Brazier himself.

"And what do you expect me to do with this startling information, Mr. Alekseyev?" Brazier had asked.

Alekseyev responded with a speech he'd rehearsed while waiting his audience. He spoke of his loyalty to the company and its goals, emphasizing that what he'd learned of the report would remain with him. When Brazier didn't respond, Alekseyev went so far as to promise to use his best efforts to obtain the report from the person who'd told him about it.

"And who might that be?" Brazier had asked.

Alekseyev hesitated. He hadn't intended to mention Marge.

But when he did, Brazier's recognition of the name was obvious. He thanked Alekseyev for coming forth, and said he would reconsider the transfer back to Moscow.

"Come in," Alekseyev said, opening the door to allow Fodorov to enter the apartment. When he was inside, Alekseyev said, forcing a smile, "Good to see you again, Yvgeny. A drink?"

"*Nyet.*"

"Okay. What's the message from Mr. Brazier?"

Yvgeny slid the weapon from his waistband so quickly and smoothly that Alekseyev wasn't immediately aware of what was happening. But when Fodorov raised the gun, a silencer extending the barrel, and aimed it at Alekseyev's face, the reality screamed out. Alekseyev's reflex action was to raise his hands in front of his face. The first shot tore through the back of his hand and into his cheek. The wounded hand pressed against the gaping hole in his face. Blood ran freely down his wrist and drizzled to the floor.

Alekseyev's mouth and eyes opened in pain and shock. Before he could do or say anything else, the second slug entered his mouth and smashed through the back of his head, carrying with it skull and brain and a streamer of crimson blood. Alekseyev's body followed, stumbling back six feet until falling into a heap on the floor.

Fodorov replaced the weapon in his waistband, looked at his watch, cast a final, fleeting glance at the lifeless body of Alekseyev, and left the apartment. Ten minutes later he was back at the Washington headquarters of Brazier Industries, just in time to join Brazier and his contingent of janissaries as they piled into cars and drove to the Capitol, where they were met in the underground garage by a staffer from International Relations. The staffer handed them visitor badges, led them past security, and up to the committee room.

Jack Emerson, majority staff director of the House International Relations Committee, left his meeting with Bob Mondrian and rode the subway back to the Capitol Building. He walked into Room H 139, where other committee staffers, and some House members, waited for the meeting to start.

"Where's Mr. Jessup?" Emerson asked.

"On the floor. He'll be here soon," an assistant answered.

Tom Krouch, Brazier Industries' chief lobbyist, entered the room. His reputation in Washington, built over years of service to House and Senate committees, as well as to individual House members and senators, was considerable and deserved. His decision two years ago to join Brazier Industries raised a few of his colleagues' eyebrows, but no one questioned his motivation. Speculation was that Warren Brazier had given Krouch an offer he couldn't refuse, making him the highest-paid lobbyist in Washington. He'd earn his pay, they knew. Not only was Brazier's autocratic, often brutal management style well known, his executives were on call twenty-four hours a day, seven days a week.

Krouch called Emerson aside. "We'll need another room, Jack, for staff."

"Yeah, I heard you were bringing an army. Why?"

"Brazier wants his troops here. You know, feed him economic data if we get into technical areas."

Emerson screwed up his face. "What's your boss doing here in the first place? The glitches in the bill don't need him to get fixed."

Krouch leaned close to Emerson's ear. "A last-minute decision, Jack. You know how he is. I wouldn't be surprised if he didn't show up. It's minute-to-minute with him. If he does show, it's probably because he wants to press the new chairman's flesh, let him know how strongly he personally feels about this bill."

"He'll accomplish that, I suppose."

"Level with me," Krouch said.

A smile from Emerson: "Of course. This is Washington. Remember?"

"Jessup. What's his view of Brazier and Brazier Industries?"

"Want it straight?"

"Sure."

"He's no Paul Latham when it comes to championing your boss's agenda."

"Against this bill?"

"You know he is."

"All of it?"

Emerson shrugged. "Enough to gut it."

"Thanks for being candid. Anything I can do to soften him?"

"Yeah."

"And?"

"Put Brazier in a box and keep him away after tonight. Jessup dislikes him even more than the bill."

"Advice noted. What room can staff use?"

"Over here." Emerson led him to an adjacent, empty conference room with a dozen chairs around an oblong teak table. "This do?"

"Perfect."

The arrival of Warren Brazier caused a speculative buzz among the staffers, some of whom had never seen him in person. Brazier's own staff hung back as he shook hands with members of the committee. Tom Krouch knew his boss's style well, and was impressed at how the generally pugnacious Brazier could, in a blink, like Khrushchev, become friendly and outgoing when the situation called for it. Twenty minutes ago, he'd been cruelly tyrannical with everyone.

"Sure you brought enough people with you?" Congressman Jessup asked.

Brazier laughed, said, "I can get another dozen here with a phone call."

Jessup, a tall, courtly North Carolinian with silvery, senatorial hair and an easy, slow southern manner of speaking, laughed. "Please don't do that, Mr. Brazier. No place to put 'em. I wasn't expectin' you personally to attend this meeting. But now that you're here, I'm sure you'd like to get down to business."

"That makes sense, Congressman."

The large room seemed smaller once the many participants took their seats. Brazier was flanked by Tom Krouch, his chief lobbyist, and a pudgy, middle-aged gentleman wearing a plastic-looking toupee, who was introduced by Brazier as the company's vice president of banking. Joining Congressman Jessup were five other members of the committee, and six of the more than eighty committee-staff members, including director Jack Emerson.

Jessup said, "This committee is in a little bit of flux, Mr. Brazier, as you can imagine. The tragic and damnable murder of Jack Latham, a good friend of yours, I know, and my good friend, too, has caused us to hold up on any further consideration of this bill."

"And I can certainly understand a certain amount of confusion," said Brazier. "I just hope that the fine work Paul Latham did all these years on this committee, and especially on this critical piece of legislation, which, I hasten to add, will advance America's vital interest in seeing Russia become a successful free-market economy and vibrant democracy, wasn't in vain."

Tom Krouch kept a watchful eye on Congressman Jessup for signs of reaction. His read as the meeting progressed was that as hard as Jessup tried to be courteous—to be political—his distrust of the truculent Brazier, indeed his dislike, was evident in subtle facial expressions and body language.

The meeting, everyone knew, was unusual. Brazier had testified on occasion before the committee and its subcommittees in the past. But to gather like this, at night, with so many interested parties present, was unprecedented, at least from Krouch's perspective, and he was surprised that his last-minute request for it had been granted by the majority and minority leadership.

As the meeting progressed, the discussion widened to include others in the room. But it was Jessup who got to the meat when he said, "Mr. Brazier, I have some serious reservations about this legislation, especially the amendments you advocate."

"I'm listening," Brazier said.

Jessup went on to cite two amendments that had been pushed by Krouch and his lobbying staff. Brazier asked his banking chief to provide figures on the financial impact of those amendments on the International Monetary Fund, World Bank, and the Russian central banking system. That prompted the banking expert to ask for two of his staff from the adjacent room to join them.

In the smaller room, the ten remaining representatives of Brazier Industries continued to while away the time. They weren't sure why they were there, but that wasn't unusual. Working for Warren Brazier often meant waiting around, killing time until summoned by the boss. But you'd best remain focused and sharp, ready to respond when the call to do something came.

Yvgeny Fodorov, glum and uncommunicative, not a usual member of the group, sat stoically, picking at skin on his hands. Resting against his chair was the slim briefcase given him by Aleksandr Patiashvili earlier that afternoon. He felt superior to the others in the room, hated them for their smug disdain of him. Inside, he felt satisfied. It had been a good evening so far.

Not so for Warren Brazier.

As the meeting in the main room droned on, he continued to present his reasons why the legislation pending before the International Relations Committee was not only good for his company, but for the United States as well. His tone answering the long, drawn-out questioning had become more arrogant and impatient, which was not lost on the others. He leaned heavily on the late Paul Latham's supposed commitment to the bill, and Latham's unparalleled understanding of its U.S.-Russian ramifications.

Krouch hoped the meeting would end soon, before Brazier allowed more of his true nature to surface. The lobbyist's professional respect for Brazier tempered his privately held personal view—that his boss was the most unpleasant man he'd ever met.

Marge Edwards took a deep breath as she stood on Independence Avenue, in front of the Rayburn House Office Building. It was twenty minutes to eight; she was ten minutes late.

She went up the steps and entered the building, relieved that the uniformed Capitol police officer on duty was not one of the regulars who might recognize her. A conveyor belt passed her bag into the X-ray machine as she stepped through the archway without causing beeps from the metal detector. She thanked the officer when he handed her bag back to her, and headed for Congressman Paul Latham's office.

She paused outside the office. Hopefully, Mondrian was alone. The click of high heels on the marble hallway floor prompted her to open the door and step inside. The door closed behind her. Latham's private office was open.

"Bob?" she called, her voice lacking strength.

"Come on in," he replied from Latham's office.

She stood in the doorway. He sat behind Latham's desk, one foot propped up on it. He was in shirtsleeves. His tie, pulled loose from his neck, was a muted montage of game birds in a green forest.

"Hi," she said, giving a little wave.

"Hi," he said, not moving.

"Well . . ." She entered the office and stood across the desk from him. "Surprised to see me?"

"No. Close the door."

She did what he asked.

"Sit down," he said. His stare was hard, his voice firm and angry.

Once she'd pulled up a chair, he lowered his foot from the desk, leaned forward, rested his chin on his clasped hands, and said, "Where is it?"

"It's safe, Bob."

"Safe?"

"Yes. Safe from you."

He cocked his head. "Marge," he said, "I don't know where you got it into that crazy head of yours, but Paul's investigation and report doesn't have to be kept from me. We're on the same side."

She locked eyes with him. "No, we're not," she said. "And you know it. That report on Warren Brazier and Brazier Industries was meant to go to the Justice Department. Paul spent the last year of his life compiling information on Brazier for Justice. And it *cost* him his life."

"It probably did," Mondrian said. "So why did you run off with it? The least we can do in Paul's memory is to make sure Justice gets it."

"Exactly. And if I left it here with you, it never would arrive there."

"Marge, I—"

She stood and placed her palms on the desk, jutted her chin at him. "Bob, I know about the overture Brazier made to you through his inter- mediaries. What were you offered? Fifty thousand? Was it more? No matter what it was, it was cheap, Bob. Cheap to sell out a man like Paul."

"I don't need a lecture, Marge. Being offered and taking are two dif- ferent things."

"You didn't take money from Brazier Industries?"

"No. Not *that* money."

"Not *that* money? What does it matter what money you took from them? Even if you took a dollar from that sleazebag Brazier, you sold Paul out. If you'd do it for one thing, Bob, you'll do it for another, in this case the report. That's why I grabbed it from Paul's safe and ran."

He glared at her.

"How could you?"

"Who the hell are you to lecture me, Marge? You ever have to scrape just to get by?"

"That doesn't justify anything." She softened. "Bob, I don't care that you sold out to Brazier Industries in the past, in some—in some god- damn moment of weakness. That's human. *You're* human. But it isn't too late. Let's take the report to Justice together, in Paul's memory, as you put it. I'll forget you ever took a nickel from Brazier."

He sat back and exhaled. "Why didn't *you* just take it to Justice, Marge?"

"I would have. But then Paul was murdered. I didn't know what to do. And there was the story that I would charge Paul with sexual harassment. Nonsense! That's all it was. But—"

"There was a diary," Mondrian said. "Wasn't there?"

"I don't care about that, Bob. Maybe it was just as well that everyone thought I ran because of the harassment rumor. No one knows about Paul's investigation and report except you, me, and the people at Justice who set it in motion a year ago."

"God, you are naive, Marge. Justice didn't set it up. It was CIA. They had Broadhurst working on this back when he was with the trade commission. *He's* the one who approached Paul. Once he and his people started putting together the case against Brazier—and God knows there was enough to make that case—he saw Paul as the perfect insider. No one was closer to Brazier than Paul. He knew every dirty deal Brazier was involved with."

"And you'd sell out to someone like that." Her tone wasn't one of disgust. Fatigue more accurately described it.

"What about Paul, Marge? He knew about Brazier for years, but kept right on working with him. How many times did you hear him defend Brazier, praise him as some goddamn gift to free economy and the democratic process? All those bills he ramrodded through. Did *he* sell out to Brazier? You bet he did. And you and I did, too, every time we advanced trade legislation to benefit Brazier."

"Paul really believed in Brazier, at least until a year ago," she said. "Sure, he knew he owed Brazier for all his support over the years, the fund-raising, the contributions, the influence on voters in Paul's district. But give Paul credit, Bob. When he realized what Brazier was really like—the huge payoffs in Russia, his covert support of the Communists, his use of mobsters—God, the man is a godfather of Russian mobsters here. Once Paul saw this, had it pointed out by Broadhurst and the others, he didn't hesitate to cooperate, to document everything he could in the report. To even consider protecting Brazier is to spit on Paul's grave."

"I never intended to cooperate with Brazier on the report, Marge. You know that. Hell, when Paul confronted Brazier at their meeting the day before Paul died, told him what he intended to do, he put his life on the line."

"Literally," she said.

"As it turned out. Where is the report, Marge?" he asked.

"Where I know it won't go to Warren Brazier."

Mondrian sighed. "Okay," he said. "Wait here." He left the office, returning a minute later with a small envelope, which he handed to her.

"What's this?" she asked.

"Open it. You'll see."

Inside was the check from Brazier Industries, written to Robert Mondrian.

"When did you get this?" she asked.

"Earlier today."

"And you—"

"Go ahead, Marge. Tear it up."

She hesitated, then tore the check into four pieces, placed them in the envelope, and handed it to him.

"Satisfied?" he asked.

She looked down at the floor, then up at him. She smiled. "I guess I get carried away sometimes," she said.

His smile was broad, but not as spontaneous as hers had been. "Look, Marge," he said, "I'm really glad you're okay, and that you're here. It's easy to get carried away in this insane place, isn't it?"

Her response was a stream of air directed at an errant strand of hair on her forehead.

"You're right," he said, coming around the desk and placing his large hands on her shoulders. "Let's take the report to Justice together. Lay it all out for them. Do right by Paul."

She nodded.

"Where is the report? You have it with you?" He glanced at her oversized shoulder bag.

"No," she said.

"Well?"

"I put it in a package of books and papers I gave Molly."

"Molly? Molly Latham?"

"Yes."

"Why? What did you expect her to do with it?"

"Nothing. Frankly, I didn't think she'd even open it."

"And if she did . . . open it?"

Marge shrugged. "I didn't think that far ahead. All I knew was that I wanted it out of here. Paul gave me the books and some of his speeches to package up for her, so I included the report in with it."

"And she's had it all along."

"Yes. She would have gotten hold of me if she had opened it and saw what it was."

"How could she? You disappeared."

"I know. The sexual harassment thing. The report. I—I just panicked, Bob. That simple. Excuse me. Nature calls."

"Molly's probably on page duty. I'll try to call her. They're still in session. We'll find her and put this thing to rest."

"Yes," Marge said. "That's what we'll do."

"It's time for your other meeting."

Yvgeny Fodorov picked up his briefcase from the floor and stood. Another young Russian also stood; he, too, held a leather briefcase in his hand. The others in the room watched with interest as they left the room. "Where are they going?" one asked.

"A meeting. A related topic," Patiashvili said.

"A security meeting?" another said, his tone skeptical.

Patiashvili trained his black eyes on the questioner.

There were no further questions.

Fodorov and his colleague from security approached a uniformed Capitol Hill police officer in the hall just outside H 139. They nodded.

"Good evening," the officer said, eyeing the official visitor badges hanging from their jacket handkerchief pockets.

They proceeded down the hall to a stairway leading to the basement, where the Capitol subway system linked the building to the House and Senate office buildings. They climbed aboard the sleek, open tram, operated by a young black man in white shirt and tie. Others boarded, too. When the cars were full, the subway left the loading ramp and, in a few minutes, came to a stop beneath the Rayburn House Office Building.

Fodorov and his partner joined the flow of passengers riding the escalator to the floor above. They paused at an intersection of hallways. Fodorov had been given a map of the building to study. Still, it was confusing.

"Where?" the other man said.

"This way," Fodorov replied, choosing one of the halls and leading them down it.

They reached the outer door to the office suite with Paul Latham's nameplate still on it. Looking left and right, they opened the briefcases, removed the weapons, and secured them in the waistband of their pants. A glance at each other, a nod, and a hand on the doorknob.

CHAPTER THIRTY-TWO

Molly Latham had returned to the Democratic cloakroom after delivering a message on the House floor to Congressman Barney Frank, when the phone rang again. Melissa looked at Molly, who'd rolled her eyes up in an expression of fatigue and frustration. Melissa laughed. "Ah'll get it, hon," she said.

Melissa wrote down the message—"For Mr. Skelton," she said, waving to Molly and heading for the floor.

Molly sat heavily in one of the many leather chairs.

"Got you running, huh?" a congresswoman said pleasantly.

"I have to get better shoes," replied Molly.

Phones started ringing again.

"Relax," another page said. "Take a break."

As her fellow pages answered phones, and ran messages to the floor, Molly picked up the wrapped package from her father, plopped it on her lap, and slowly began to undo it.

"Present, Molly?" a congressman asked.

She smiled and shook her head. "Just some dull reading," she said, wondering whether she dishonored her father by saying it.

The ringing phones were now a discordant chorus. Molly dropped the partially opened package to the floor and started answering calls again. She hoped the House finished its business soon. A pile of homework awaited her back at the dorm.

This was shaping up to be a longer night than she had thought.

"Democratic cloakroom," she said, answering yet another call.

"I'm trying to reach Molly Latham."

"This is Molly."

"Molly. Bob Mondrian."

"Oh, hi, Mr. Mondrian. You're looking for *me*?"

"Yes. I—I'm in your dad's office with Marge Edwards."

Molly's eyes widened. "Marge is there?"

"Yes. It's very important that we talk with you."

"Right now? I'm real busy."

"Is your supervisor around?"

"Yes."

"Molly, do you remember a package Marge gave you?"

Molly's hand went to the scarf she wore, Marge's gift to her at lunch. "I'm wearing it," she said.

Mondrian's momentary silence testified to his confusion. "Wearing it?"

"The scarf she gave me."

"No, Molly. Another package, with books and—"

"From my dad. I have it here with me. Mom dropped it off this morning."

"Have you opened it?"

Molly laughed. "I started to, but the phones went crazy again and—"

"Look, can you hop on the subway and come over here to the office? Bring the package with you."

"All right. Where has Marge been? Is she all right?"

"She's just fine, Molly. Put your supervisor on."

"That was wonderful," Smith said, sitting back and admiring his empty plate. He'd opted for a porterhouse steak. Annabel had chosen a smaller version.

"I'm stuffed," she said. "Nothing but apples and water for the next few days."

Smith made a face. "Dessert?" he asked.

"You jest, of course."

"No, I—"

Their waiter came to the table. "An after-dinner drink, compliments of the manager?" he asked.

They looked at each other.

"We really shouldn't," she said.

"No, we shouldn't," he said. To the waiter: "That is, cognac, please."
Annabel laughed.

The manager, whom they knew, joined them. "Still planning your trip
to Russia?" he asked.

"Planning it," Annabel replied. "Whether we'll ever get there is another question."

"I can put you in the mood," the manager said.

"Oh?"

"A special after-dinner drink. The Commissar. Equal amounts of
vodka and Triple Sec. Very smooth."

"No, I—"

"Try it," said Mac.

"All right."

"And as long as we're going this far—"

"Bread pudding with whiskey sauce?" the manager asked, knowing of
their fondness for the restaurant's special dessert.

"Mac!"

"Just one to share," Mac said.

And so they lingered over their cordials, and dipped spoons into the
heavenly pudding, content to be together sharing the meal, one hand
occasionally touching the other's, the problems of Washington, especially
of murder, kept at bay by the window separating them from Connecticut
Avenue.

"I'm getting sleepy," she said.

"I'll be tucking you in very soon, Annie," he said. "How's the Commissar?"

"Good. He sends his best."

She delivered the message with a light kiss on his lips.

CHAPTER THIRTY-THREE

From the private bathroom in Paul Latham's office suite, Marge Edwards heard the door open, and close. "Damn," she said softly. It didn't strike her as strange that someone else had arrived at that hour, but it was dismaying. She wanted to talk alone with Bob Mondrian. She reacted by putting on lipstick and fluffing her hair.

Yvgeny Fodorov and his colleague, Vladimir Donskoi, stepped into Latham's private office, where Mondrian had just hung up on Molly Latham.

"Can I help you?" Mondrian asked, standing behind the desk.

Fodorov and the other man, Donskoi, answered by drawing their weapons.

"Who the hell are you?" Mondrian said, starting around the desk.

"Where is the report?" Donskoi said in almost flawless English.

"Report? Hey, come on. Put those down. I'm—"

Fodorov swore in Russian as he squeezed the trigger, sending three bullets into Mondrian's chest. The chief of staff fell back against the desk, his hands desperately attempting to stem the sudden rush of blood and searing pain.

Donskoi turned to Fodorov. "Fool," he shouted. "Imbecile."

Fodorov ignored him, pushed Mondrian's lifeless body to the floor from where it was sprawled over the desk, and started going through piles of paper in a frenzy, sending files flying.

Donskoi was tempted to shoot him. Their orders were to go to the office and demand of the man and woman who would be there that they turn over the report. Donskoi was in charge. He'd been shown photographs of Marge Edwards and Robert Mondrian, and had been briefed on the nature of what they were looking for. It was only after they'd gotten their hands on the report, or couldn't, that they were to kill both people.

In frustration, Donskoi joined Fodorov in his haphazard search.

The sounds from the office froze Marge Edwards in the bathroom. What could be happening? Should she remain there until the intruders left? She decided she couldn't. They might search the entire office. Who'd been shot? Bob Mondrian? Why? Who?

She opened the bathroom door an inch and peered through the gap. Sounds came from Latham's office—muttered voices, things being thrown about.

She opened the door farther, wide enough to slip through, drew a deep, desperate breath, and crossed the office to the door leading to the hallway. Should she stop to see what had happened to Mondrian? No. There was nothing she could do by herself. She had to find help, the Capitol police, let them know.

The door to the suite had a heavy latch bolt that made a loud metallic sound whenever the door was opened and closed. Marge Edwards paused, held her breath, and opened the door, the noise sounding to her like a cell door in prison movies. She glanced at Paul's office. No one responded, thank God.

She stepped into the hallway and allowed the door to slam shut behind. "Oh, God," she gasped, again gripped with inertia as she tried to decide in which direction to run. She looked back at the door. It opened. A face appeared—and a revolver.

She bolted toward an intersecting hallway, slipped as she turned the corner, retained her balance with one hand on the marble floor, and ran as fast as she could to a stairway leading down to the building's main lobby. She was afraid to look back, but did, only for a second. A man holding a weapon stood at the intersection of hallways. He'd stopped there. No matter. Marge stumbled down the stairs two at a time, grasping the railing to keep from making the descent headfirst.

She reached the main floor and went to where the uniformed security guard sat behind a table.

"Please," she said. "There are men with guns in Congressman Latham's office."

He stood. "What are you saying? Men with guns?"

"Yes." She looked over her shoulder, then back at the officer. "Someone's been shot there. Mr. Mondrian, I think."

"Slow down," the officer said. "Who are they?"

A puff of exasperation came through her lips; she slapped her hands against her thighs. "Call for help," she said. "Please."

The officer took a battery-powered radio from his belt and spoke into it, giving his name and location: "Report of armed individuals in the building. Congressman Latham's office. Request immediate backup to investigate."

A wave of relief caused Marge to relax. Help was on its way. She shut her eyes tight and said a silent prayer that Bob Mondrian was all right—that everyone was all right.

"Did you see them up close?" the security officer asked.

"No. I was in the bathroom and—"

The front doors to the building opened and a half-dozen members of the Capitol police, armed with M-249s, burst through. The building security officer told them the problem had been reported by the young lady standing next to him, and that it had occurred in Congressman Latham's office, one floor up.

"How many armed men?" the group's leader asked Marge.

"I don't know. I only saw one, but I think I heard two. Talking. I think there were two different voices."

"What sort of weapons?"

"I don't know," she said, wishing they would just go and see for themselves.

The group leader used his radio to call the communications room, asking for a CERT team to secure the building. That request delivered, he said to the other officers, "Let's go, but slow." To Marge: "You'd recognize the one you saw?"

"I think so."

"Stick close. Keep quiet. If you see him, say so."

Marge fell in behind as they made their way from the entrance lobby, the stone eyes of former Speaker Sam Rayburn peering down at them.

Vladimir Donskoi made an instant decision after seeing the woman disappear down the stairs. He ran past Latham's office door in the direction of stairs on the other side of the building, leaving Yvgeny Fodorov alone. He'd no sooner rounded the corner when Molly Latham approached from the opposite direction, carrying the package Mondrian had asked her to bring.

She paused to knock at her father's door, placed her hand on the knob, and opened it.

"Bob?" she called as the door closed behind her. "Marge?"

Fodorov appeared from the inner office. The sight of him caused Molly to start. "Where's—?"

He pointed his gun at her. "Shud up!" he said in broken English.

"Where's Marge—and Mr. Mondrian?"

The sound of multiple footsteps outside captured Fodorov's attention. As he listened, Molly backed away and reached for the doorknob. But Fodorov was too quick. He grabbed her arm and pushed her against the door.

The thud of Molly's body stopped everyone outside in their tracks; anxious looks were exchanged.

"Who's in there?" the officer in charge asked Marge.

"I don't know."

But then it hit her: Mondrian had said he would try to call Molly. Did he reach her while Marge was in the bathroom? *Was Molly Latham in there with a killer?*

"It might be Congressman Latham's daughter," Marge said. "She's a House page. She was coming here tonight."

More armed officers arrived. The leader of the second group conferred with the initial force's leader. They turned to Marge.

"She knows you?" one asked.

"Yes."

"Call her name."

"I—all right."

Marge put her mouth close to the door. "Molly," she said, too softly to penetrate the wood. "Molly," she repeated, louder this time.

Two shots splintered the door inches from Marge Edwards's head, accompanied by an agonized female scream from inside.

Marge fell to her knees; the officers pressed themselves against the walls. "Jesus," one said. "Who the hell is in there?"

"It's Molly," Marge said, crawling to where a knot of police congregated. "What are you going to do?"

"What's the phone number in there?"

Marge gave it to him. After ordering another officer to contact headquarters to declare an emergency alert for the entire Capitol, he dialed the number Marge had given him on a cellular phone. They heard it ring in the office. It went unanswered. The officer slid along the wall to the door, checked the position of his fellow officers, then said in an authoritative voice, "This is Lieutenant Shuttee. Capitol police. You can't leave. There are dozens of armed officers here in the hall. The building is surrounded. Put down your weapons, open the door, and come out with your hands raised."

They waited for a reply. There was none.

The officer repeated his order.

Seconds that seemed like minutes passed.

The door slowly opened.

Molly was the first to be seen. Her eyes, red and wet, were wide with fright. Fodorov stood directly behind her, one hand gripping her blond hair, the other pressing his weapon against her temple. He said something in Russian, then again in fractured English: "Away! Ged away! This girl dead if you do not go away."

"Molly," Marge said.

Molly's mouth opened, but no words came out.

"Back off," the officer in charge said.

"I will kill her," Fodorov said.

"Who the hell is he?" an officer whispered to Marge.

"I don't know. He's Russian."

"His accent. You sure?"

She thought of Anatoly. "Yes," she said softly.

Fodorov slowly maneuvered Molly through the door and into the hall.

"It's the congressman's kid," an officer said.

"I know, I know," the lead officer said. "Everybody stay calm. Calm, cool, and collected."

Another officer at the rear of the pack called communications to order a hostage negotiation team be sent to the Rayburn Building. The phone at communications was immediately handed to Capitol Police Chief Henry Folsom.

"What's the status?" he asked.

The officer on the scene gave him a capsule rundown.

"What's he doing?"

"Just standing there with a gun to the kid's head."

"Any ID on him?"

"No. He's got an accent. He's Russian, we think."

Folsom immediately thought of the meeting going on in House committee room H 139: a dozen official visitor badges issued, most to a group of Russians from Brazier Industries.

"What's he doing now?"

The officer in the hall looked over others blocking his view. "He's starting to move with her. Down the hall. Real slow."

"No chance of getting a clean shot?"

"No. He's got her pressed right up against him, walking in lockstep. Got her by the hair, gun up against her head. He's got a crazy look about him."

"Don't spook him," Folsom said. "Hostage team'll be there in a few minutes."

The now sizable contingent of Capitol police followed Fodorov at a distance as he moved with Molly to stairs leading to the first floor. Two officers entered Latham's office and found Mondrian dead on the floor. They quickly passed word that the man holding Molly Latham hostage had already killed, and would kill again if cornered.

"Keep a distance," everyone was quietly instructed. "Don't push him."

It was assumed that Fodorov would take Molly to the lobby and out into the street.

Instead, he proceeded to another set of stairs leading down to the subway connecting the building with the Capitol.

"What's he going down there for?" an officer asked, not expecting an answer.

By now, Fodorov's route was lined with armed police. Their increasing presence visibly unnerved him. His eyes darted from face to face, blinking rapidly, mouth working as though chewing something. Molly's face, too, reflected the stress and tension. Her eyes seemed to plead with every other set of eyes to help, to do something for her.

By the time they arrived at the subway platform, a contingent of Capitol police were there, along with special agents of the FBI. The young black man running the subway that night had been shocked to see members of the CERT team swarm into the area. At first, he thought they'd come for him. "What'd I do?" he asked.

"Just stay where you are," he was told.

Seconds later, Fodorov and Molly appeared.

"Do what they tell you to do," the driver was ordered.

Fodorov, still with a painful grip on Molly's hair, stopped on the platform. His pinched, pale face mirrored his confusion. He was surrounded by heavily armed men and women wearing flak jackets, a hundred of them, maybe more. If he didn't have this hostage, he knew, he'd be gunned down. Despite the situation, he felt a certain superiority. He wouldn't hesitate to kill the girl, and they knew it. He'd take some of them down, too. Any fear he might have been feeling at the moment was tempered by a certain euphoria. They would never accuse him of being a coward. Not Yvgeny Fodorov. The adrenaline pulsing through his body was palpable.

He maneuvered Molly onto the empty subway car, and, in Russian, ordered the operator to move.

"Go on, take him," a senior officer said.

The operator tentatively activated a control, causing the small train to move away from the platform on a cushion of air. Police lined the pedestrian walkway and watched the car make its short, virtually silent journey to the Capitol. Other police, led by Chief Folsom, waited on the platform beneath the Capitol for its arrival.

Fodorov forced Molly from the car. Folsom instructed his men to step back and allow them access to the door. They went through it and moved to where two elevators stood with open doors. One had a sign above it indicating it was for the exclusive use of members of the House of Representatives. Fodorov shoved Molly into it. As he did, he created a momentary gap between them, prompting some police officers to raise their weapons. But the moment Fodorov and his hostage were in the elevator, he grabbed her again and pulled her to him. He pushed a button. The door slid closed.

"He's going to the floor," Folsom said. "What's the status there?"

"Secure, sir. They're still in session, but all entrances are secure, heavily guarded."

"Which won't do anybody any good as long as he has the Latham girl," Folsom said, more to himself. He spoke into his radio: "Suspect and hostage on their way up in members' elevator. Might be heading for the floor. Do nothing—repeat—do *nothing* to cause him to injure the hostage." Folsom headed for the stairs, dozens of officers following on his heels.

The elevator door opened, and Fodorov peered out at a circle of armed police. "Get back!" he shouted in Russian, then in English. He waved his gun for emphasis. "Back! Get back!" He moved in tandem with Molly from the elevator and in the direction of one of the doors leading to the floor of the House of Representatives.

"Does he know where he's going?" an officer asked Chief Folsom.

Folsom shrugged. Then, he saw the four officers guarding the door brace themselves, and raise their automatic weapons. "Stand down!" Folsom said in a booming voice. To one of his lieutenants: "Get around to another entrance. Clear the floor. Get the members out of there, into cloakrooms, whatever. Now!"

But it was too late to vacate the floor. Fodorov, who'd paused as though to gather his thoughts, made a sudden lunge toward the doors leading to the House chamber. The officers stepped back as the Russian assassin, Molly still in tow, pushed open the doors and disappeared behind them.

Folsom got on his radio. "They still there?" he asked an officer assigned to a three-person squad at Room H 139, where the House International Relations Committee met with Brazier Industries' Warren Brazier.

"Yes, sir."

"Get Mr. Brazier and put him on."

"Get—?"

"Damn it, just do what I say."

"Yes, sir."

Those attending the meeting had been told there was an emergency situation in the Capitol, and that they were to remain in the room until it was resolved. Questions of the officer went unanswered. "Orders are for you to remain here," he said. "That's the order."

"What's the emergency?" he was asked again.

"Orders are to remain here," he repeated. He walked from the room, a buzz of speculation following him.

Folsom waited until Brazier said, "Hello? Brazier here."

"This is Capitol Police Chief Folsom, Mr. Brazier."

"Yes?"

"Sir, there's an armed man holding hostage the daughter of Congressman Paul Latham."

"Molly Latham?"

"Yes, sir."

"Good God!"

"Sir, we believe the gunman is Russian. He's already killed Mr. Latham's chief of staff, and he's holding a gun to the girl's head."

"I can't believe this."

"I know you have a number of Russian executives with you at the meeting."

"Yes?"

"Have any of them left you this evening?"

"I—I don't know. Some of my staff is in a separate room. You aren't suggesting that—?"

"All I'm suggesting is that I'm trying to save the girl's life, Mr. Brazier. Has any of your staff left the area?"

"I'll see," Brazier said.

A minute later he spoke into the radio again. "I'm afraid one of them is gone."

"Who?"

"One of my security men. Fodorov. Yvgeny Fodorov."

"Thin, pasty face, thick glasses?"

"Yes."

"Mr. Brazier, I'm afraid he's the one."

"I can't imagine . . . Why would he? What can I do?"

"I'd like you to come down here, sir. I'll have one of my men escort you."

"Yes, of course. This is shocking."

"Yes, sir, it is. Put the officer back on."

"Bring Brazier down here," Folsom said. "On the double."

At first, those inside the House chamber were unaware of Fodorov and Molly. Congressman J. C. Watts, former football star and second-term representative from Oklahoma, spoke from the well on a bill he'd sponsored that was being debated on the floor. Fifty or so other members milled about, and chatted with one another at their seats. The visitors gallery contained a few onlookers. C-SPAN's cameras transmitted the debate live; the cable channel was pledged to carry every session of the House of Representatives gavel to gavel.

The realization that something was amiss started with those nearest Fodorov and Molly Latham, and spread in a ripple. At first, the response was quiet shock, and disbelief. But as it expanded, voices became louder. A woman screamed. A member slid down to the floor in front of his chair. The Speaker *pro tempore,* Democratic representative from Hawaii Neil Abercrombie, unaware of what had caused the upset, repeatedly rapped his gavel and called for the House to be in order.

"Get down!" the clerk, seated in front and below Abercrombie, shouted. The Speaker disappeared behind the raised desk, the gavel flying from his hand.

The C-SPAN camera operator couldn't believe what he was seeing. Nor could those members of the press who'd stayed late to follow the evening's debate. They rushed out of the expansive congressional press room to the press gallery, overlooking the House floor. "The guy's got a gun." "The kid he's holding. She's a page." "That's Paul Latham's kid." "What the hell is he up to?"

Fodorov, uncomfortable with the small area to which he was confined just inside the door, moved toward the center of the huge, ornate chamber, 139 feet long and 93 feet wide, one of the largest legislative rooms in the world. Everyone else in the chamber froze, a few peeking through spread fingers at what was happening, the way they would watch a violent movie. Others refused to look. Still others were too stunned to do anything but gape open-mouthed.

Initially, Molly had struggled against Fodorov's grip. Now, she was like a rag doll, drained, empty, literally being dragged by him from place to place.

Fodorov reached the well. He looked up to the visitors gallery, where a few people sat with their arms on the railing, their attention focused on the macabre scene playing out below them.

The setting was not lost on Fodorov. Since being in the United States, he'd seen C-SPAN's coverage of the House of Representatives. He was scornful of those who spoke: "Windbags," he said to himself in Russian.

Still, the majesty of the House chamber was not lost on him. Pomp and officialdom had always impressed Fodorov. The grandiose rituals of the Soviet Union, particularly those involving the military, stirred his blood. And now here he was, center stage in America's symbol of its arrogant democracy, all eyes on him, fear on the faces of those witnessing Yvgeny Fodorov's moment.

Those watching the spectacle in the House chamber included Ruth Latham.

She'd been in the kitchen, filling the dishwasher after dinner. Martin was in the family room clicking through channels on the television. He went right by C-SPAN, then went back to it. He came forward to the edge of his chair and extended his neck. It couldn't be. *"Mom!"*

Warren Brazier, accompanied by one of his staff and by Capitol Police Chief Henry Folsom, entered the chamber through the Republican cloakroom.

"That him?" Folsom asked.

"Yes," Brazier replied. "He must be insane."

"Think he'll listen to you, Mr. Brazier?"

"I don't know."

"Only if you don't think it'll set him off."

Brazier turned to his young staff member. "You are his friend. Right?"

"Yes."

When Folsom had asked Brazier why he was bringing the young man with him, Brazier had replied, "He and Fodorov are friends. He might be helpful."

Folsom said to the young man, "You want to talk to him?"

"Yes. I will talk to him." He looked at Brazier.

"Go ahead," Brazier said. To Folsom: "They work together in my security office."

Folsom looked around. Instinct told him time had run out.

The cloakroom door behind them opened, and two hostage negotiators joined them. Folsom looked to where Fodorov continued to hold Molly, his gun pressed to her temple. "This guy's going to try to talk to him," Folsom told the negotiators. "They're friends."

"Go ahead," Brazier said. "Go on!"

Folsom glanced at the industrialist, taken slightly aback at his having taken charge.

Vladimir Donskoi, who'd returned to the meeting in H 139 after running from Latham's office, walked slowly in Fodorov's direction. As he did, he spoke in Russian, his tone friendly, almost joking. "Hey, Yvgeny, calm down, man." He raised his hands to show they were empty. "It's all worked out. We can leave here. Diplomatic immunity. No problem."

"What's he saying?" Folsom asked one of his negotiators.

"Beats the hell out of me."

Donskoi continued toward Fodorov. "Hey, Yvgeny, cool it, man. Brazier worked everything out. We're out of here, on his private goddamn jet back to Moscow."

He stopped six feet from Fodorov and Molly. Fodorov's eyes were open wide—frightened, confused eyes. He stared at Donskoi, then said, "Brazier? We can leave?"

"*Da.*"

Donskoi broke into a wide smile. "Everything's okay, man. Everything's cool."

He closed the gap between them and stood at Fodorov's side.

"Who's he?" one of C-SPAN's camera operators asked another as they zoomed in, Donskoi's face filling the screen.

"I don't know. Widen the shot."

It happened so fast no one saw it coming, especially Yvgeny Fodorov. Donskoi's hand came up holding a revolver. In one continuous motion, it moved from his belt to beneath Fodorov's chin. The weapon's discharge was picked up and magnified by the microphone at the podium. Simultaneously, Fodorov's jaw and a portion of his face erupted in a vivid red cloud of blood. The hand holding the gun next to Molly's head flew up in the air, Fodorov's finger squeezing tightly against the trigger in a reflexive action, sending a hail of bullets from the automatic weapon up to the visitors gallery, where onlookers dove for cover.

Molly Latham, now free of her abductor's grasp, slumped to the floor, on top of Fodorov's lifeless body. They were immediately surrounded by Capitol police, two of whom lifted Molly and ran with her to the front row of the Republican side of the aisle. They gently laid her across the seats. "Get a doctor!" one yelled.

Molly opened her eyes. Her fingers went to her bosom, then came away with Yvgeny Fodorov's blood on them. She shuddered, allowed a cry of anguish that had been bottled up to come forth, and then began to sob.

Vladimir Donskoi handed his weapon to Chief Folsom.

"Nice going," Folsom said. He turned to Warren Brazier. "Thanks for the help, Mr. Brazier."

"I'm just glad the girl wasn't hurt. Her father was one of my best friends."

CHAPTER THIRTY-FOUR

"Wonderful, as usual," Mac Smith said to the manager as he and Annabel prepared to leave the restaurant.

"Always good to see you," the manager said. "Safe home."

The Smiths had parked their car a half block away. They stepped out onto the street and took deep breaths. "Lovely evening," Smith said.

"Delightful. Care to carry me to the car?" Annabel asked. "I'm so full I'm not sure I can walk."

"Of course," he said, grabbing her around the waist and pretending to try and lift her.

"I was only kidding," she said, giggling. "Mac, stop it!"

The two men who'd waited across Connecticut Avenue for them to leave the restaurant crossed the street and approached. They held weapons.

But before they could reach the couple, four armed men emerged from a car parked two removed from the Smiths' Chevy. They ran into the street: "Drop the guns," one commanded.

The two men crossing stopped in the middle of the avenue.

"What the hell—?" Mac said.

He was interrupted by the sound of a single gunshot, then the sting of a bullet entering his thigh. As he fell to the sidewalk, the usually peaceful Connecticut Avenue became a battleground. The four men opened fire on the other two. One fell to the street, mortally wounded. The other attempted to flee, but was cut down by a fusillade of bullets ripping across his legs. His weapon flew from his hand and skidded across the avenue. He swore in Russian.

Annabel crouched over her husband. "Mac, are you all right?"

"My leg," he said, grimacing against the pain.

Annabel stood and shouted, "Help! My husband's been shot!"

Two of the four men came to her side. "We've called for an ambulance, Mrs. Smith," one said.

"Good. You know who I am?" she said.

"Yes, ma'am." He held out his badge for her to see. "FBI."

"FBI? You just happened to—?"

"Annabel," Smith said. He was now in a sitting position, his hands gripping his thigh.

"Yes?" she said, her hand lightly resting on his cheek.

"It was a good dinner."

"Yes, it was," she said, a large lump in her throat. "A very good dinner."

CHAPTER THIRTY-FIVE

Mac Smith was taken to the George Washington University Medical Center, where emergency room physicians treated his wound. The bullet had passed cleanly through the fleshy portion of his thigh; no damage to muscles or nerves. He wanted to go home, but doctors prevailed upon him to stay overnight.

He sat up in bed. Annabel perched on its edge and held his hand. They watched the news on TV. Footage from C-SPAN had been provided to other stations, which ran special programs on the events that evening at the House of Representatives.

The station they watched reported that the murderer of Robert Mondrian, and abductor of Molly Latham, Yvgeny Fodorov, had been killed by another employee of Brazier Industries, Vladimir Donskoi. Donskoi was hailed as the hero of the evening. He declined to be interviewed. But Warren Brazier faced reporters outside the Capitol:

"This has been a tragedy of immense proportions," he said. "That an employee of Brazier Industries would turn into such a demented villain is beyond my comprehension. I'm just thankful that another of my people bravely intervened, and that the daughter of my good friend, Congressman Paul Latham, was spared."

The replay of how Yvgeny Fodorov's threat to Molly Latham was resolved was run over and over as interviews continued to be aired. One was of Ruth Latham, flanked by Martin and Molly.

"I just thank God that it ended the way it did," Ruth said.

"Does it bother you that an employee of your late husband's good friend Warren Brazier almost took your daughter's life?" a reporter asked.

"No," she replied. "A crazy person can work for any company. All the shootings in post offices by disgruntled employees proves that."

Another question: "Your husband was murdered, Mrs. Latham. Now his chief of staff. And your daughter is kidnapped. Do you see a pattern here?"

"No. Please, we just want to get home."

Melissa had been standing just behind Molly. She said quickly, leaning into the camera, "When I heard Molly—she's my roommate at the page dorm; we're both pages—when Ah heard what was happening to her, I could just have died right on the spot."

The program shifted to a statement by Capitol Police Chief Henry Folsom, who said all circumstances of the evening would be investigated thoroughly by the appropriate law enforcement agencies.

Smith shifted his position in the bed and growled, "Ruth doesn't see a pattern? What else can you see?"

"Once the attack on *you* becomes part of the mix, Mac, that pattern will become painfully clear."

A doctor entered the room. "How are you feeling?" he asked.

"Not bad," Smith replied.

"Up to some visitors?"

"Who?" Annabel asked.

The doctor consulted a piece of paper. "A Ms. Belle and a Mr. Broadhurst. There are two FBI agents with them. I assume they're with the Bureau, too."

Mac looked at Annabel and smiled. "At least they're not asking me to meet them in a rowboat on the Potomac." He said to the doctor, "Sure, send them up. But have them check their guns at the door."

An hour later, Belle, Broadhurst, and the two special agents left Mac and Annabel alone once again. They sat silently, each trying to sort out what they'd just been told. It was Annabel who broke the silence.

"The man is evil incarnate," she said of Warren Brazier.

Smith nodded.

"He tried to eliminate every person who might know of his criminal acts. Paul. Bob Mondrian. Marge Edwards. And then you. Even Molly Latham."

"I know."

Annabel shook her head and sighed. "I never understand rich and powerful people resorting to crime to become even more rich and powerful."

"*Avaritia,*" Mac said.

"Spoken like a true lawyer, reverting to the Latin," said Annabel.

"I'd say it in Russian if I knew how. Greed. Money corrupting. Egos running amuck. What surprises me is the claim that Brazier is actually a major figure in the Russian mob, here and in Moscow, laundering their dirty drug money and God knows what else. A man can be brilliant, even brilliantly criminal, brilliantly corrupt, and then finally stupid. What did he think—because he was in a meeting at the Capitol when the mayhem went on that he had a perfect alibi? Or had he stopped thinking? From what Giles and Jessica and the agents said, all the strings lead right back to Brazier. They have him dead-to-rights—the money laundering, payoffs, contract killings, the works. And he's not the least impenitent."

"Giles is confident that the FBI will make a solid case against him, based upon what the CIA has come up with over the past year, and Paul's investigation and report. I hope he's right."

At eleven, Annabel prepared to leave. "You'll be okay?" she asked.

"It's you I worry about," Smith said. "Hate to see you alone in the house."

"I'm never alone, not with the Beast there."

He smiled. "Give Rufus an ear rub for me."

The eleven o'clock news came on, updating the events in the House that evening. Annabel stopped to watch.

"We have two important additions to this ongoing story," the anchor said in dulcet tones. "First, we've learned that another murder attempt took place tonight in Washington, this also involving Russians. An attempt was made on the life of Mackensie Smith, former noted criminal attorney and professor of law at George Washington University. Smith was also counsel to murdered congressman Paul Latham. The incident took place outside a restaurant on Connecticut Avenue, when two men, Russian national citizens with alleged ties to organized crime, attempted to kill Smith and his wife. The FBI, which had been quietly protecting Smith because of his link to Latham, killed one of the assailants and severely wounded another. Smith, according to our source, received a superficial wound, and is spending the night in the GW Medical Center."

"The FBI protecting me," Smith muttered.

"I'm glad they were there," Annabel said.

"You were right."

"About what?"

"About not getting involved. If I hadn't, there never would have been any need to 'protect' me."

Their attention returned to the screen. The newscaster said, "In still another related development, an employee of Brazier Industries, Anatoly Alekseyev, was found shot to death in his Georgetown apartment. His body was discovered following the tense scene at the Capitol by Marge Edwards, an employee in Congressman Latham's office, who disappeared after it was rumored she intended to charge President Scott's nominee for secretary of state with sexual harassment, a rumor she emphatically denied tonight. Ms. Edwards, it's reported, was romantically involved with the murdered Brazier Industries employee, Mr. Alekseyev. She has been admitted to a local hospital."

Smith used the remote to click off the set. "It seems the cold war didn't end, Annabel," he said. "We've been invaded by the Russians."

"No, Mac. The invader was a sick individual named Warren Brazier. And he's been defeated." She kissed him on the lips. "Get some sleep, which is what I intend to do. I'll be back first thing in the morning."

The Smiths made their trip to Russia, where he met with a variety of legal experts. The corruption in the judicial and law enforcement communities there was more pervasive than he'd ever imagined from his research. There was much to be done before the former Soviet Union would become a true democracy, and where a free people and a free market could flourish. Mac and his colleagues promised to return to the United States and draw up a list of recommendations for their Russian hosts to consider.

They enjoyed the trip, although the ghost of Warren Brazier, and the havoc he created, followed wherever they went.

They returned to Washington and settled into their routines, Mac back to teaching at the university, Annabel to managing her art gallery.

Federal charges, ranging from money laundering to racketeering to murder, were filed against Warren Brazier and some of his associates. Brazier vowed to fight them, but the overwhelming legal opinion was that despite his money, the case against him was strong enough to assure a conviction.

Smith met with Marge Edwards only once, the day before she was to leave Washington to live with her father in Indianapolis: "Just until I put the pieces together," she told him.

"A smart move," he said.

"You know I never intended to hurt Paul," she said.

"Of course I know that. He was a good man. I miss him. The country misses him."

"Well, I'm sorry for all the upset I caused. I acted like a silly school-girl."

Smith smiled, said, "It's all in the past, Marge. Say hello to your father. I like him. It's a good place for you to be right now. And it will brighten his life."

Molly Latham, according to her mother, had settled back into being a House page, and was thoroughly enjoying the experience. "I think she'll run for Congress one day," Ruth said.

"She'll have my vote," Smith replied. "Provided Annabel and I move to Northern California."

Senator Connors fired his AA, Dennis Mackral, who returned to California to attempt to build a base for his own run for Congress. His prospects were considered to be 15-watt, although it was, after all, California.

President Scott put up another nominee for secretary of state, a former ambassador to the Soviet Union whose reputation had been carefully built over the years to preclude the ruffling of feathers—anywhere, with anyone—including Senator Frank Connors. The nominee passed Senate scrutiny with ease.

That evening, Mac received a call at home from Jessica Belle.

"Hello, Jessica," he said.

"Hi, Mac. Giles and I were wondering if we could get together."

"Get together?"

"Maybe dinner? Our treat. There's something we wanted to bounce off you."

A twinge of pain in his thigh where he'd been shot caused him to wince. He slowly recrossed his legs.

"Mac?"

"Yes, I'm here."

"Dinner? Tomorrow?"

"I, ah—I'm tied up, Jessica. Will be for quite a while."

"Sure. I understand," she said. "How about giving me a call when things ease up?"

"A good suggestion."

Rufus placed his large canine head on Smith's lap. Smith scratched him behind the ears, smiled, and said, "I'll get back to you, Jessica."

"In a year or so," he said to Rufus after hanging up. "And maybe later. Come on, big guy. I've got a few things to talk over with you. Need your advice. Need a walk."

ABOUT THE AUTHOR

MARGARET TRUMAN is the author of a dozen best-selling novels of life and death around Washington's monuments, as well as two bestselling biographies, one of her father, the former president, and one of her mother. She lives in New York City with her husband, former *New York Times* editor Clifton Daniel.